Published by Autumn Day Publishing
Copyright 2015
Cover by Toby Gray
Other work by L.S. Gagnon,
Witch: A New Beginning
Witch: The Spell Within
Original release, 2013
ISBN 978-0-9962305-4-4
All characters in this book are fiction
and figments of the author's imagination.
If you want to receive our monthly newsletter, text the
word, 'witch' to 42828 to sign up.

WITCH: THE SECRET OF THE LEAVES

by L. S. Gagnon
Facebook/TheWitchSeries

I dedicate this book to two of the most amazing women I have ever known. The first is my mother, Ana Delia. Not a day goes by that I don't think of you. I will never find the words to express how my heart aches for you every day. I miss you with every passing moment. I love you, Mom.

The second is the most amazing witch I have ever had the pleasure of knowing. Connie Ouellette, your heart was an ocean of love. You gave so much and asked for nothing in return. I will always remember that smile of yours. I miss you.

Special thanks to Toby Gray for designing the cover. You are an amazing artist.

Table of Contents

Prologue

Precious things grow only in the sun. Evil things thrive only in the shadows.

I have seen the beauty of both worlds, tasted the sweet nectar of both sides. Today I would choose which side would control me, decide which side carried less heartbreak. Both sides had failed me. Both sides had taken it all away. It was time to take my life back, to pull myself out of the darkness.

The question was: Did I really want to leave?

I could guess what Simon would do next. I felt his evil thoughts run through me as though they were my own. The darkness had wrapped its arms around me, just as it had done with Simon so long ago. We shared the same dark eyes, and now the same dark desires.

Chapter 1
My Favorite Spot

I awoke to the rumbling sound of the snow plow on the street below. Winter had arrived early this year, blanketing Salem in white and creating a hush over the town. The temperature had dropped suddenly, halting the tourist season almost overnight. The streets were often empty, and most shops opened for only part of the day. The peaceful sounds of winter could be truly appreciated only by those who embraced life in a place where it snowed several months out of the year. Winter was my second-favorite season. Cars sounded as though they drove on cotton. Footsteps were muffled, nearly silent.

I rolled out of bed and shuffled to the window. It was still dark. The salt trucks followed the plows in full force. I spotted my husband's truck parked across the street. He'd soon be out there brushing it clean of snow so he could take me to work.

I was grateful that Norm had given me my old job back. He had been ecstatic to see me when I walked into the bakery a few weeks ago. We were well into November now, and in a few short days, people would be flooding the bakery to place orders for holiday pies.

The bakery would likely be the only shop open today. Norm refused to close no matter the weather. I had planned on leaving early so I could visit my favorite spot before my shift. The lake, now frozen into a sheet of ice, called to me. The surrounding trees looked brilliant flocked in snow.

But Cory's insistence on driving me to work had foiled my plans.

He'd tried talking me out of going to work altogether. There was over a foot of snow on the ground, and he didn't want me out in it. His overprotectiveness wasn't necessary, but I understood his worry. I hadn't been myself for the better part of a month. Like any caring husband, Cory worried.

A few weeks earlier, while I was walking home from my father's house, Simon's warlocks had struck me with a powerful spell. My father explained that it was a wizard's spell—one Simon had taught them. Since then, I'd been having trouble recalling certain past events. My mind was still foggy, but my memories were slowly returning, the pieces falling back into place.

I knew Simon wanted me to kill my husband, cut out his heart, and bring it to him. But Cory had encased my mother's heart in his own to stop the enchanted heart from stealing my thoughts. My father wouldn't divulge to me what secret the heart held, only that I didn't need to worry about that anymore.

One thing I did remember was the lie I'd told Simon: that I had taken the heart and placed it in a crystal. I warned Simon that if he touched Cory, my spell would kill him. It was the only way I knew to keep my husband safe. Simon had bought the lie and also believed that the crystal he desired to get his

~ 3 ~

hands on was located in Magia, the magical world from which my father, the wizard, had come.

Simon also presumed that I was under his control, that his spell had changed me. I had done the impossible: I had convinced Simon that I loved him. Truth be told, it wasn't difficult to pretend I was happy around Simon. Each minute by his side felt like mere seconds. Our meetings always left me wanting more. I couldn't live without him. At least, that was what I wanted—needed—him to think.

I was doing well so far fighting off the effects of Simon's spell. I could even be with Cory without wanting to kill him. My father continued to insist that we not live together. "Still too dangerous," he warned. But Cory was never but a whisper away. My apartment was on the third floor, while Cory and the boys lived on the first and second floors. Cory spent most of his days with me.

I couldn't remember our wedding day, but I knew in my heart that it must have been perfect. We had married just before the nightmare had begun, before Simon came and destroyed our lives. Cory and I had never bonded after we married. Even now, he refused to touch me. "Not until you can remember why you fell in love with me," he said.

I tried telling him that it didn't matter whether or not I could remember. I loved him now, and that was all that mattered. But he wouldn't hear it. He needed to know that we were together because I was truly in love with him. How could I not be in love with him? Why else would I have married him? After four hundred years of waiting, Cory was back in my life. The past was behind us. What did it matter that I couldn't remember why I had fallen for him?

The only thing that mattered now was getting Simon back to my father's world. The dragons would break Simon's spell and set me free. If the spell was broken in the human world, I would die—a detail Simon had somehow overlooked.

For weeks I had been clandestinely meeting with Simon at night. He did things to me I couldn't even think about—his way of testing the strength of his spell.

But as much as I feared it, he never took me. He never let things get that far. Just before the point of no return, he'd push me away and tell me to return the next night.

I was relieved to be let go. Simon's touch made me want to vomit; the façade was getting harder to fake.

But I felt the spell taking me over at times. Some nights, when I stared into Simon's cold, calculating eyes, I actually wanted him. Fortunately for me, he limited our meetings to a few minutes at a time. For reasons I hadn't yet figured out, he seemed unable to be around me for too long.

I felt guilty keeping secrets from Cory. But how could I explain Simon's intoxicating effect on me? Cory would never understand how hard it was for me not to give in to him.

Sometimes several nights would pass without Simon sending for me. He no longer seemed in a rush to get to Magia—his previous urgency seemingly all but gone. His demeanor was calm now, placid even. At times it seemed as though the worst was over. I had even been tempted to let my guard down. But I knew he couldn't be trusted. No matter how tranquil he appeared on the surface, Simon was always working on some sinister plan.

On my nights alone, I hunted warlocks. I was determined to deplete Simon's army before taking him to my father's world. I feared Simon was on to me. He had mentioned to me that many of his men had gone missing. As it was, the warlocks were getting harder and harder to find. My frustration rose with every unsuccessful hunt.

The leaves remained my biggest obstacle. The dragons had ordered me to find and destroy them before bringing Simon to Magia. But Simon had yet to utter a single word about them, and I was at a loss. Those leaves had the power to extinguish the wizards' magic, and Simon planned on using them to destroy all the wizards in Magia. Time was running out. Simon had told me his tools were almost ready. What those tools might be, I hadn't a clue.

During our encounters, Simon would caress my cheek and tell me how we would rule Magia together one day. His eyes lit up when I shared stories of what I'd seen in my father's world. I told him everything. Everything, that is, but the detail of the dragons, or the two wizards who were helping me.

I had traveled back to Magia and briefed Martin and Morgan on the situation, warning them that I planned to bring Simon there soon. My father had sent orders for them to remain in Magia, stating that he needed them there. Martin had become upset. He and Morgan wanted to come to the human world to help my father. Nonetheless, Martin respected my father's wishes, and the two had secured a safe place to hide from the other wizards.

I had asked my father why he refused the help of his friends. For reasons he could not—or would not—share, he explained that wizards could not cross into this world. At least, not yet. I wondered if this was why he never ventured outside. I had a gut feeling it all had something to do with the leaves Simon had taken from Magia—the leaves I sought to destroy.

My father and I had agreed not to tell anyone that he was the king of Magia, or that I was a princess. There was simply no need for anyone in the human world to know. I couldn't get over my father's recent transformation. He actually listened to me now. He took my advice and didn't argue when I sent the Spanish warlocks home. I was doing this all on my own, placing only myself in danger. That my father and I were on the same page took me by surprise. In fact, my father seemed interested in one thing only: feeding me. He placed food in front of me at every possible opportunity.

"Good morning."

Cory's voice broke me from my thoughts. I turned to find him looking down at me with his beautiful blue eyes, a symbol of love I never tired of.

I smiled. "I didn't hear you come in."

He pulled me into his arms. "I didn't want to scare you." He tilted his head, surveying my nightclothes. "You're not dressed yet?"

"Care to help me?" I asked.

"Behave, Thea. You know how hard this is for me."

I ran my fingers through his hair. "Is that a yes?"

"No." He leaned into me, smiling his golden smile. "But I will kiss you if you want."

Cory was beautiful, with a Polish nose that suited him well, extra-long lashes, and a body like a

Greek god. I had a hard time being good when we were close.

I squinted up at him. "Why do you always ask me first?" He never gave me so much as a peck on the cheek without asking.

"Because I want to make sure it's what you really want."

I leaned into him and pulled his lips toward mine. I sighed as our tongues met. Weaving my fingers through his hair, I kissed him harder before pulling away. "Does that answer your question?"

He smiled. "Sure does."

As our lips met again, I attempted to push him toward the bed.

"What are you doing?" he asked between kisses.

"Trying to get you into bed. Do you object?"

"That depends."

"On what?"

He stiffened. "Do you remember why you fell in love with me?"

I closed my eyes. Just like all the other times he'd asked, I didn't have an answer. I couldn't remember where or how I had fallen in love with him. I only knew that I did, in fact, love him. Cory believed that this simple little thing stood between us.

When I didn't answer, he combed his hand through my smooth, straight hair. "That's what I thought."

Just as a male witch's eyes turned blue, a female witch's hair became tangled and knotted when she was in love. It was a sign to others that she was taken and in love. I tried to explain to Cory that my untangled hair was only because I had lost some of my memories. I was sure of that.

I turned away from him. "I don't like when you do that."

He placed his hands on my shoulders and turned me around. "Don't be angry. I don't want you with me just because you were told that we were married."

"But that's silly. Why would I marry you if I didn't love you?"

He looked into my eyes and then at my hair. "I'm going to go clean off the truck. I'll wait for you downstairs."

I reached for him. "Don't you want me?"

He took my face in his hands. "Thea, I've never wanted anyone like I want you. I just wish you could look into my eyes and say the same thing."

"I only want you," I whispered.

He smiled and pulled me back into his arms. "I'll tell you what. If in two months you still feel the same, I'll marry you again and give you forever."

"Why two months?"

"Seems like the proper time to wait. No one can accuse me of taking advantage if you truly fall in love with me."

I pushed him away. "You don't think I love you?"

"It's not that." He dropped his hands to his sides. "But I need to know you feel the same way about me as I do about you."

I felt a pang inside that I couldn't quite define, and promptly ignored it. "But I'm telling you, I love you."

"No, you're telling me what you presume you felt back then, not what's in your heart now. There's a difference." He glanced at my hair and turned toward the door. "I'll be waiting downstairs."

As usual, his words left me confused and lost. I decided to let it go for now. To dwell on the situation would just put me in a bad mood, and I didn't want the others telling me that the "old Thea" was back. I could hear Fish's voice in my head: *You're crabby again.*

Their assertions irritated me; I could never tell if they were meant as compliments or insults. I stepped into the shower and allowed the hot water to pour over my face for several minutes. After the shower, I searched through my closet and selected my usual loose, dark attire.

As I walked into the kitchen, I heard the boys outside in the hall.

"Is Cory in there?" Fish asked through the door to my apartment.

I opened the door, and there stood my three guards, the angels sent from heaven to protect me. They had watched over me for many years, putting their own lives aside to stay by me during the time when my memory of who I was had been washed clean.

There was only one problem: an angel was missing. My precious Sammy had been killed the night of the Halloween Ball. He had died trying to protect me. I put on a brave face around the boys, but the pain and guilt returned every time I looked at them. I could still see the anguish in their eyes over his loss. No one could even talk about him; it was too painful. I would never forgive myself.

Joshua was having an especially hard time. He became visibly upset when my father and Fish insisted that Delia stay with the boys and take Sammy's room.

Furthermore, Fish wouldn't let Delia out of his sight. He didn't trust that Simon wouldn't come after her, even though I had assured him that Delia was now safe. He went as far as to beg Norm to give her a job at the bakery, and had boarded up Delia's house, ordering her to stay away from there.

When Delia had come to live here, I'd suggested informing the landlord about the tenant change. I had been surprised when Cory announced that *he* was the landlord. Somehow, in all these years, no one had ever bothered to tell me that he and the boys owned the building. "We bought it so we could keep an eye on you," Cory had explained.

Even more confounding had been Delia's annoyed response: "Cory, you keep slipping."

I smiled at Fish's boyish face. He was still beaming from Delia having said "yes" to his proposal. It made him nearly impossible to be around at times. He wanted everyone else to be as happy as he was and found humor in the most evil of things. He'd been counting the days to their wedding and kept telling Delia to rest up for their wedding night. "Take some vitamins," he would say. To which Delia would roll her eyes and laugh when he wasn't looking.

Delia wanted a simple and traditional witch wedding. Fish was making more of a fuss.

"No tuxedos," Delia warned. She wanted only a few guests and simple attire. She begged Fish to wear just a nice shirt and some slacks, but Fish had other plans. After several lively negotiations, Delia had finally agreed to a reception. "But not too big," she insisted.

But she always gave in to his boyish face. "He's impossible," she told me. "Right now, he's out there trying to find a spell that can draw out our wedding night for three whole days."

I had laughed on and off for a week just imagining Fish scurrying about town in search of such a ridiculous spell. But who could blame him? Delia was an extraordinary woman, and beautiful—black hair, milky-white skin, dark eyes. It was no wonder Fish couldn't wait to take her.

Javier was pretty much back to his old self. He was still dating human girls exclusively, but I knew he would find love with a witch someday. He still had his signature Mohawk, one of his best qualities, he thought. I always felt that his wrestler's body was what made him popular with the ladies.

Fish peeked into my apartment. "Has Cory put his clothes back on yet?"

I smiled. "He's outside, Fish."

Fish nodded. "I'll go help him clean the snow off the truck."

"I'll come with you," Javier said, following Fish down the stairs.

I smiled at the red-headed Joshua—my gentle giant. His heart was the biggest part of him.

"You want to come in?" I asked, opening the door wide.

He shook his head. "No thanks, but I do want to ask you a question."

"What is it?"

"Do you think Meaghan likes me?" His face flushed, and he bowed his head.

My poor Joshua, so nervous and shy. Meaghan was a girl I had healed. A warlock had cast a spell on her when he learned her mother had married a human. Joshua was completely in love with her.

"How could she not?" I replied.

"I don't know." He shrugged his shoulders. "She never calls me back."

"Maybe she's shy," I suggested.

He looked up at me, a ray of hope appearing on his face. "You really think that's it?" He looked over his shoulder when he heard someone climbing the steps. "Never mind." He turned away and headed down the hall.

"Morning, sweetie," Delia said, passing him.

"Hey, Dells," Joshua replied flatly.

Delia walked into my apartment. "Are you ready yet?"

I watched Joshua make his way sluggishly down the stairs.

"What's his problem?" Delia asked.

I knew Joshua had been calling Meaghan, but I hadn't realized she wasn't returning his calls. "Nothing. Let's get out of here."

I grabbed my coat, and we headed for the truck.

"This is silly," Delia said on our way down the stairs. "The bakery is only a few blocks away."

"Try telling Cory that."

"Why does Norm want us there so early, anyway?"

When we stepped outside, the snow-covered town took my breath away. It looked like a picture postcard, too beautiful to be real. Although it was still dark, the moon beamed off the snow and lit up the sky. The fluffy white ice crystals that covered every inch of Salem sparkled like diamonds. The trees had come to life, gently cradling the snow in their graceful branches.

The boys had already shoveled the front walk,

and Delia hurried ahead to the truck. I lingered on the path, mesmerized by the beauty around me. I wished I'd been able to convince Cory to let me walk to work today. I could have slipped off to my favorite spot to clear my head before starting the workday. I could fly there in less than a minute's time and usually return before anyone missed me.

Cory didn't like me going to the lake. I couldn't understand why. I came alive there; the emptiness that tugged at my heart disappeared when I stood among the trees and by the water's edge. The moment I left, the black hole inside me would return.

I'd lost some memories, but I'd lost something else, too. I didn't have a clue as to what, but I did know that it filled me with pain. For weeks now, I had cried at the drop of a hat. I broke down often, and for seemingly no reason. I had no answer for Cory when he asked what was wrong. What could I say to him? "There's an empty hole inside me, and being near you doesn't make it go away." I couldn't possibly explain the hollow feeling in my heart without Cory using it to confirm his doubts about our marriage.

As much as it pained me to admit it, Cory was right to be cautious.

I broke away from my thoughts and headed for the truck. Cory pulled up in front of the bakery less than five minutes later. It really was silly of him to insist on driving us practically every morning. I loved walking to work. I often left early so I could take my time and enjoy the sights of the town.

We were barely inside the bakery when Delia made a beeline for the coffee machine. Now that she knew how to use it, she drank coffee all day long.

"Will you start the pumpkin pies?" Norm

shouted from the back.

I shrugged out of my coat. "Sure, Norm." I breathed in the smell of freshly baked bread and glanced at the thermostat. The heat from the ovens had already warmed the building to a cozy seventy-five degrees.

Delia handed me a steaming mug. "Geez, can he at least let us drink a cup of coffee first?"

I had missed this place. It was here that I had seen Cory for the first time, when he'd returned to Salem after his long absence. He'd come in asking for directions. Even then I'd known I belonged to him.

"I'm bringing back your friends," Norm called. "Too many deliveries to do on my own."

"Great," Delia said, rolling her eyes. "Now Fish will be here all day, yammering on and on about the wedding."

I smiled and reached for an apron.

Again Norm's voice boomed from the back: "Thea, can you come here a minute?"

When I reached the ovens, I stifled a giggle. Norm was covered in flour, his mustache holding evidence of whatever baked item he'd chosen for his breakfast.

He turned to the counter and began rolling out more bread dough. "The delivery truck didn't make it because of the snow. I'll have to run to the store and buy some sugar. I shouldn't be long."

I smiled to myself: a chance to get away. It would be daylight soon, but I could fly to the lake without being spotted. "You might want to get the bank out of the way, too," I said, looking for a way to extend my little break. "They might close early because of the snow."

~ 15 ~

He scratched his mustache and nodded. "Good idea."

Yes!

After removing the last batch of bread from the ovens, Norm headed out into the snow. He left Delia with the job of calling the boys and asking them back. Fish was, of course, ecstatic. She pulled the phone away from her ear, letting his cries of joy reverberate through the bakery.

Delia drained the last of her coffee and sighed. "You know, the only good thing about working in this damned place was getting a break from the over-eager Fish. Now what am I going to do?"

I smiled and shook my head.

As Delia trudged back to the machine to pour her second cup of the day, I grabbed a bag of trash from under the counter. "I'm going out to the dumpster," I called, walking out the back door.

In the alley, I pulled my father's wand from my pocket. The dragons of Magia had presented me with it, and it was unlike any I had ever seen before. It could transform into any object I needed, whatever the situation called for. I didn't even need to wave it; it simply read my mind. It always knew exactly what I needed. I smiled when the wand changed into my stick.

In seconds, I was off and flying. I was but a flash in the sky to human eyes, and the snow provided good cover. I shaded my eyes against the blinding light that beamed off the snow from the rising sun. Nonetheless I flew, unworried, and soon landed. I threw the stick to one side and gazed at the lake. I lowered myself to the snow-laden ground as tears filled my eyes. A mysterious sense of loss washed over me. But despite the heartbreak, the lake made me happy.

What is it about this place?

I sighed and looked around. My favorite red spruce, draped with snow, sparkled in the morning light. My heart raced just to look at it, though I couldn't understand why. I got to my feet and compelled myself to walk toward the giant evergreen. Halfway to the tree, a stinging gust hit my face as I caught the stench.

Warlocks.

I held out my hand, and my stick immediately obeyed my silent command. Seconds later, I was flying through the trees, following the warlocks' scent through the forest. There were five of them, that much I knew. I was reasonably sure they hadn't sensed me, but I couldn't know for sure. When the stench intensified, I landed on the forest floor. I scanned the area as my stick took the form of a glass sword. I ducked behind some bushes and held up the weapon, waiting for my prey.

Their heartbeats thrummed in my ears. They were close. Behind me I heard a sound like the striking of matches. I turned to find all five of them smiling at me, spells spinning in their hands.

"You looking for us?" the shortest of them asked. "I thought you were on our side."

Another of the group—this one dark-eyed and balding—stepped forward. "Simon will not be happy to hear about this."

I raised my sword. "Who said he was going to find out?"

Before I could strike, a flash of gold sliced one of the warlocks clean in half. The other four had no time to react before their heads were sheared off and sent flying. When the last of the heads rolled to a stop and turned to dust, I searched the area but saw no one.

"You shouldn't be out here."

My head snapped in the direction of the unfamiliar voice. This was no warlock.

I raised my sword higher. "Who's there?"

"If I come out, will you promise to put the sword down? You look quite scary, you know."

A mild and pleasant scent hit me. It brushed against my face and sent my heart racing. I let the sword drop to my side. To my right, a tall, good-looking man emerged from behind a tree.

I turned, stunned.

He could be Simon's twin.

As the stranger approached, I saw that he was actually much younger than Simon. He was broader, and presumably stronger. He was also a half-human witch.

"I didn't need your help," I said.

He held up his weapon and gave it a shake. The whip disappeared into the handle. "I beg to differ, ma'am." He glanced at my sword. "That's quite a weapon. Do you always carry a sword?"

I hoped the sword wouldn't revert to wand-form in front of him. I had no idea who this witch was, and it was clear he didn't know me, either. If he knew who I was, he'd have known that I didn't need his help.

When I didn't respond, he smiled and crossed his arms. "A simple thank you will do."

"I told you, I didn't need your help."

He shook his head and chuckled. "You're welcome."

Who is this arrogant, self-important witch?

"You should leave, before my sword thanks you up close."

He eyed my weapon again. "Yes, it does look quite menacing. But I would feel better if you would allow me to escort you out of the forest. You don't seem to be aware of the dangers that lurk here."

I stepped forward and pointed the sword at his chest. "Actually, I believe it's you who is unaware of the present dangers."

He smiled. "What a bad temper for such a pretty face."

The point of the sword hovered inches from his heart. "Do you want to test my temper?"

"No, ma'am." He threw up his hands playfully. "I've had enough excitement for one day." His expression turned serious. "But it's only fair to warn you, since you're obviously new in town, that warlocks walk these woods."

"I can take care of myself." I spun on my heel and started to walk away.

"So I take it we're not friends?" the stranger called out.

"So I take it you're not stupid?" I replied over my shoulder.

The sound of his laughter followed me. *Rescue me, indeed. How dare he?*

As soon as I was out of his sight, the sword changed back into my stick. That idiot had ruined what was supposed to be the best part of my day. I could have killed those warlocks and still had time to enjoy a moment to myself. Since when did I need help killing a measly five warlocks? *Doesn't he know who I am? What I am?*

My bad mood followed me all the way back to

the bakery.

Chapter 2
The Wedding Cake

"Where have you been?" Delia asked as I walked through the front door of the bakery. "I thought you were taking out the trash."

"I ran into trash instead." My eyes darted toward the back room. Was Norm back?

"You can relax, Miss AWOL," she said, pouring chocolate batter into a cupcake pan. "The boss-man's still out. What do you mean, you ran into trash?"

I didn't have the energy to explain to Delia what had happened. I was still too angry. "I'd better get on those pumpkin pies." I disappeared into the back and drew the pumpkin puree from the fridge.

By the time Norm returned, the ovens were filled with pies. I was prepping more pie shells when I heard Delia arguing with someone at the front counter. Delia's customer service left a lot to be desired, but she wasn't usually prone to snapping at customers. I wiped my hands on my apron and went to check up on her.

My confusion cleared when I spotted Helena on the other side of the counter. Salem's meanest witch was a strikingly tall, blond beauty with legs that went on forever. She was also unbearably arrogant and condescending. Delia couldn't stand her.

"I'm sorry," Delia was saying, "but I don't think we can help you, witch.

Helena stepped back, flipping her long, silky hair over her shoulder. "Oh? Well, I guess I'll just take my business elsewhere, then."

Norm stepped up to the counter. "Now ma'am, I'm sure that won't be necessary." He turned to Delia and spoke quietly through a strained smile. "This is my bake shop, Delia. And we don't turn away customers." He faced Helena and smiled sweetly. "Whatever it is that you need, ma'am, I'm confident we can help you."

Helena looked past Norm to Delia, a smug expression on her face. "Thank you. And I'll have you know, I'm willing to pay double for good service."

Norm's eyes grew wide. "Thea!"

"Right here, Norm," I said, waving from the sidelines.

He hurried over and drew me toward the counter, pushing the still-seething Delia aside in the process. "Thea will be happy to take care of you." With that, Norm was gone, banishing himself once again to the back room.

I groaned inside. *If Norm wants this witch's business so badly, why doesn't he take care of her himself?* I mustered a smile. "Hello, Helena."

She gave me a tight-lipped smile and glared over my shoulder at Delia. "Do you mind? I wish to speak to Thea alone."

"Tough luck, witch." Delia folded her arms across her chest. "I'm not going anywhere."

"Very well," Helena said, returning her icy gaze to me. "I want you to make my wedding cake."

"You hag!" Delia shouted. She lunged across the counter.

I intercepted Delia's hand, which was reaching for Helena's perfect head of hair. "Delia, what are you doing?" I yelled, mystified. I didn't like Helena either, but violence?

"Let me at her, Thea," Delia begged. "Just let me at her for one second."

Helena threw her head back and laughed. "Why don't you explain why you don't want her making my wedding cake, Delia? Go ahead, tell her why."

Delia's chest heaved. "You've gone too far this time, hag."

Helena narrowed her eyes. "I've only just begun, witch."

Delia lunged toward her again. "I'm going to kill you!"

"You're going to get yourself fired," I said, stepping between Delia and the counter. "Go help Norm. I've got this."

Delia gave Helena one last steely glare and stormed off toward the back room.

Helena looked pleased with herself as she redirected her gaze to me. "I suppose I could have flown a French pastry chef here to make my cake," she said, "but I'm afraid there's no time. My fiancé can barely wait another day to bond himself to me forever, much less the time it would take to fly in a foreign chef."

I ignored Helena's gloating. "What kind of cake do you want?"

"Well, money is no object, of course," she replied, flipping her hair again. "My fiancé said I could spend however much I wish. But I suppose that's not really an issue in a place like this. You're clearly not capable of making a cake of that . . . caliber."

Rolling my eyes, I pulled out a book of cakes I had made in the past, set it on the counter, and opened it to the first page. "Do you want to look through this?"

When she didn't answer, I glanced up.

She was looking at the book with disdain. "I doubt you'd have anything in there I'd want."

I slammed the book shut. "Do you want me to make the cake or not?"

"Does it bother you to make it?"

What kind of question is that? "I don't care either way, Helena."

"That's too bad," she replied.

She was starting to annoy me. Helena was hopelessly conceited and cared more about money than anything else, but this was over-the-top, even for her. That she bragged about her rich, adoring fiancé didn't surprise me. That she flashed her giant diamond ring in my direction at every opportunity was entirely predictable. But her demeanor toward me was decidedly personal today, and I'd had just about enough.

"I'm busy, witch," I said, shoving the book back under the counter. "Make up your mind."

She looked at me with such hatred, as though she wished she could kill me with her icy stare alone. "I think it would be perfect if you made my wedding cake," she finally answered.

"Fine," I replied through gritted teeth. "Come back and we'll do a cake tasting."

She laid a stack of bills on the counter. "I'll take a sampling of each of the pastries you have in the display case here. I'm meeting my fiancé later, and he loves sweets."

I rolled my eyes and boxed up her pastries.

When I set them on the counter, Helena shook her head. "You can bring those to my car."

What is this witch's problem? "It's only two boxes."

"Should I call your boss?" She glanced toward the back room. "Norm, is it?"

I snatched the boxes from the counter and headed for the door. "Where are you parked, witch?"

She fell in behind me. "It's the white Mercedes right out front there." She pointed her keys at the car, and the trunk popped open. "Isn't it pretty?" she asked. "It was an engagement present from my fiancé."

I was tempted to toss the boxes into the trunk and slam it shut. Instead, I placed them in gently and hurried back toward the bakery door. "Have a nice day, Helena."

Delia was peering through the front window when I walked in. "I really hate that witch."

"You're acting like this is some new development, Delia." I took a seat at one of the tables and rested my chin in my hand. "Helena's always been tough to take. Why are you letting her bother you so much?"

The fury in Delia's eyes was unmistakable. "Oh, I don't know. Maybe because she's getting a happy ending she doesn't deserve."

"What do you care?" I asked flatly. "Feel sorry for the poor soul who's going to marry her."

She glanced out the window, watching as Helena pulled away from the curb. "Yeah, I pity the idiot who would want a woman like that for someone they loved."

She stormed off to the back and didn't speak to me for most of the day. I knew better than to question her. When it came to Delia's temper, it was better to just let it go and let her come to me.

By my count, that was two friends I'd unwittingly managed to alienate. Justin still wasn't speaking to me. His two brothers had been killed the night of the Halloween Ball, and Justin blamed me for the tragedy. I tried calling and sending flowers, had even mailed countless letters begging for his forgiveness. But they had all come back marked *Return to Sender*. If he continued to ignore my calls, I would make the trek to Fall River and meet with him face to face.

I breathed deep in an effort to clear my head and started making éclairs—Delia's favorite. A little while later, I presented her with a freshly baked éclair with extra chocolate frosting.

Delia snatched it from the plate. "You're impossible."

I took a seat on Norm's stool. "So, what was all that about this morning?"

"You know I hate that witch," she replied, her mouth full of éclair.

"Yeah, but what did you mean when you said she'd gone too far?"

A nervous smile appeared on her face as she licked the chocolate from her lips. "Did I say that?"

"Don't play dumb with me, Delia."

"I don't know what you're talking about." She shoved the last of the éclair into her mouth and wiped her hands on her apron. "You going to see your father today?"

She was hiding something, but I decided not to push it for now. There was still a lot of work to do, and I didn't want to risk setting her off again. "Yeah, I'm going after work," I finally answered. "You want to come with me?"

She set a carton of eggs on the counter and gave me a strange look. "Answer me a question: Have you ever met the man your father works for?"

I hopped off Norm's stool and started cracking eggs into a bowl. "No, he never seems to be around when I visit. Why?"

"So you've never even seen him?"

"I just told you, no."

Delia gathered the other ingredients for the custard pies. "What has your father told you about him?"

"Nothing," I replied, whisking the eggs. "He never talks about him." I glanced at her. "Why are you asking me all these questions?"

"I just don't understand how you've never met the man your father works for."

I shrugged. "I'll meet him at your wedding. Isn't he Fish's best man?"

"Oh yeah," she replied thoughtfully. "He will be there, won't he?"

"How does Fish know him so well, anyway?"

Delia bit her lip and poured sugar into a large mixing bowl.

She could pepper me with one strange question after another, but I couldn't get an answer to one simple question? My irritation rising, I pressed on. "For that matter, how well do you know him?"

"Very well," she answered curtly. "That's why I'm surprised he's marrying Helena."

I stopped whisking and stared at her. "Helena's fiancé is my father's boss?"

She glanced at me from the corner of her eye. "Crazy, isn't it?"

I went back to whisking the eggs. Nagging questions began to plague me. My father had been in this man's service for years. How could it be that we'd never met? "Delia, how long have you known this guy, and why have you never mentioned him before?"

She seemed nervous as she looked at me. "I have. You just can't remember."

Maybe Delia was right. Maybe this man was just another of my lost memories. "At any rate," I said, returning to the eggs, "what kind of man would marry someone like Helena?"

"That's just the thing," Delia replied. "I don't see him being happy with her."

"Why do you say that?"

"Because he prefers brunettes," Delia muttered.

"So do I." Fish breezed into the bakery with Cory in tow. He made a beeline for Delia and kissed her cheek. "Norm called a bit ago and told us to come get the van ready."

I looked at Cory. "Don't I get a kiss?"

"No," he replied, winking. "You get two."

I dropped the whisk into the bowl. "Feeling generous, are we?"

He pulled me to his lips. "Extremely."

Fish drew Delia toward him. "Come here, baby. Let's show them how it's really done."

Delia dabbed some chocolate sauce on Fish's lips. "There," she said. "Now you're ready."

Fish dipped Delia and kissed her.

Cory rolled his eyes and looked at me. "You

two looked deep in conversation when we walked in. Did I hear Delia say something about brunettes?"

"We were talking about Helena's fiancé," I replied.

Cory eyed Delia suspiciously. "What about him?"

"Nothing," Delia replied, avoiding Cory's gaze. "It was nothing."

Cory looked back at me. "Do you know him?"

"No, I was just telling Delia that I've never even seen him. Don't you think that's a little strange?"

Cory flashed Delia a look I didn't understand. "Wondering about that, are ya?"

"Not really." Delia measured the vanilla, her fingers trembling as she poured it into the bowl. "I . . . I need to get something from the front."

Cory's gaze didn't waver. His eyes remained on Delia until she left the room with Fish in hot pursuit.

Cory had been hurt when Fish asked my father's boss to be his best man. Cory didn't realize that Fish and this guy were even close. To make matters worse, Fish's best man had insisted on helping with all the wedding arrangements. Cory felt shut out. It was hard to fathom how Fish couldn't see that.

"You did what?" Delia's shrill voice rang through the bakery.

"What could I do?" Fish replied.

Cory and I glanced at each other and quickly went to see what the problem was.

Delia was poking her finger into Fish's chest. "If that hag shows her face at the wedding, you can forget about me saying 'I do.'"

"What's going on?" Cory asked.

Delia put her hands on her hips. "Brainiac here

told James he could bring a date to the wedding, and guess who he's bringing."

Cory stifled a chuckle. "Nice going, Fish."

Fish reached for her hands. "Delia, baby, come on—"

"Don't you 'baby' me," she shot back, slapping his hands away.

"What can I do?" Fish asked. "I can't go back now and tell him not to bring her."

Delia crossed her arms. "Actually, you can and you will. That hag is not going to ruin my special day."

"I can't do it, Dells."

"Then the wedding is off!" Delia yanked off her ring and threw it at Fish. "Maybe Cory can spare you one of his girlfriends!"

Before Fish could catch her, she stormed out the front door. Fish scooped the ring off the floor and ran after her. "Delia, please!"

I hurried to the door and looked out. Delia was already halfway down the street with Fish at her heels.

I closed the door and leaned my back against its cool, hard surface. "What's gotten into those two?"

Cory shrugged. "I'm not sure."

I looked at Cory and tilted my head. "What did she mean, one of your girlfriends?"

Cory's face went pale. "I . . . I don't know."

"And who is James?"

"Um, Helena's fiancé."

I nodded knowingly. "Oh, that makes sense, then."

"What makes sense?"

"Have you forgotten that Delia can't stand Helena?"

"Oh yeah," he replied absently. Cory's eyes

wandered the room as though his mind were somewhere else.

I eyed him curiously. "Are you okay?"

Several awkward moments passed before his eyes settled on me again. "I . . . I'd better go after those two."

"Yeah, okay. Tell Delia she's not done working yet. She needs to get back here."

"I'll tell her," he said, slipping out the door.

After Cory left, I returned to the back and finished the custard pies. What was taking Delia so long? I couldn't help but smile, wondering how many blocks Fish had chased her before she relented. Those two seemed to thrive on drama.

The bells on the bakery door jingled. "Anyone here?"

I smiled, happy to see Jason Corser with his military haircut and big, soulful eyes—the police officer who, for years, hadn't known he was a witch.

I stepped around the counter and hugged him. "It's so good to see you."

"It's great to see you, too, Thea," he replied, pulling away. "But how about nixing the public show of affection? Simon's men might see us."

I nodded knowingly. "Of course."

Now that Jason's mother, Kym, had broken her spell and Jason knew who he was, he was always eager to help. Jason was a full-blooded witch—a "warlock," as the boys called him. I had warned him to steer clear of the ongoing war between Simon and myself, but when Jason walked into the bakery a couple of weeks ago holding orders from Simon, I knew it was too late.

Jason had made a point of tracking down warlocks when he first found out the truth about his origin. The warlocks took Jason to Simon, suggesting that Jason would make a good spy, since few knew who he was. Simon agreed, viewing Jason as untainted and willing to serve.

Simon was not aware of my friendship with Jason.

My father was thrilled to hear of Jason's willingness to play spy for our side; he was relieved to have someone watching out for me during my meetings with Simon. He had even taught Jason some wizard spells. He instructed Jason to use them if he ever witnessed Simon forcing himself on me. Jason had become one of Simon's right-hand men in a short amount of time. It was Jason whom Simon had sent to reveal the times and locations of our meetings. We never met at the same place twice; Simon still didn't trust me.

Kym was furious that Jason had fallen in with Simon and his men. She hated her son having any association with the likes of the vile so-called warlock. I couldn't say I blamed her. I didn't want anyone risking their lives for me. I had enough blood on my hands already.

But Jason wouldn't listen—to anyone. His mother had kept him sheltered and out of danger for so many years that he felt it was his turn to step up. What Jason didn't realize was that it was my father who had warned the witches about Simon. He had advised them all, including Kym, to send their sons away before they were tricked into becoming servants for Simon. My father knew that Simon wouldn't hesitate to kill any and all who refused him.

Jason had the most beautiful blue eyes, and not because he was in love; he'd been born with those eyes.

"Is it safe to talk?" he asked, looking toward the back room.

Jason understood that, aside from my father, no one else in my circle knew about my meetings with Simon.

I nodded. "You know, you don't have to keep doing this."

"Yes, I do." Discreetly he handed me a small slip of paper with an address.

I looked down at the note. "He wants to see me at midnight?"

Midnight was my usual hunting time. Jason often gave me a heads-up on where I could find warlocks. I sighed. If I had to meet Simon so late, I wouldn't get much sleep.

"He's been acting strange," Jason said. "Moody, mostly varying degrees of anger."

"Why don't you just kill him?" Jason asked.

"I can't," I replied. "I have to find the leaves first."

"I haven't seen any leaves, Thea. Maybe he doesn't have them anymore."

If that were the case, I would have dragged Simon to Magia long ago and had Attor break the spell and set me free. I would have long since secured the energy my father needed for restoring his powers.

My father had originally tried to trick me into bringing him the energy so he could transfer Simon's spell onto himself to save me. My father knew the spell would eventually kill me, and Simon, too. But the dragons had given me a way out. We agreed to keep the energy from my father until I brought Simon to them. They would then kill Simon and break the spell, saving me in the process.

The bakery door opened again. Jason straightened and did his best to resemble one of Simon's real underlings. "Hurry up, witch. Get my order."

A voice rang out behind him. "Jason, my son."

Jason's face reddened. "Mother," he said, slowly turning toward the door. "What are you doing here?"

"I had to see you." She stretched out her arms.

As Jason embraced his mother, I saw the anguish on Kym's face. Her curly black hair looked as though it had gone uncombed for weeks. Dark circles lined her eyes. Her cats waited impatiently, as they always did, outside the bakery door. I noticed that her feline brood seemed to have grown exponentially since her last visit.

"Mother, it's not safe for us to be making contact. It's too dangerous."

She stroked his face. "I would face the devil himself for you, my son."

He softened. "Soon, all of this will be over, and we'll be together again. I promise."

Kym shot me a look, her sunken eyes suddenly coming to life. "If he dies, I will never forgive you."

"This wasn't her choice, Mother."

Kym looked at Jason and sighed. "You have your father's blue eyes, and his stubbornness, too." She touched his face again. "I love you," she whispered before quietly slipping back out into the snow.

I watched as the parade of cats followed her. Jason closed his eyes and sighed.

I stepped back behind the counter. "Can't you see what you're doing to her?"

"Can't she see what she did to me?" he replied, opening his eyes.

"She's a mother. It's what any mother would have done."

"I'm not a coward, Thea. I would have fought by your side. All the boys who were sent away feel the same."

"The witches sent you away because Simon would have killed you all. Can't you understand that she was trying to protect you?"

He bowed his head. "He didn't kill your friends."

I stepped out from behind the counter again and approached him. "Simon didn't know who they were. He had no way of knowing they were witches."

"And he knew I was?"

"No, he knew your mother was. That's why he would have killed you all."

When Delia walked in, Jason left without another word.

"Is he still weird about the whole witch thing?" she asked, reaching for an apron.

I ignored her question. "Where have you been?"

"Hiding from Fish."

"He didn't mean any harm, Delia."

"Don't defend him," she said, filling her coffee mug. "He knows how much I hate that witch."

I wanted to ask her what she meant by Cory's girlfriends, but she stormed off to the back, muttering about Fish the entire way.

By closing time, she seemed calmer. Fish never came back to the bakery, but I caught Delia glancing out the front window several times that afternoon. I knew she had hopes that Fish would return and say he was sorry, but that never happened.

At five o'clock, we put on our coats and waved as we ventured out into the bitter cold. "Night, Norm," I said, over my shoulder.

Chapter 3
Déjà Vu

I'd been to see my father many times, but this was the first time Delia had come with me. During the walk from town to my father's place of employment, I had a nagging sense that we'd been on this walk before. It felt eerily familiar to tread this path with her, almost like a dream.

"Whoa," I said, shaking my head.

Delia pulled the collar of her coat tightly around her neck. "What is it?"

"I'm not sure, but I think I'm having déjà vu." I stopped walking. "Did we forget a tart?" I asked.

Delia stopped and turned. "What?"

I inspected my hands. "I have this odd idea that I should be carrying a tart."

Delia began walking again. "Come on, let's keep moving."

Ten minutes later we arrived at the mansion, an old Colonial with divided-light windows. A towering wrought-iron fence teeming with clematis vines surrounded the home. Above the six-car garage hung a sign with the name *Wade* imprinted on it.

I opened the front gate and stepped inside the fence, motioning for Delia to do the same. She followed me around to the back of the house; my father always left the kitchen door unlocked when he knew I was coming. I was taken aback when Delia breezed in as though she'd been there a hundred times. My father stood hunched over the stove, stirring a pot of something that smelled delicious.

"There you are," he said, looking up from his work. His green eyes sparkled when he smiled. His thin nose—a trait he had passed on to me—and salt-and-pepper hair gave him a distinguished look.

"Hello, Father." I wrapped my arms around him. "You look well."

He released me and smiled at Delia. "Young Delia, how go the wedding plans?"

Delia's face fell. "There isn't going to be a wedding."

My father offered her one of the tall stools at the counter and turned back to the stove for the kettle. "No wedding?" he said as he filled the kettle at the sink. "Then why do I still see you dancing in your wedding dress?"

A glimmer of delight passed through Delia's eyes. "There's going to be dancing?"

My father smiled as he drew two teacups from the cupboard.

"William, have you seen my—"

We all turned in unison toward the kitchen doorway. It was him—the man from the forest.

"You," I gasped.

His eyes widened. "Forest girl."

My father set the cups beside the stove. "You two know each other?"

A smile broke across the man's face. "Did you come to thank me properly?"

"I wouldn't have come at all if I'd known you were here."

He laughed.

Delia and my father exchanged puzzled glances.

After an awkward silence, my father stepped forward. "Allow me to introduce my daughter. James, this is Thea. And Thea, this is James Ethan Wade, my employer."

"Your daughter?" James asked. "I never knew you had a daughter."

My father's face reddened. "I'm sure I've mentioned her at least a few times, sir."

James regarded me curiously, took two steps forward, and extended his hand. "Please, call me James." He stole a playful glance at my father. "And I'd like to think that William here thinks of me as a friend and not just his employer."

I looked down at his hand, not bothering to offer my own.

"Thea," my father said, "don't be rude."

James dropped his arm. "You're still angry with me," he said seeming amused. He straightened and smiled that same self-important smile he had displayed earlier in the woods. "The next warlock I come across, I promise to save him for you."

My jaw tightened. This entire encounter was setting me on edge.

My father stepped between us. "I don't understand what's going on here. How do you two know each other?"

James tore his smug gaze away from my icy stare and placed his hand on my father's shoulder. "It's nothing, William. I ran into your daughter at my favorite spot in the woods earlier today, that's all.

There

were a few warlocks giving her a hard time, but lucky for her, I was there."

What did he mean, *his* favorite spot? And why did he smell so odd? If he hadn't annoyed me so much, I would have said that his scent was rather appealing.

"Thank you, master," my father said, giving James a short nod. "I'm sure Thea is more than grateful for your help."

"Thea is not grateful," I said.

When James returned his attention to me, my eyes were drawn to his dark eyebrows, liquid brown eyes, and thick brown hair. He was very tall, and built. I had to admit, he was extremely attractive. But his resemblance to Simon was decidedly unnerving. I hated myself for noticing how good-looking he was.

"Again, I'll take that as a thank-you," James said playfully. He tilted his head. "Hey, don't you work at the bakery?"

"Yes."

He looked at my father. "I'm sorry, William. I never knew she was your daughter. I feel so foolish now."

"It's my fault for not introducing the two of you sooner, master."

"Yes," James muttered, his eyes wandering back to me. "It's a pity." He turned his attention to Delia. "Excited for the big day?"

"There isn't going to be a big day," Delia replied through clenched teeth.

James furrowed his brow. "I don't understand."

"Let me clear it up for you, then." Delia got to her feet and approached James. I feared she might hit him. "When I found out you were bringing your *dog* to my wedding, I called the whole thing off."

"My dog?" he asked, stifling a chuckle. "You mean Helena?"

Delia leaned toward James. "Bow wow."

James stood motionless for a moment before bursting into peals of laughter.

Delia rolled her eyes and crossed her arms, waiting for James to compose himself. "I'm glad this amuses you."

"No, no," he said, waving his hand. "It's just that, well, this is perfect."

Delia drew back. "Perfect?"

"What I mean to say is, I didn't know how to tell Fish that Helena doesn't want to go to your wedding. This is all a huge relief, really."

Delia uncrossed her arms. "So she's not coming?"

"Apparently no one is," he replied. "Didn't you say you called it off?"

When Delia didn't answer, James put his arm around her. "Fish didn't want to be rude, Delia. I'm sure that's the only reason he invited Helena. He was just trying to show his appreciation for my wedding gift."

"Gift?" Delia said, perking up. "What gift?"

He pulled his arm away, suddenly seeming nervous. "I was told you've agreed to a reception, yes?"

"Yes . . . why?"

"Well then, I plan on giving you both the finest reception ever. We can have it here in the ballroom. I'll take care of everything: the food, the wine, the flowers, the music . . . everything your heart desires. It's the least I can do as the best man."

Delia opened her mouth to protest.

James placed his finger in front of her lips. "No arguments. Besides, I've already hired the caterers, ordered the flowers, and booked the musicians. It's a done deal."

When he pulled his finger away, Delia smiled. "Thank you."

James looked at me. "You see, that's how you thank someone."

I stifled an impulse to giggle and instead rolled my eyes.

"How is it that we've never met before?" he asked. Suddenly his smile was less self-important and more dazzling.

"I was just wondering the same—"

"What's the holdup, James?" Cory asked, walking into the kitchen. He froze when he saw me. "I'm sorry, this was an unexpected stop." Although he was looking at me, I sensed his apology was directed at my father.

"You two know each other?" James asked.

Cory put his arm around me. "I should think so," Cory replied. "This is Thea . . . my wife."

"Your wife?" James asked.

"I told you I was married," Cory replied.

James' bewildered stare was starting to make me uncomfortable.

After a moment, he looked at Cory. "Yes, of course."

My father cleared his throat. "You asked about the holdup?"

Cory glanced at James. "Yeah, I was wondering what was taking James so long."

James was staring at Cory's arm. When Cory

noticed this, he kissed me on the head. James took a step forward but quickly caught himself, a confused expression washing over his face.

"I'm sorry," James said. "I'll be outside waiting."

After James left, Cory pulled his arm from my shoulder and told my father he was sorry.

Why is Cory apologizing to my father?

"Cory," my father said. "James is waiting for you."

"Right," Cory replied, pecking my cheek. "See you back at the apartment."

My frustration grew. Even Cory knew James. Everyone, in fact, seemed to know James—everyone except me, that is. James and Cory hung out together. Fish had asked James to be his best man. James was giving Delia the finest wedding reception of all time. Where was I when all these friendships had formed? Either Simon's spell had really done a number on me, or I was losing my mind. But then, James didn't know who I was, either. Could it all just be one huge coincidence?

After Cory walked out, Delia shook her head. "I never knew James could be so funny."

My father nodded. "It's amazing how someone can change when they're not tortured with worry."

"What are you guys talking about?" I asked.

Delia avoided my question and instead asked if I'd mind if she left. When I said no, she quickly went off in search of Fish. The news that Helena wouldn't be attending the wedding had changed Delia's attitude in a hurry.

I claimed her vacated stool. "Father, why do you call James 'master'?"

"Because that's what he is." My father poured a cup of tea and set it in front of me. "Now, drink."

Now that we were alone, I could bring him up to speed on Jason's latest communication. "I'm meeting Simon at midnight tonight."

"Has Simon mentioned the leaves yet?"

"No, Jason suggested that he may not have them anymore. I think I agree with him."

"Rubbish. He has them." He sat next to me and pointed at my cup. "Drink."

I brought the steaming cup to my lips and sipped it carefully.

"How are things going with Cory?" he asked. "I trust he's still staying downstairs?"

"Yup, you know how he is. He says he won't move in with me until I can remember why I fell in love with him. I think it's silly of him."

He nodded, looking relieved. "And that's exactly how it should be. You shouldn't try to rush things, Thea. Respect his wishes and don't push him."

I set down my cup. I really didn't want to talk about my sex life with my father. "Can I ask you something? Does James know you're a wizard?"

"No, he believes I'm just a witch. And I think it's best if you don't use your powers around him; he may grow suspicious."

I don't know why my father would worry about that; I had no plans to be around James again.

"He didn't see anything, Father. He got there before I could strike down the warlocks."

I took another sip and thought of how impossible it seemed that James didn't know what my father was. I sifted through what was left of my memories, but it was no use: I always drew a blank

~ 44 ~

when it came to remembering things about my father.

"What does James say about you never going outside?"

"James does not notice such things." He grinned sheepishly. "After drinking my special tea, that is."

I laughed, bumping his shoulder with my own. "I should have known."

"Where are you meeting Simon?" he asked.

I handed him the note Jason had brought to me. My father always wanted to know when and where I was meeting Simon.

He handed the note back to me. "Does Simon ever ask about your husband?"

"I do my best to avoid the subject," I replied. "He has asked about my bond to Cory, though, always wanting to know if it's been broken yet. Thankfully, he doesn't seem to know that Cory and I have never bonded."

"And you must never tell him." My father's look of grave concern was one I knew well.

"I know. You've told me that many times."

He pointed to the note. "Simon is getting desperate. He's trying a spell, but it's not working."

"Jason said something about him being in a real bad mood lately."

"Jason was right. Simon is furious. And dangerously frustrated."

"What kind of spell is it, Father?"

"It's a changing spell, but not for himself."

"Then for who?"

Without answering, he got up from the counter. "Your cup is empty," he said, heading for the stove. He refilled the cup and set it in front of me. "How have you been feeling?"

"Fine. I just wish I knew where Simon was hiding those leaves. I told Attor, Martin, and Morgan that I would bring them news."

"I'll have orders for them when you go tomorrow."

I kept feeling his eyes on me. He seemed a little unsettled. When I drained my second cup of tea, he again refilled my cup.

I stared down into the steaming liquid. "Are you trying to keep me up?"

"Are you hungry?" he asked, ignoring my question.

"A little, I guess. But I'm leaving soon. I'll make something when I get home."

It took mere moments for my father to set a plate of reheated lasagna in front of me. "Eat."

I looked up at him. "Why are you so pushy today?"

"It's my way of spending more time with you," he said, winking.

I eyed him suspiciously. "I don't buy it, but this smells and looks too good to pass up." I picked up my fork. When I began to eat, he sat next to me again.

"I have a favor to ask. Two, in fact."

"I knew it," I replied, setting down my fork. "I knew you wanted something."

He didn't bother to justify his tactics. "First, on the night before Delia's wedding, I want you to come here and stay with her. The ceremony will be in the garden out back, and James has offered Delia a room so she can get ready here."

I opened my mouth to protest.

He held up his hand. "I'm not finished."

I relented, shoving a forkful of lasagna into my

mouth.

"James has gone to a lot of trouble to make this wedding perfect for Fish and Delia. I won't have it ruined because they're worried about you. I'm asking you to put your personal feelings for James aside so that young Delia may have the wedding of her dreams."

"Why would they be worried about me?"

"Thea, your intense dislike of James is rather obvious."

I couldn't argue with that. "Fine. Next request?"

"I want you to stop hunting warlocks."

I halted my fork halfway to my mouth. "I can't do that."

"Actually, you can. Simon's army has been depleted to the point where they no longer pose an imminent threat." He reached under my chin and turned my head to face him. "I want you to stay out of those woods and focus on finding the leaves."

"Are you sure you don't see Simon's army growing?"

"I'm sure," he said, looking away.

He was lying, of course. My father always looked away from me when he was about to lie. I knew him better than he thought I did.

"I'm not lying," he said. "And thank you for bringing that to my attention."

I closed my eyes in frustration. He could read my mind again. Attor had placed a fireball in my head to protect my thoughts, but it had obviously worn off.

"Not fair," I said. "You keep your mind blocked from me all the time."

"Life is rarely fair, Thea." His green eyes twinkled. "But you'll survive."

He got up and poured himself some tea. "And please try to refrain from being rude to James. He is my employer, after all, and he's been very generous to Fish and Delia."

"I have to be nice to James, too?"

"I'm only asking that you not be rude."

I pushed my plate away. "Anything else?"

He set down his cup and lifted my chin with his finger. "Yes. Do not forget how dangerous it is to lie with your husband. You need to stop goading him. He's a man, and he won't always possess such self-restraint. Until the spell is broken, you will act like a lady."

I bowed my head. He was referring to this morning.

"Be a lady with my own husband," I muttered, shaking my head.

"You can kill him if you'd rather."

I gave him my word and agreed to comply with everything he'd asked of me. It was the least I could do; he had been saying "yes" to me a lot in recent days. He didn't argue when I sent Ciro and his brothers away. He wasn't even putting up a fuss about my meetings with Simon. In the past he would have begged me not to put myself in that kind of danger.

No, my father was being very patient and understanding about my concern for those around me. He understood my determination to keep others from putting themselves in harm's way on my behalf. It was bad enough that I couldn't get Jason to relent. I didn't need to worry about the others, too. One way or another, I was going to do this on my own. I even planned to erase Jason's memory if I couldn't talk him out of what he was doing. He would forgive me one day, after Simon was dead.

I said goodbye to my father and headed for home. I was delighted when the snow started falling again. So much snow was unusual this early in the year, but I welcomed it. I took my time, allowing the soft flakes to hit my face as I walked. Two blocks from my apartment, a black sedan pulled up beside me. Its dark, tinted windows made it impossible to see inside.

The back door opened and Jason stepped out, looking nervous. "Simon wants to see you, witch."

I glanced into the car and spotted a warlock sitting in the back. "The note said midnight," I said, looking back at Jason.

"I'm not here to answer questions," Jason replied.

He was trying to tell me something. I watched him carefully, trying to read his expression.

I kept my voice low. "Is everything okay?"

"Just get in!" the warlock inside the car shouted.

Without looking away, Jason discreetly opened his coat to reveal two odd-looking guns, each tucked into its own holster. "Don't worry about it, witch. Just get in the car."

I tore my eyes away from his and climbed into the backseat between Jason and the other warlock. The warlock driving the car kept watching me in the rearview mirror. I didn't recognize these warlocks. They were bigger than most, and said nothing during the entire ride. The tension rose as we continued deep into the woods. I'd never been through this part of Salem before. These particular back roads were mostly used by hunters.

The car pulled onto a long, winding driveway.

As we rounded the second turn, a ranch-style house came into view. It looked like a normal home, complete with two lawn chairs left sitting in the yard, covered in snow. When the driver stopped the car, the warlock sitting to my right yanked me from the backseat and practically dragged me up the walk.

Jason stepped between us. "Simon said not to hurt her."

The warlock glared at Jason. "Don't defend this witch."

The warlock had the most unusual gray eyes and a shaved head, making him more intimidating than the others I'd come across. His hand hovered over a large dagger secured to his belt.

"Simon is waiting," Jason said, taking my arm.

"What does he want?" I whispered.

Jason kept his eyes straight ahead. "I don't know."

Chapter 4
The Spoiled Ginger Root

Simon walked into the living room, which was lit only by the fire, and stood facing the hearth, his hands clasped behind him. He said nothing as he stared into the flames. The hiking boots and torn jeans he wore were out of character for him, to say the least. Simon was usually dressed impeccably, and always in dark colors. The room was devoid of furniture, save for a single chair sitting in the center, draped with something I couldn't make out.

"Leave us," Simon ordered over his shoulder.

I gave Jason a subtle nod, letting him know I was okay. He glanced toward Simon and stepped onto the front porch with the other warlocks. Simon remained facing away, his gaze locked on the fire as I approached him from behind. He seemed deep in thought. I glanced at the chair. I could see now that a shawl had been thrown over it. It looked handmade.

Simon turned to face me. "I have a gift for you."

Once again I was stunned by the resemblance between Simon and James. Simon had darker eyes—almost black. But he had the same thick, dark eyebrows and the same golden smile. He was easily as tall as James, and just as handsome.

"A gift?"

He drew the shawl from the chair and wrapped it around my shoulders. "I hope you like it."

Before I could thank him, I began to feel weak. I tried to remove the shawl, but my hands were useless. I couldn't move my arms.

Simon laughed. "Did you really think it was going to be that easy?"

I tried with all my strength to raise my arms, but they wouldn't move. When my legs began to give out beneath me, Simon swept me up and set me in the chair.

He looked down and smiled. "A wonderful thing, those leaves." He began pacing the room while I continued trying to free myself.

"It's pointless," he said.

Panic rose inside me. "Why are you doing this?"

"I want to see how good an actress you are."

"What are you talking about?"

He stopped in front of me. "Where have my men gone? What have you been doing to them?"

My stomach lurched. He knew I'd been hunting them.

"Where is my army, witch?"

Now I was confused. I hadn't killed that many of Simon's men—ten at most. "I don't know."

Again he paced the floor. "Tell me: Why have you tampered with your memory?"

I stared at him, confused.

"Did you think I wouldn't find out?"

I glanced down at my useless hands, trying to make sense of his accusations. "I haven't a clue what you're talking about, Simon."

"Is that so?" He stopped pacing and leaned over me. "I've been watching you, witch. Did you think I'd believe that you would do anything for me?"

I lifted my head to meet his icy gaze. "I *would* do anything for you," I lied.

"And yet you order your friends to hunt my men. You tamper with your memory to hide things from me."

"I hide nothing from you, my lord. And I haven't instructed anyone to hunt your men."

"Do you think me stupid, witch?"

I drew a deep breath and exhaled. "No."

"Did you think I wouldn't find out?"

"Find what out?" Annoyance was starting to replace the panic.

"Why doesn't he remember you?" He weaved his finger through a lock of my hair and yanked. "What is he hiding?"

"I don't know what you're talking about."

"Why can't *you* remember him?" he shouted.

"Remember who, my lord?"

His slap came down hard on my cheek. I'd barely had a chance to recover when Simon wrapped my hair around his hand and yanked my head back, making me look at him. "Does your bond to him really break when he gets married?"

"When who gets married?"

Another slap. "Do you remember telling me that you put a spell on your husband, that if I hurt him in any way, I would die?"

"Yes."

He leaned closer, his face inches from mine. "Then tell me, who is your husband?"

~ 53 ~

"Simon, why would you—"

His fingers curled around my neck. "What is his name?"

I swallowed hard. "Cory."

He straightened and turned toward the fireplace. "Bring him in."

I scanned the room, my heart racing. I fought in vain against the shawl's power. My arms wouldn't budge. I stopped trying when two warlocks entered the room, dragging Fish in with them. He'd been beaten badly. His face was covered in blood, and welts lined his back. They threw Fish at my feet and pushed him down on his knees.

"H . . . hey, Thea," Fish said, trying to keep himself upright. "Fancy meeting you here."

"Let him go!" I ordered.

Simon turned, a self-satisfied smile on his face.

I glared at him. "If you kill him, I won't stop until you're dead. I don't care if I die with you."

"That's all very well and good, my dear. But have you forgotten? My spell prevents you from hurting me in any way."

Fish doubled over, his hands holding his ribs.

Tears welled in my eyes. "Are you okay?"

"Never better," Fish replied, coughing. "Me and the guys here were just playing a little game of marbles."

I looked again to Simon. "I'll do anything you want. Please, just let him go."

"I'm afraid I can't do that," Simon replied, walking toward me. "You see, you've done something with your memory, and I need to know why." He plucked a single strand of hair from my head, met my eyes, and smiled. "I told you I've been watching you."

~ 54 ~

He caressed my face. "I don't know if you remember this, but I sent a warlock to look for Delia. I knew you would find him, and I knew you would teach me something new. All I had to do was sit back and watch." He looked down at Fish.

"Don't you touch him," I hissed.

He sniffed and examined the strand of hair. "Now how does this work? Oh yes, I remember." He held it to my mouth. "Spit," he ordered.

When I turned away, Simon kicked Fish in the face. I closed my eyes, and tears rolled down my cheeks. Again he held the strand to my mouth. "Spit, or I will cut off his leg . . . and I won't stop there."

I glanced at Fish, who nodded slightly. I obeyed Simon's order. The hair came to life, twisting and squirming. Simon held the strand to Fish's nose. Fish turned his head away, but one of Simon's minions seized Fish's jaw and turned him to face Simon.

Fish moaned as the snake-like hair slithered into his nose. His head twitched several times. When his eyes opened, they were red. The enchanted strand was strangling the part of Fish's brain that was capable of lying. He was now at Simon's mercy. The warlocks sat him up and stepped back.

A wicked smile spread across Simon's face. "Hello, Cory."

Why does Simon think that Fish is Cory?

Fish looked up at him. "Hello, scumbag."

"Do you know who I am?" Simon asked.

"Yeah, you're the asshole."

Simon ignored his comment. "I need you to answer some questions for me, Cory."

"They call me Fish."

"Very well . . . Fish. Are you Thea's husband?"

~ 55 ~

Fish wiped the blood from his mouth. "Do I look like her husband?"

"Well, no. But why would Thea think you're her husband?"

"I don't know," Fish replied, squinting up at Simon. "Maybe she's confused."

"Do you know who her husband is?"

"Yeah, he's a buddy of mine."

Simon gestured to me. "And does he know who she is?"

Fish hesitated, glancing nervously in my direction.

"I have all day," Simon whispered.

"He kind of knows her."

"What does that mean, young man?"

Fish closed his eyes. He was trying hard to fight the effects of the enchanted hair.

"Cut off his leg!" Simon ordered his men.

"No!" I screamed. I looked down at Fish. "Answer him."

"I can't, Thea."

"Please, Fish."

Fish sighed. "He just met her. He doesn't know Thea is his wife."

I looked at Fish, confused. *How is he able to lie?*

"I see," Simon said. "And why did Thea erase all trace of him in her mind? Does he know something she wishes to hide from me?"

Fish bowed his head and gripped his side.

Simon stepped behind me and held a knife against my throat. "Answer me!"

"I'm sorry, Thea," Fish said, looking beyond me to Simon. "He doesn't know anything. Thea wanted to kill him, you know, because of your spell. But the spell was working both ways. He began to hate her, too. When his love for her was gone, he would die. So she erased herself from his life and gave him to Helena. It was the only way to keep his heart loving, the only way to stop the spell from affecting him."

Simon slowly pulled the knife away from my neck. "The spell was working both ways?"

"Yeah," Fish replied. "He wanted to kill her, too."

"That's very interesting. And why did she choose to forget him?"

"Because it would kill her to watch him marry Helena."

I couldn't tear my eyes away from Fish. Somewhere in my mind, I knew he was telling Simon the truth.

Fish stared back, regret in his eyes. "I'm so sorry, Thea."

I was still absorbing the shock. "W . . . what are you talking about?"

"James is your real husband."

"But how . . ." I turned away and gazed into the fire.

Simon cupped my chin and tilted my head to face him. "Trust me, James is your husband." He turned to Fish. "Young man, if I were to kill James, what would happen to me?"

Fish stared at Simon, his face solemn. "You'd die."

Simon's face went pale. When he had composed himself, he asked, "What else do you know?"

"She no longer wants to kill James, but only

because she can't remember who he is. Your spell is still intact, in that it's making her love you and compels her to do your bidding." Fish coughed, and a trickle of blood escaped his lips. "She'd do anything to protect you."

"Well then," Simon said, "there's some good news." He stroked my face. "And here I thought she was pretending."

I shrank away from his touch. What kind of mess had I made here? Had I somehow placed my loved ones in danger again?

"Tell me something," Simon said, kneeling beside Fish. "If she would do anything for me, why has she ordered you to hunt my men?"

Fish stared him down. "I don't know what you're talking about."

Simon eyed Fish suspiciously and stood.

I thought of Cory and how he was pretending to be my husband. Why would I ask that of him? How could I have asked my friends to live a lie?

Simon squatted down in front of me. "So you erased him because of heartbreak." He brushed the hair from my face. "I can live with that."

When I looked into Simon's eyes, I saw James staring back at me. "Are you James' father?"

"Yes, my angel."

I turned away, thoughts spinning in my head.

Simon got to his feet and looked down at Fish. "If you're not helping Thea, then who is?"

My heart sank. I willed Fish not to mention my father.

"She won't accept any help," Fish answered. "She insists on doing this alone."

"So she's not lying to me," Simon said, mostly

to himself.

A sense of relief washed over me. I closed my eyes and leaned my head back on the chair.

"Do you know if it's true that Thea's bond to James will break when he gets married?"

Fish shook his head. "I don't know anything about that."

"And the wedding is still on?" Simon asked.

"Well, there's a little problem with Helena, but I'm working on it."

I bit my lip; Fish assumed Simon was asking about his wedding.

Simon smiled. "Perhaps I should let you live, then. We can't have the happy couple arguing and calling off the wedding, can we?"

Fish formed his mouth into something resembling a sarcastic grin. "Thanks."

Simon was clearly pleased with Fish's answers to his questions. He knelt down in front of me and stroked my face. "I'm sorry, but I had to be sure you weren't lying to me."

"Please don't hurt him," I said, tears streaming down my face. "Let him go, Simon. Please let him go. I'm begging you."

He reached for my hand and held it to his lips. "Anything for my angel." He kissed my hand.

"Simon, please don't kill him."

He wiped my tears. "Come now, didn't I just say I would do anything for my angel?"

I held his gaze. "I want to see him walk out of here."

Simon stood. "So be it." He called for Jason and the others, who appeared in the room seconds later. To Jason he said, "Find out who is killing the men, and bring the scoundrel to me."

Jason nodded and glanced at Fish.

"Wait for me outside," Simon added.

After Jason left, Simon directed his attention to the two warlocks towering over Fish. "Do with him what you will, but don't kill him. I've given my word to my princess."

"Simon, please don't do this!" I cried.

Simon smiled his wicked smile. "I said I wouldn't kill him. I never said I wouldn't hurt him."

I tried kicking my way out of the shawl. "Please, I beg you!"

He looked away and waved over his shoulder to his men. "Just cut out his tongue or something."

"No!" I screamed. "You can't!"

He opened the front door and walked out.

"Simon!"

When he was gone, a warlock pulled out a dagger and leaned down.

"No!" I screamed, trying to free myself.

Fish tried to drag himself toward me.

"Where you going?" one of them said as they grabbed his legs and yanked him back.

"Leave him alone!" I shouted.

The smaller of the warlocks pulled out a flask and poured the contents down Fish's throat. A moment later, Fish began to shake violently, and his eyes rolled to the back of his head. When his head hit the floor, I screamed.

The chair scraped the floor as I tried to free myself. "I'm going to kill you both!"

They lifted Fish's head. "Open wide," the bald one said, holding up his dagger.

Fish slowly raised a finger and pointed to me.

The warlocks looked my way, expressions of shock washing over their faces.

I looked down to see what they were looking at. Fish's hook sat poised on the shawl. With one quick yank from Fish, the enchanted garment slipped from my body. I sprang to my feet and waved my hand, sending both warlocks flying across the room and into the wall. When I waved my hand again, their tongues flew from their mouths and landed on the floor. With one last wave, their skin soon followed.

I kicked down the front door and searched the area. No cars—for the moment, anyway. But my senses told me more warlocks were on the way. I'd have to act fast. I ran back to Fish, who was writhing on the floor.

I dropped to my knees and felt his forehead. "You're burning up." I placed my hands on his chest. "Heal."

"Still there," he said, twisting in pain.

I waved my hand, but Fish's pain seemed only to worsen. He grasped at his stomach and groaned. *Why isn't he healing?* I pulled out my father's wand. I had to get Fish out of here.

I was trying to drag him onto the stick when I felt something cold and hard on the back of my head.

"Move and I'll shoot." Another of Simon's underlings.

Unable to wave my hand, I willed my mind to do the job. But it was no use; I was too worried about Fish to focus. A car screeched to a halt in the driveway.

Jason's voice boomed as he stormed into the house. "What's going on in here?"

"That was fast," the warlock with the gun said.

Jason batted the gun away from my head. "I came back as soon as I could." I turned to see him removing several strange-looking guns from the bag that hung over his shoulder.

"What are those?" the warlock asked.

Jason answered his question by aiming one of the guns at the warlock and sending out two spells. The warlock flew across the room, where his skin cracked and peeled away from his frame. He screamed in pain until he was nothing but a small pile of dust on the floor.

I went back to Fish and continued struggling to drag him onto the stick.

Jason came to my side and pulled Fish's body onto the stick with relative ease. "What happened to him?"

"They gave him something; he's not healing." I positioned myself behind Fish's body. "Go tell Cory and the others to meet me at my father's house."

I flew through the night like a bullet. There was no time to think about what had happened. Fish didn't look very good at all. When I arrived at the mansion less than a minute later, I kicked open the back door and dragged Fish into the kitchen.

"Father!"

My father burst in and spotted Fish on the floor. "What happened?" He dropped down beside Fish and waved his hand.

"They made him drink something," I explained. "He's not healing."

He opened Fish's mouth and sniffed. "Poison."

Panic gripped me. "What can we do?"

"Nothing," my father replied, "until the poison is out." He turned Fish onto his side and wedged his fingers into Fish's throat until he gagged and threw up.

"Very good," my father said. "Keep it going, son. Get out as much as you can."

I was crazy with worry. I tried again to heal him, trembling as I waved my hand. "It's not working."

"What's going on?" James asked as he appeared in the kitchen doorway. He ran to Fish's side. "What happened to him?"

"James," my father said, "call Cory and tell him to locate the witch Donna. We need some spoiled ginger root."

James pulled out his phone and did as my father asked. "I don't know," he said into the phone. "A lot." He set the phone on the kitchen floor, looked down at Fish, and chanted a healing spell.

"I'm afraid that won't work," my father said. "I can still smell the poison."

"Poison?" James asked. "Who poisoned him?"

My father didn't answer. Again he shoved his finger down Fish's throat, but this time, Fish didn't respond.

"Fish!" I placed my hands on his chest. "Heal!" I chanted over and over.

My father turned Fish onto his back, and I gasped. He was turning blue.

As my father pumped his chest, James pushed me aside and breathed into Fish's mouth. "Breathe, damn it!" James yelled.

Panic flooded every part of me as they worked on him. When Fish finally gasped for air, I could smell the poison. I tried again to heal him, but without success.

The kitchen door slammed open. "Fish!" Delia

screamed. She dropped to her knees, grabbed his shoulders, and shook him. "Don't you dare die on me!"

Cory arrived seconds later, practically dragging Donna behind him.

"Give me the bottle," my father ordered, holding out his hand.

Donna stepped forward and handed him the remedy. "You'll have to remove his clothes."

My father uncorked the bottle, poured it down Fish's throat, and closed his mouth. He looked up at Donna. "He's been poisoned."

She nodded. "I assumed as much." Donna knelt beside Fish and began pulling off his clothes. "He'll need some fresh air."

My father reached for Delia's hand and placed it under Fish's head. He stepped away from the back door as Cory opened it wide.

"Help me drag him outside," Donna ordered.

I was in awe of Donna's composure. The tall, blond, gentle witch worked quickly. She had a special talent for healing. Although her spells and potions didn't work on me, my father was obviously confident that she could help Fish.

James and Cory reached their arms under Fish and carried him onto the back patio.

"When he starts throwing up," Donna instructed, "blow as much air as you can at him."

"What's that going to do?" Cory asked.

"The ginger will make him sweat, and the poison will exit through his pores. We'll need to blow it away before it can find its way back in."

Cory snatched up my stick and tossed it to me. He glanced at James, who was eyeing the stick with obvious curiosity.

He returned his attention to me. "Go."

I resumed my earlier position at the back while Cory and James draped Fish's body over the front of the stick. He convulsed as the poison began to make its way out.

"Go!" Delia screamed.

I took to the sky and flew toward the ocean. Fish writhed in pain as the grayish-green poison oozed from his skin. When the wind hit him, the toxic liquid turned to vapor and drifted into the air. As we neared the water, Fish moaned and threw up again.

I ran my hand along his back. "It's going to be okay, Fish. Just hang in there."

I flew fast over the ocean, unworried about Fish falling. As long as he was touching me, he would remain glued to the stick. When the cool ocean air hit his face, his color returned. The seeping green poison had dissolved completely. I waved my hand, but my ability to heal him remained hampered.

After Fish threw up one last time, I headed back. As we approached the mansion, our loved ones came into view. Javier and Joshua had arrived to join the others. Cory paced on the patio. Poor Delia sobbed in James' arms. She pushed away when I landed and rolled Fish gently over onto the snow.

"Fish!" she screamed, running to him.

After a careful and thorough examination, Donna wrapped Fish in a blanket. "He's going to be okay. We should get him inside."

A loud sob escaped Delia's lips as she wrapped her arms around her beloved. Cory and Joshua lifted him from the ground and carried him into the living room.

When everyone had gone inside, I took to the sky again. Simon had given me his word that he wouldn't kill Fish, and I wouldn't give him another chance to harm someone I loved.

Simon would answer for this.

Chapter 5
Time to Wake Up

The wizard in me rose to the surface, and my heightened senses zeroed in on Simon's location. I lamented my inability to maintain this amplified sense of magical power; it seemed only to arise during times of extreme rage. Once calm, my lesser witch senses would return. Thankfully, in this case, my rage was only just beginning.

As I flew through the night, I debated my options. I thought about killing Simon, but first I needed to free my father. If those leaves were indeed the only thing weakening my father's power, I would find and destroy them. Once that was done, I would take pleasure in slashing Simon's throat.

I had no intention of taking Simon to Magia now. He had harmed someone I loved. I couldn't allow him to go on manipulating the situation and torturing the very people willing to protect me at the expense of their own lives. I would have to find a way to end this. Simon would die, and I would die with him. My loved ones would be free at last, and the trouble I'd caused them would die with me.

My heart pounded as I approached a house in the center of town, not far from the Salem Witch Museum. I knew the house well and had walked by it many times on my way to the bakery. I presumed it to be owned by the elderly man who sat on its front porch most mornings of the week, no matter how cold or how hot.

I glided over the porch and burst through the front door. Simon jumped to his feet, as did the two warlocks he'd been sitting with. The stick transformed into a sword, which I held to Simon's throat. He stumbled back onto a sofa and warned his men to stay back. His spell was working hard to stop me, and it pained me to fight against it. But Simon's magic was no match for my wizard power. My rage, now at its zenith, was running the show.

"How did you find me?" Simon asked.

I pushed the sword against his skin. "I always know where you are, scum."

He swallowed hard, looking down at the blade.

I fought the urge to pull the sword away. Part of me longed to protect him, but the wizard part of me wanted him dead. "Give me one good reason why I shouldn't kill you."

"I thought you loved me, my angel."

I made a small incision above his collarbone and squeezed the sword reflexively when my own neck suffered the pain. "I said I loved you. I never said I wouldn't hurt you."

His men brandished their weapons.

"Stop, you fools," Simon shouted.

My neck throbbed. Each time I pressed the sword against Simon's throat, the pain immediately transferred to me. Now I knew: I would feel every agonizing slash I rendered to Simon.

I didn't care. I would gladly suffer whatever pain came my way if it meant I could save my loved ones from Simon's wrath.

Masking the pain as best I could, I pushed the blade further into Simon's skin. "Why did you lie to me?"

"What did I lie about?" Simon asked, his breath coming in short gasps.

His men moved closer at the sight of blood trickling down Simon's neck.

I positioned the sword at the base of his throat. "You poisoned him," I hissed.

The fear in Simon's eyes revealed his true nature. He wasn't the arrogant master he made himself out to be, but merely a coward willing to sacrifice the lives of many for his own pleasure.

Fighting against the pain, I stared into Simon's dark eyes. "If you touch any of them again, I will hunt you down and burn you." The tip of the sword sank into his neck, sending a jolt of searing pain through my own neck.

Simon's eyes darted to the sword. "I thought you loved me."

I etched the tip of the sword along the side of his face. "I love them more," I growled.

His men stepped closer.

"Move again, and he dies," I said, my eyes never leaving Simon.

Simon's eyes widened in terror. "Listen to her, you fools." Sweat dripped down his face, mixing with the blood already drying on his neck.

I held my sword at the ready. "If I find one hair on any of their heads out of place, I will hunt you down like an animal." I pushed the sword into his neck just below the right ear. "Do you understand?"

A thick stream of blood trickled from the wound. I drew a deep breath, absorbing the pain. Simon seemed not to notice the pain this was causing me, somehow unaware of the far-reaching effects of his own spell. If I hadn't hurt him, I wouldn't have known myself.

"If you kill me, you die, too," he reminded me.

I sniffed. "Does it look like I care?"

"I'll make you a deal," he offered.

I ran the tip of the blade along the opening of his ear. "No deals."

He closed his eyes. "Very well. I'll leave them alone."

"And why should I believe you?"

His eyes shot sideways toward the sword. "Because I'm convinced now that you would kill me, even if it meant that you'd go with me."

I pulled the sword away, and Simon sighed in relief.

"This is between you and me, Simon. I'll do whatever you want, but leave them out of it."

He rubbed his neck with his hand. "Between you and me."

I waved the sword at the warlocks. "That goes for your men, too."

Simon nodded. "I'll keep my word, witch. Besides, I have no use for your friends."

I turned to leave.

"Wait," he called.

I stopped without bothering to turn around.

"Tell me something: Why didn't my spell stop you?"

"I already told you," I said over my shoulder. "Because I love them more."

"I'll take that into consideration, witch."

I stepped over what was left of the door and took to the sky. I rubbed my neck, trying to soothe the stinging pain. The guilt I felt for what had happened to Fish was still very much with me. No amount of threatening Simon could take that away. How could I have erased James from my life and presumed to keep it from Simon? Fish never would have gotten hurt if not for my foolish choice—a choice I planned to fix.

All was quiet when I arrived back at the mansion. I entered through the back door to the kitchen, hoping to find my father. I was also hoping to avoid James; I wasn't ready to deal with all that yet. I was still processing the fact that he was my husband. For one thing, he didn't seem like the kind of man who would look twice at someone like me.

I was nothing like Helena. She was tall, slender, and elegant. I wasn't exactly short, but Helena towered over me. Her silky blond hair cascaded gracefully over her shoulders, and her speaking voice sounded like a choir of angels compared to mine.

I looked down at my clothes—old, loose, dark. My hands showed the telltale signs of having fought one battle after another. Helena's, of course, were soft and smooth. My nails were short and jagged from years of biting them, while Helena's were long and manicured. My face was plain and simple, while Helena's was stunning and flawless.

It wasn't hard to guess why I had chosen her for James. He must have wanted her at some point. He must have realized what a mistake he'd made in choosing me. What other reason would I have for wanting her by his side?

"You're back." It was James.

I gasped and stepped back. "Y . . . you scared me."

"I scared you?" James asked, raising an eyebrow. "I'm not the one who can fly."

I bit my lip and looked away.

He crossed his arms. "I'm not sure what to make of you, forest girl."

"How is Fish?" I asked, hoping to change the subject.

"He's resting upstairs. Delia and the others are with him." He paused. "Where did you learn the flying spell?"

I could barely bring myself to look at him. But I could feel his eyes on me, intense and unyielding. "I don't remember."

"What happened with Fish today?"

I looked past him to the door. "Can I go up and see him?"

"Who poisoned him?" James asked, stepping toward me.

I finally willed myself to meet his penetrating gaze. "Can I go up or not?"

His liquid brown eyes stared down, as if he could see right through me. He truly was a beautiful man. With sweat beading up on my forehead, I made for the kitchen door.

He grabbed my arm. "Why do you hate me?"

I struggled in his grasp. "Let go of me."

"What did I ever do to you?"

I closed my eyes as his sweet scent hit my face. His touch sent my heart racing. I could see now why I'd fallen in love with him.

He loosened his grip, and I slipped my arm away. "Nothing."

"Do you not like meeting new friends?" he asked.

I looked back into his dark, soulful eyes. I wanted badly to touch him. He seemed almost like a dream. I felt like nothing standing next to him. What could he have possibly seen in me?

"I have plenty of friends already," I replied.

"So you won't consider me for a friend?" He leaned toward me.

My face suddenly felt warm. "No," I said, walking out.

I hurried through the foyer and up the stairs, wondering what to do about Cory. He deserved to be happy—they all did. Now, more than ever, I accepted that killing Simon was the only way to make things right. The only thing standing in the way was finding the leaves that would set my father free.

At the top of the stairs I paused. There were so many rooms; I hadn't a clue which one Fish had been taken to. I knew where my father's room was because I'd been there many times. It was there that I would put on his ring and travel to Magia.

"Delia?" I called down the hall.

The third door on the right opened, and Joshua popped his head out. "Over here."

When I walked into the room, my father was examining Fish. His eyes were still closed. My heart sank. I suddenly found it difficult to breathe. His boyish face had an angelic quality. Delia sat at the end of the bed, tears rolling down her cheeks. Cory looked strained, and seemed to be going out of his way to avoid eye contact with me.

I approached the bed. "Is he okay?"

My father nodded. "He's sleeping."

Donna walked in with a stack of towels. "Everyone out," she ordered. "I'm going to treat those welts on his back. It seems my magic is working very slow on him. I think it's the effects of the poison."

"Why doesn't he open his eyes?" Delia asked.

My father placed his hand on her shoulder. "He's exhausted, young Delia. He needs to rest."

Try as I might to get Cory's attention, he still refused to look at me.

"Thea," my father said, "we'll give you a moment with him before Donna begins."

I nodded, and the others filed out of the room. As Cory passed, I reached for his hand, but he shook me off. What had I done? The possibilities began to spin in my mind, but I quickly shut them down. This was no time for my own problems. I set my worries aside for the time being and sat beside the now peaceful-looking Fish.

My father, who hadn't left the room, pulled up a chair next to the bed and sat.

"They're gone, Fish," he said.

Fish's eyes popped open. "Man, I thought they'd never leave."

I nearly slipped from my place on the bed. "Fish, you're awake!"

"Take it out, Thea," Fish said, sitting up.

"What?"

"The hair—take it out. It's still in there working its magic, and I don't think I need to explain why that's a problem."

"He would have found out anyway, Fish," my father said.

I drew my hand to my heart. "Cory. That's why."

Fish nodded. "He knows everything. I managed to spill the beans and let the cat out of the bag in one fell swoop."

"I can explain everything to you," my father said, placing his hand on my shoulder.

I gave him an angry look. "You don't have to. I don't care."

My father eyed me. "I see."

Fish reached for my hand. "I'm so sorry, Thea. I didn't mean to tell you about James."

I ran the back of my hand gently across his cheek. "Close your eyes."

Fish did as I asked. I tapped his nose with my index finger and called for the strand. He moaned as it slid out of his nose. My father snatched it and quickly took a match to it before dropping it into an empty teacup sitting on his desk.

Fish leaned back and opened his eyes. "It's out?"

My father smiled. "It's out."

A look of worry crossed his face. "Is my brain dead now?"

My father chuckled. "Your brain is fine. What little damage was done will heal itself in time, thanks to Donna's remedies."

Fish leaned back, sighing in relief. He looked at me. "Are you mad?"

I rolled my eyes and wrapped my arms around him. "Don't be stupid."

Fish pulled away. "I'm just glad he didn't go after Delia."

I brushed my fingers along his face. "You won't have to worry about that anymore. I'm going to take care of things."

"What are you going to do?" he asked. "About James, I mean?"

I looked down at my lap. "Nothing. He's found his place with Helena."

"No, he hasn't," Fish said seeming upset. "I know things are a mess right now, but you and James belong together. You can't give up on him."

"I don't even know him, Fish. I'm not giving up anything."

Fish looked at my father. "You can't let this happen. We have to tell her the truth."

I gently pushed Fish back onto his pillow. "You need to calm down. You're still recovering."

"No," Fish said, batting my arms away. "This isn't James' fault. You cast the spell, the one that erased you from his memory. He never wanted to be with Helena. That was all your doing."

"What does that matter?" I replied. "What's done is done."

Fish shook his head. "It doesn't work that way."

I could feel my father's eyes on me, but I didn't care. What could he do? He had no power to stop me. He was imprisoned in this house. I no longer cared that he could read my mind and would find out I was planning to kill Simon.

"I see," my father said again.

I ignored his comment and kept my attention on Fish. "Why did Simon think you were Cory?"

Fish threw up his arms and slammed his back against the headboard. "I was on my way to ask Helena if she would mind bowing out of going to the wedding—Delia was so pissed. As I was leaving Helena's house, two guys approached me and asked if I was Cory. I wanted to know what they were up to, so I said 'yes.' After that, things get a little hazy."

My father leaned forward. "And why did you tell Simon he would die if he killed James? Thea never told anyone about that lie."

Fish looked from me to my father. "He *would* die. Because if he ever hurt James, I would kill him."

I couldn't help but giggle.

Before my father could question Fish further, Delia walked into the room. When she saw that Fish was awake, she nearly knocked me out of the way to get to him. I stood and stepped back, smiling at their happy reunion.

My father got up and quietly left the room.

When Donna returned and asked me to leave, I decided to go down the hall to my father's room, where I knew he'd be waiting. Cory was leaning against the wall outside Fish's room. Tension hung in the air as our eyes locked. When Cory cast his eyes to the floor and headed for the stairs, I took a deep breath and kept walking.

A variety of unusual items filled my father's room: jars of multicolored seeds, dried leaves clipped to strings that hung from one side of the room to the other, an ancient spell book with a torn cover lying open on the table in the center of the room.

My father stood facing the opposite wall. "We need to talk."

I already knew what he was going to say.

"I'm sorry, Father, but my mind is made up."

"I get no say at all?"

"There's nothing to say."

"I thought as much."

He sighed and turned to face me. He held a tiny, luminous, sparkling gem in the palm of his hand. I swear I spotted miniature clouds floating inside it.

"I've made many mistakes," he began, turning the stone in his hand while looking into my eyes. "But the biggest was erasing James from your life. I wiped clean the one thing that kept you strong, the one thing that kept you fighting. At the time, I thought it was the right thing to do. I couldn't stand to see you suffering, and I gave in to your pain." He paused, taking a deep breath. "I'm done sparing your feelings."

"Good, then we have nothing to—"

"I lied to you. I told you that it was Simon who cast the love spell on James." He drew another deep breath and exhaled. "But it was me."

I stared at him, mystified. "Father, what are you saying?"

"I was trying to keep his heart loving, trying to keep him alive. What I didn't realize at the time was that James never would have stopped loving you." He bowed his head. "I see that now."

"I don't understand what you're trying to tell me."

"I'd always told James you would cast that spell and make him forget you. He refused to believe me. He believed in you completely. He said your love for him would stop you from casting the spell. But I knew your love for him would make you do it. I didn't have enough faith in him to allow him to do things his way—a mistake I don't plan to make twice."

I crossed my arms. "What are you going to do?"

He gazed at the stone in his hand. "Something I should have done a long time ago. I have to learn to look the other way, to allow you your own failures and triumphs. I instructed James to do the same, but it was I who fell victim to your suffering."

"But I'm not in pain, Father. You don't have to worry about that anymore."

"You're also not in love," he replied. "And love is a powerful weapon, more powerful than any spell I know. James had faith in your love, but I doubted him. I should have listened to him, and trusted him."

I opened my mouth to speak, but he continued.

"I thought you had discovered the wizard part of you, Thea. I was wrong. You can't access it completely, not without James. A heart without love is an empty shell." He lifted his head and stared deeply into my eyes. "You will lose yourself to Simon without your love for James."

I was starting to feel nervous about my father's intentions for that stone. "Why are you telling me this?"

He turned the gem in his hand. "It's time for me to turn the other way. The only way for you to fight is through pain. You need to suffer in order to find what makes you strong. I wanted to spare you that, but I see now that it's the only way. I can't show you the way. No one can. Only your mistakes have the power to do that."

I stared back at him, incredulous. "I'm sorry you have regrets, Father. But I won't let you trick me. I'm not taking that stone from you."

He smiled again. "You won't have to."

Before I could reply, he tossed the stone to me. I couldn't fight the instinct to reach up and catch it. When he waved his hand, clouds flew out from the stone. As more and more clouds escaped and were reclaimed by my memory, a searing pain grew in my heart. It was like a bad dream. I remembered everything. I clutched at my chest as though my heart were dying all over again.

Darkness filled my head, and I dropped to the floor.

Memories swarmed in my head as I lay with my cheek on the floorboards. I kept my eyes tightly closed as my life with James flowed back into my mind. I saw myself casting Attor's spell on him.

I heard his voice begging me to stop. "Please don't do this to us!"

I seized my chest again, this time from pure elation. My heart was broken, yes. But I could feel it again. The black hole had vanished. The emptiness that had plagued me dissolved. I felt more alive than I had in my whole life.

Tears of joy streamed down my face. *James.*

My father crossed the room to the door. "You're on your own now, Thea. I'm not going to interfere with your decisions, and you will have to fix your own mistakes."

I was tempted to yell at him, but I knew he'd done the right thing. I was glad to feel my pain, the pain of loving James. I wouldn't trade my memories of our marriage for anything. A broken heart had made me beg my father to erase James from my life. Now I wanted nothing more than to remember James always.

My father turned the knob and paused. "You have a choice to make: die and save your friends, or live and save the world." He slammed the door behind him.

I lay on the floor, unable or unwilling to get up. I held my hand over my heart as the tears flowed freely. What had possessed me to believe my life would be happier without my memories of James? For that matter, how could I have thought that erasing myself from James' memory would give him a better life, with Helena of all people?

I pulled myself up from the floor and drew a ragged breath, nervous about leaving the safety of my father's room. What was I going to do? I couldn't just run to James and tell him who he was or, for that matter, what I was. He wouldn't remember me, and he'd probably think I was crazy.

My father's words reverberated in my head: "Die and save your friends, or live and save the world."

The words struck a nerve. My father wouldn't have said them if they didn't hold meaning. This was much bigger than I had imagined. I knew in my gut that killing Simon was the wrong thing to do. My father was right; I had to stop thinking foolishly and concentrate on what I had to do.

My thoughts drifted back to James. *What did you do, Thea?*

I couldn't let him marry that witch, but how was I going to stop it? Why her, of all people? I had to find some way to fix this. If James couldn't remember me and instead fell in love with someone else, I could live with that. But I couldn't let him marry Helena. She would never love James the way he deserved; she was too busy loving herself.

I inched slowly toward the door, taking one deep breath after another. I couldn't undo what I had done, but I would find a way to make things right.

Chapter 6
My Brother, My Friend

I opened the door of my father's room and stepped out into the hall, feeling stronger and better able to face up to my mistakes and do what was necessary to set things right. First and foremost, I had to find Cory. I needed to tell him that my father had restored my memories of James. There were no words good enough to thank Cory for what he'd been willing to do. But it was time to let him go. I was never going to make him happy or love him the way he deserved.

My love for Cory was real, but I understood now that it was not the kind of love Cory needed from me. I could never love him the way I loved James. I could never give myself to him the way I had to James. I had leaned on Cory so much, but it was time for me to lean on myself and allow him to move on and find his own happiness.

I found him—not surprisingly—in Fish's room. What I hadn't counted on was that James would be there. I feared that his presence would bring forth a rush of anger, but thankfully that didn't happen. Instead, I felt calm. There was no rage like before. Simon's spell seemed not to be working, and I couldn't understand it.

Fish had fallen asleep and was resting peacefully. Delia sat on the bed with Fish's hand in her own. So much had happened in such a short space of time that our ordeal with Simon and his men seemed far in the past.

Cory sat in the chair next to the bed as James talked to Delia.

I knocked quietly on the door frame. "May I come in?"

When Delia turned to me, her expression changed from one of surprise into something I couldn't decipher. Cory also gave me a strange look when he looked at my hair. I remained in the doorway, growing more and more uncomfortable.

Delia stood and faced me, looking as though she might lay into me. I braced myself to absorb her wrath. In a second's time, she closed the distance between us and threw her arms around me. "Thank you, old friend!"

I sighed in relief and hugged her tightly. "Is he okay?"

She pulled away, nodding. Her joyful tears flowed freely. "He's going to be fine."

I glanced at James, who quickly shifted his eyes to avoid mine. I recalled our earlier discussion, in which I'd been impossibly rude. I thought of Simon's spell and prepared for the inevitable onslaught of murderous rage.

James headed for the door. "I'll give you all a moment alone."

"No, wait," I said.

He stopped and looked down at me, his brown eyes catching me off guard. I hesitated and searched for the right words.

"Yes?" he asked. "Did you want something?"

"I'm sorry . . . about before. When I was rude to you. I was just upset."

He smiled. "There's no need to apologize. I understand."

His eyes drifted to my hair, and a confused look appeared on his face. He glanced at Cory before walking out. Delia squeezed my hand and looked sympathetically in Cory's direction before reclaiming her seat at Fish's side. Cory was still refusing to look at me, but we had to talk. It was time.

I approached him cautiously. "Would you mind taking me home?"

Without bothering to look up, he nodded. "I just need a quick word with William first."

After Cory stood and left the room, I pulled the chair closer to Delia and took a seat. Delia's gaze remained fixed on her beloved as a seemingly endless supply of tears flowed from her eyes.

I reached for her hand. "He's going to be okay."

"Look what they did to him," she replied.

I looked at Fish and wondered why Delia hadn't chanted a spell to make his wounds disappear. Whip marks lined his shoulders. His cheek was bruised from where Simon had kicked him.

"How do you do it?" Delia asked.

"Do what?"

"Simon. He's done so much to you, tortured you like an animal. How do you hold back? How do you keep from killing him?"

I sighed, and my gaze moved to the window. "His day will come."

"Fish told me what happened after Simon sent the hair into his brain. It must have been hard for you, learning the truth that way."

I leaned back on the chair. "Not half as hard as learning the rest of the story."

She tore her eyes away from Fish and studied my face. "Your father broke his spell?"

"Yes."

"Does Cory know yet?"

I glanced toward the door. "I think he's about to find out."

"As difficult as that conversation is going to be," she said, returning her gaze to Fish, "it's time."

I nodded. There was no disputing this. "Are you going to be okay?"

Tears welled in her eyes. She shook her head. "Forgive me, Thea."

"Forgive you? For what?"

"I understand now why you did all those things to save James." She brushed her hand across Fish's cheek. "I would have made a deal with the devil himself if it meant saving this man. I've never felt that way about anyone in my life—except maybe you, that is." She grasped my hand. "I thought I would die if I lost him tonight. I promise never to judge you again."

I squeezed her hand. "Thankfully you didn't need to make that deal with the devil." I looked lovingly at Fish, "because he's going to be just fine."

"He'd better be, because I'm going to kill him when he wakes up."

"Why would he tell those warlocks that he was Cory?" she asked.

"You know about that?"

"Fish told me. Cory too."

I was relieved not to have to relive the ordeal.

"Can I ask you something?" Delia said.

"I suppose."

"Why'd you pick her? What in the world possessed you to hand James over to a conceited, self-absorbed witch like Helena?"

I looked away. I didn't want to tell Delia how I felt. I didn't want her to know that I was well aware that I'd made the biggest mistake of my life. Worse, that it was probably too late to do anything about it. The deed was all but done.

The door opened before I could answer. "May I come in?" James asked.

I felt my face flush. "Please, of course," I said, getting to my feet.

"I wanted to offer you and Cory a room for the night," James said. "You're more than welcome to stay. I can have William prepare a room for you."

Delia grabbed my hand. "Please stay."

"I don't know," I said, glancing at James. I knew it wasn't a good idea. I wasn't sure why Simon's spell wasn't affecting me. I was also fully aware that Simon was watching me, and I was wary of giving him any reason to bother James.

"It was just a suggestion," James said.

I smiled. "Thank you for such a generous offer. But we'll be going home."

Cory walked in with Joshua and Javier in tow.

"You ready?" Cory asked, his voice cold.

I nodded and thanked James again. His scent brushed against my face as I passed him. It was as sweet as I remembered.

"I'm not working tomorrow," Delia said over her shoulder.

"I assumed as much. I'll come by after work to check on Fish."

Joshua approached me. "Would you mind if Javier and I stayed here for the night?"

"James offered us the guest house," Javier added.

I gave Joshua a hug. "Of course. You should stay and be here for Fish, and for Delia." I followed Cory out of the room.

Out in the hall, Cory asked, "Did you want to stay?"

I shook my head. "I want to go home."

"With me?"

"Do you want me to walk home?"

"You know what I mean, Thea."

Our eyes met. "Let's not do this here, Cory. Let's go home and talk."

The bitterly cold night air blew against my face on the way to Cory's truck. Even after he turned up the heater, I sat shivering in the passenger seat. I couldn't wait to get home and wrap myself in a blanket. The temperature seemed to have dropped another ten degrees.

I gazed out the window. "Do you think it's going to snow again?"

"Are we really going to talk about the weather?"

"My father told you."

"Yes, and I don't care."

I looked at him. "But I do."

"This doesn't change things, Thea. I still love you."

"He's my husband, Cory. I will never love you the way you deserve."

"I'm not asking you to."

I didn't know what to say. I wasn't expecting him to say that. I bit my lip when we got stuck behind a snow plow. I couldn't get home fast enough.

"Just answer me this," Cory said, frustration in his voice. "Did you ever truly love me?"

"Yes, but not like I love James."

"Does this mean you're going to tell him he's your husband?"

"Maybe. I don't know. He probably wouldn't believe me anyway."

Cory shook his head. "And where does that leave me?"

I wanted to tell him that I still wanted him by my side, just not the way he wanted. I reached across the seat and placed my hand over his. "The day my father erased James from my life, I didn't realize he'd asked you to pretend to be my husband. I never would have allowed it if I'd known. I've taken so much from you already. I'm not going to lie and say we'll be together someday."

"Your father didn't ask me. I asked him."

I pulled my hand back. "But the day my father erased James from my memory, I heard you telling him that you would do everything he asked of you."

He gave me a nervous glance. "He asked me not to bond with you. He told me that if you truly fell in love with me, he wouldn't stand in the way. He knew the chance he was taking by sending you with me, but he couldn't bear to see you suffer."

I bowed my head. "I'm so sorry."

When we arrived in front of the apartment building, Cory threw the truck in park and let out a big sigh. After a moment, he finally spoke. "Look, Thea, you don't have to decide now. Just think it over. Maybe after James' wedding you'll feel differently."

I shot him a look, got out of the truck, and slammed the door. I hurried up onto the porch and into the building, and began climbing the stairs to the third floor.

On the second-floor landing, Cory caught up to me and grasped my hand. "Why are you getting mad? Isn't this what you wanted? Are you not the one who chose Helena? No one forced you to do what you did, Thea."

"I made a mistake!" I said, yanking my hand away.

"A mistake you can't change."

"What if I can?" I continued up the stairs and down the hall.

Cory followed me to my apartment door. "Didn't your father explain it to you?" He looked deeply into my eyes. "James is never going to remember you."

I shoved my key in the lock. Cory grabbed me from behind and pulled me to him. There was anger in his eyes. "I regret the day we sat up in that tree together. The day you told me you once loved me." He pushed me away. "Why in the hell would you say that to me?"

Without waiting for an answer, he stormed back

down the stairs and out of the building. I entered my apartment, hurried to the window, and watched as he drove away.

A shiver ran through me. I turned up the thermostat and wrapped a blanket around me while I waited for the heat to kick in. The drafty old building was having a hard time keeping pace with the cold temperatures outside. I didn't bother to turn on the lights. I sat on the couch in the dark and thought about Cory, of all he'd been willing to risk for a chance at love with me. What a mess I had made of things. What was wrong with me that I repeatedly hurt the ones I loved? I wanted to cry, but the tears wouldn't come. A numbness settled over me. I felt only guilt and emptiness. I'd never felt more alone.

What if I'd lost my dearest friend in the world? Cory meant more to me than I could ever adequately express to him. His friendship had seen me through countless dark days. I hated myself for hurting him like this, but living a lie would be worse. I thought back to when we were kids; Cory had practically lived at our house. I thought of his big white smile shining from his dirty little face.

Cory's parents had been killed by warlocks. The circumstances were still horrifying to recall. Cory's father had been dragged through the forest for falling in love with a human. They had burned his mother alive. Sharron had taken Cory in and given him a home when no one else would. He had regularly bounced between our house and Sharron's. Together, we had become the family he needed.

After Cory grew into a man and took in the rest of the boys, they too had become part of the family. They were the unwanted half-human witches no one respected, much less loved, and they soon had become the most important people in my world. After I taught them a few spells, the other witches had begun to accept them. They blended in with the others in the community and didn't feel so out of place.

Those were happy days—some of the best in my life.

I sat up when I heard keys jingling in the hall. I hurried to the door and flung it open. There he stood, key poised where the lock had just been.

Cory bowed his head. "I'm so sorry."

I threw my arms around him. "I don't want to lose you, Cory."

"Not a chance of that," he said, squeezing me tightly.

I took his face in my hands. "Your friendship is the most important thing in the world to me. You're my family. I would die if I lost you."

"You'll never lose me, Thea."

I buried my face in his chest. "I wish I could love you the way you love me. Sometimes I wish I could rip James out of my heart and make you happy."

I felt his fingers in my hair. "Yeah, good luck with that."

I looked up at him. "I never wanted to hurt you."

"I'm not suffering like you think I am, Thea," he said, pulling away.

I looked at him, confused.

He closed the door and sat down on the couch. "Come here," he said, patting the cushion next to him. "Sit next to me."

I sat beside him, waiting for his explanation.

"Remember when we were kids?"

"I was just thinking about that, actually."

"Back then, I loved you like a sister."

"I remember," I said, smiling. "We were joined at the hip."

Cory chuckled and draped his arm around my shoulder. "As we got older, my love for you grew into romantic love. But I still remember the brotherly love. It's still in my heart. My heart was free back then, and I think it's time I set it free again."

"I'm not sure I'm following you."

"When I became friends with James, I stepped aside. I let go of the dream of being with you. And I was actually pretty happy. But when you told me you had once loved me, too, I allowed myself to dream again." He looked into my eyes. "It was a mistake. I should have never begged your father to let me play the part of your husband."

I stared at him, unsure how to respond.

He sighed. "It's never going to be me, Thea. It's always going to be him." He tousled my hair. "I mean, look at you."

My hand drifted to my head. When had my hair become so tangled and knotted again? So that's what everyone was staring at. A troubling thought appeared in my mind. "You're not leaving, are you?"

Cory smiled. "No, but I am letting go. I did a lot of thinking tonight, and the thing is, I don't love you the way James does, and I don't think I ever could. For one, I would have never waited so long for you. So you see, I'm not the suffering soul you think I've been."

He drew a deep breath and exhaled. "There have been other women, lots of them. You know I've dated human girls before, and . . . well, I never stopped dating them. I never stopped looking for the warmth of a woman."

My eyes grew wide.

He leaned back. "Just the other day I was with a human girl. Her lips were sweet, her bed warm. I didn't think of you once. I actually felt happy for a change. I have no love for her, but her touch made me feel like a man again."

I looked down into my lap. "I see."

He lifted my chin. "I want you to know that if you'd fallen in love with me, I would have walked away from that life in a heartbeat. But somewhere inside myself, I knew that was never going to happen. And if I'm being honest, I'm pretty sure I could be happy with someone else."

"If you had so many other engaging options, why were you waiting for me?"

He stared up at the ceiling. "I asked myself that same question earlier tonight. I love you, no question about it. But I can also see that my love for you doesn't compare to how James loved you." He leaned forward, resting his elbows on his knees, and looked back at me. "I have loved you for so long that it never occurred to me till now to stop and analyze my feelings. But when I did, I realized that although I do love you—very much—your ambivalent feelings toward me through the years have slowly diminished the intensity of that love, the romantic part of it, anyway."

As he spoke, his eyes began to change color, from blue to gray to hazel.

He reached for my hands. "I don't love you like I thought I did, Thea."

I enjoyed a short wave of relief before a

disconcerting thought occurred to me. "You're not just saying this to give me an easy out, are you?"

He shook his head. "No. But to be honest, I didn't believe it myself until just now."

I leaned forward until our foreheads met. "Are you going to be okay?"

"As much as I hate to admit it, Fish was right. If I loved you so much, I wouldn't have kept up my"—he cleared his throat—"*friendships* with the other women."

I drew back. "Fish knew?"

He nodded. "Fish, Javier, Josh, even Delia. You remember her comment to Fish about giving him one of my girlfriends."

I closed my eyes and sighed. I felt better knowing that Cory hadn't been lonely during our time together, and I appreciated that he had finally been honest with me.

"How about us?" I asked. "Are we going to be okay?"

"We're going to be fine. In fact, I feel better now than I have in months."

I opened my eyes. "You know what? Me, too."

We shared a laugh and hugged.

"So you remember everything, huh?" Cory asked, pulling away.

I nodded, looking down at my hands. "I really screwed things up this time, Cory."

"What are you going to do?"

I leaned back on the couch, blowing a tangled wisp of hair off my forehead. "I haven't got a clue."

Chapter 7
War Zone

A knock at the door woke me in the morning. I had fallen asleep in Cory's arms. As I carefully lifted his arm and crawled out of his embrace, his eyes flickered open.

He stretched his arms above his head. "What time is it?"

"Not sure," I replied, shuffling toward the door. "But someone just knocked."

"Probably the guys," Cory said, yawning.

On the other side of the door was Jason, looking extremely nervous.

"Hey, Jason," Cory said. "What are you doing here so early?"

Jason kept his eyes fixed on me. "I need a word with Thea."

Bad news.

"You're in luck," Cory said, getting to his feet. "I'm heading down to grab a shower." He kissed my cheek. "After I clean up, I'll go and check on Fish."

I thanked him and watched as he walked down the stairs. He seemed normal, chipper even. My heart swelled. I had my friend back. Things between us were going to be okay.

"What happened to your hair?" Jason asked.

I tore my eyes from the stairs. "Oh, it's nothing. What's going on?"

"He wants to see you—now."

My stomach lurched. "What does he want?"

"Don't know," Jason replied, checking his watch. "But he's ecstatically happy."

"Happy?" My apprehension escalated. "What did he say?"

"He said something about finally understanding the spell."

"The spell?" I dragged Jason inside and closed the door. "What did you see?"

He shrugged. "Not much. When I arrived, I overheard what I just told you. When he noticed I was in the room, he shut up fast and told me to come and get you. He was practically beaming."

I bit my lip, trying to imagine what horrible thing Simon was up to this time. "You have no idea what spell he was talking about?"

"I don't know, Thea. But there are about fifty warlocks waiting there with him."

I mulled over my options. I had to get word to my father. I opened the door and called down the stairs to Cory.

"What do you want me to do?" Jason asked.

"Nothing." I reached for the pen and pad by the phone. "Just keep your eyes and ears open."

"What's up?" Cory asked from the doorway.

I kept my voice calm and relaxed. "Would you mind giving a note to my father when you check on Fish?"

"Sure thing."

I hurriedly scribbled down what Jason had told me and sealed the note in an envelope.

"Everything okay?" Cory asked.

"Everything's fine," I replied. "Oh, would you also mind calling Vera and asking her to work for me? She'll know what to do."

Cory eyed me suspiciously. "And you're not going in because . . ."

"I'm going to help Jason talk to his mother," I lied.

His eyes darted from Jason to me. "You're sure you're okay?"

"I'm fine, Cory." I smiled, rubbing his arm. "Really."

After Cory left, I changed clothes and tucked my father's wand safely into its place in the inside pocket of my jacket. I snatched his ring from my nightstand and slipped it into the pocket of my jeans. As I passed the mirror on my way out of the bedroom, I stopped. I waved my hand and watched as my tangled mass of hair reclaimed its previously straight, silky appearance.

I met Jason at the front door. "If you see Simon set down anything next to me, pull it away."

"Like what?"

"Anything at all, anything that arouses your suspicion—and anything that doesn't, for that matter."

We drove to the same house in the woods, which I thought was strange. Simon had never met me in the same place twice. About fifteen cars were parked outside. Simon stood on the lawn, waiting, surrounded by his men. He wore a scarf around his neck, no doubt trying to hide what I had done to him.

"There's my angel," he said as I stepped out of

the car. Like the night before, he wore jeans. He extended his arms toward me. "Come, my dearest."

I didn't know what to make of him wrapping his arms around me. I pulled away. "I'm not falling for your tricks, Simon."

He threw back his head and laughed.

"Come now," he said, draping his arm around my shoulder. "Do you see me holding anything?"

He guided me toward the porch. His men parted, making a path for us. His good mood was unsettling. Yesterday I'd almost killed the man, and today he was acting as though none of it had ever happened. When Simon stopped short of going into the house, I grew anxious. On the porch, he took a seat on an aging and creaky rocking chair. Several of his men had followed us and stood just inches behind me.

Simon smiled and rocked in the chair.

I threw a glance over my shoulder. "Tell your men to get back."

"Do they make you nervous?"

I waved my hand and sent his men flying into the woods. "No."

He smiled. "You never cease to amaze me, witch. You've never shown fear. No matter how many men you face, you stand like a warrior." The chair creaked each time Simon rocked forward. He smiled wider. "I can only dream of what else you can do."

"What do you want, Simon?"

"Are you still angry with me?" His voice was sickeningly sweet, mocking.

My blood boiled. "Do you want to find out?"

He stopped rocking, and his smile evaporated. "Now don't be upset, my angel. I just wanted to check something."

"Yeah, and what's that?"

He slowly rose from the chair, which let out one last grating screech before coming to a halt. "You gave me a lot to think about last night, witch." His hand drifted to his neck. "You made it clear what I've been doing wrong."

I was becoming impatient. "What are you talking about, Simon?"

"You said you loved them more." He walked toward me and stopped about a foot away. "The night of the Halloween Ball, your friends tried to kill me. But you fought like a warrior . . . for me. You took down everyone who came within five feet of me." He closed the gap between us and caressed my cheek. "That night, you loved me more.

I leaned away. "What are you getting at?"

He didn't answer. His eyes drifted above my head, and he yelled for one of his men. The warlock with the gray eyes walked up onto the porch. A sinister smile broke across Simon's face as he stepped back and ordered, "Hit me."

Panic flooded me. The mere thought of the warlock hurting Simon sent a sharp, searing pain through my heart. I jumped in front of Simon and faced the warlock. When the warlock reached around me and attempted to strike Simon, I kicked him in the stomach and sent him flying off the porch.

Simon called to the remaining warlocks on the lawn: "Attack me!"

Try as I might, I couldn't fight the urge to protect Simon. I waved my hand repeatedly, sending one warlock after another soaring toward the surrounding woods. As more and more warlocks ran at him, I bounded off the porch, keeping Simon safely behind me.

"Kill me!" Simon shouted at his men. He was enjoying himself immensely, practically giddy with delight.

A force had risen inside me that I couldn't control. I waved my hand at the ground and sent hard clumps of dirt pummeling the warlocks. Jason was nearly killed while jumping out of the way of the rising earth.

Simon burst into peals of laughter.

I spun around. "Are you hurt, my lord?"

His arms encircled my waist. "It seems I've found your weakness, my sweet."

Self-hatred consumed me. Bile rose in my throat. His spell seemed to have grown more powerful than before. I had no will of my own—at least, not when Simon was in danger. What was I going to do?

I locked my eyes onto his. "What have you done to me?"

He grinned. "Just making sure you love *me* more."

His eyes were so tender, I thought he might kiss me. I was startled when he pushed me away.

He walked to the front door. "Come inside."

His men walked close behind as I followed him into the house.

"Leave us," Simon said over his shoulder.

I glanced nervously at Jason as Simon closed the door. The chair that had occupied the middle of the room the night before had been replaced by a table.

While Simon strolled to the fireplace, I tried to make sense of what I was feeling. The spell had paralyzed me with the fear of Simon getting hurt. I couldn't access any of my power, save for the strength

I used to defend Simon.

The spell had become more powerful than my ability to fight it, more powerful than me. Worse, Simon's little experiment had intensified my romantic feelings for him, making me want him more.

Simon turned, beckoning me with his finger. "Come."

I walked across the room slowly, stopping only when I could feel his breath on my face. My heart started racing. I hated myself for wanting him right now.

"I'm very angry with you," he said, stroking my face. "You nearly killed me last night."

I was losing myself in his eyes. "You hurt someone I loved, my lord. I couldn't stop myself."

"Do you love me?"

From somewhere inside, the real Thea screamed, *No!* But Simon's spell had trapped her beneath the surface. I fought back tears. "Yes, I love you."

He stared without blinking into my eyes. "Prove it."

I fought against my own will as I pressed my body to his and kissed him.

Simon moaned. "Love me, witch."

He crushed his lips to mine again, and our kiss grew more passionate. He clutched the back of my neck as if he couldn't get close enough. I struggled to breathe as his tongue explored every part of my mouth. When I tried to pull back, he forced my lips to his.

My body warmed with desire. I ran my fingers through his hair as his hands traveled my body. In my head, I screamed at myself to stop before it was too late. It was clear the spell was more powerful than me.

"Thea," Simon whispered.

All my efforts to fight Simon's spell ceased when he whispered my name. Our lips never parted as he gathered me in his arms and walked to one of the bedrooms. Simon laid me on the bed and stepped back, unbuttoning his shirt. He tossed it aside, followed by the scarf, and climbed on top of me.

His lips felt like an angel caressing my neck. I closed my eyes and gave in, knowing all the while that I was about to bond myself to a monster. I knew my life was over now.

He began pulling off my jacket. "My love," he whispered into my ear.

My eyes shot open. A wave of my hand sent Simon soaring across the room and into the opposite wall. I leapt off the bed and made for the door.

"I'll kill myself!" he shouted, picking himself up off the floor.

I stopped dead in my tracks, as though I'd slammed into an imaginary brick wall. The thought of him hurting himself froze me. Breathless, I turned to him, fighting the urge to run back into his arms.

He pulled a dagger from his belt and held it to his neck. "Get back on that bed."

My breathing became more labored as I fought the power of the spell. I kept my eyes on the dagger, desperate to save Simon from himself. I had to get out of here.

Simon's eyes lit up. "You're not bonded anymore, are you?"

I was out of breath as he inched closer.

"You want me, don't you?" he said, the knife still pointed at his neck.

"Don't," I pleaded. "Please!"

With his other hand, he pointed. "Get back into that bed."

Frozen halfway between the bed and the door, I searched for some part of me strong enough to fight the spell. I thought of my father's wand. I would use it to fly out of here. With what little strength I had left, I slipped my hand into my pocket and felt his ring instead. I quickly pulled it out and slipped it onto my finger.

"No!"

The sound of Simon's anguished protest faded as I spiraled into the vortex toward Magia. I slapped my hands to my head, horrified by what I'd been about to do. I had been so confident in my ability to fight Simon's spell.

I thought how Simon had spoken the words— James' words—that had snapped me back to reality. My father was right; my love for James made me strong. Simon's poor choice of words had saved me from a life of misery. I heard James' voice in my head. "My love . . ."

When I felt earth under my feet, I opened my eyes. I was in Attor's cave. I breathed deeply, feeling more myself. The cave seemed different somehow. I searched for any sign of Attor, but the cave was empty. I ventured outside and gasped.

Magia looked like a war zone. The trees that had once radiated beauty had been destroyed, as though someone had set fire to them. When the light dimmed, I looked up; Magia's unusual sun appeared to be losing its power. The water in the lake beside Attor's cave was no longer crystal clear, but murky and full of sludge. Curiously, or perhaps not, the forest—the one that had once made me so weak—

remained untouched. Not a single tree or even a leaf had been damaged.

Suddenly my problems seemed small and insignificant. Something was terribly wrong here. I reached inside my coat for my father's wand and gasped as something seized my shoulders and lifted me into the air.

"Don't scream, witch."

Attor. A wave of relief washed over me.

I craned my neck but couldn't catch a glimpse of him. Though I could feel his talons gripping my shoulders, I couldn't see them. A strange sensation tingled through my body. I looked down at my hands but couldn't see them. A quick scan of my body revealed that it, too, had become invisible.

"Hold on," Attor said, soaring over a mountain.

My mouth fell open when I spotted the waterfall. Its sparkles of light ceased to exist; the water that had once cascaded over giant boulders had slowed to barely a trickle. The river below was as muddy and silt-filled as the lake by the cave. The flowers had withered and died on their stems. Everything looked dead. The grass looked dried and burned. My heart sank. What was happening here? Was Magia dying?

Attor flew to a part of my father's world I'd never seen before. Trees towered over the area, clearly unaffected by whatever had destroyed the rest of Magia. Here, the forest was still dense and green. Mountains constructed of strange-looking stone—full of holes, like hundreds of little caves—surrounded the forest.

A voice came from out of nowhere. "Don't panic, Princess."

My eyes darted to my right. "Who's there?"

"I'm concealing you from the wizards."

"Martin?"

"Yes, it's me. But you must stay silent, Your Highness. Do not speak a word until it's safe to do so."

Attor silently glided over another mountain and toward a forest. Then hundreds of wizards came into view, hovering in the air at the forest's edge. I realized that we were going to sneak by them. I held my breath as Attor sailed by Wendell, whose eyes, which were darker than I remembered, remained fixed on the forest ahead. He hovered from side to side.

"Even if a bird flies by," he shouted to the others, "kill it!"

"Are we to kill everything in Magia?" one of them shouted back.

"There will be no Magia if we don't find them!" Wendell replied.

Attor was searching for an opening in the miles-long queue of wizards along the forest's perimeter when he flapped his wings, catching the attention of Wendell. The wizard's eyes narrowed, and a moment later, he locked onto Attor's position and threw a spell.

A loud gasp of pain escaped Attor's lips.

"There!" Wendell shouted, pointing. "Throw your spells there!"

A deafening horn sounded, followed by hundreds of dragons dashing out from the trees and taking to the sky. Attor flew through a wall of fire with the wizards on his tail. I waved my hand and sent spells in every direction. My mouth dropped open when the giant trees came to life. One reached for the wizards, and began picking them off.

One wizard was knocked off his staff when the tree-like giant simply slapped him away. Another giant caught the falling wizard in midair. Cries of pain sounded through the area as the giant clutched the wizard in his hand until he aged into an old man. When the old wizard died, the giant hurled him to the ground and reached up for another.

When Wendell gave the order to abort, the wizards retreated to an area well behind the forest's borders and remained there as we continued on. Leaving them behind, Attor flew to the other side of the strange-looking mountain. I wondered why the wizards didn't follow us.

"We're almost there, Your Highness," Martin whispered.

The forest grew more and more lush, each cluster of trees more beautiful than the last. I could see nothing below.

When Attor began his descent, he drew his talons up and held me close to his massive body. "Look out for branches," he warned.

I remained in awe of the giant, towering trees. Nearly every inch of forest floor was consumed by their massive trunks. A single leaf could cover my entire body. Their odd scent wafted around me, making me feel pleasantly drowsy. A tingly sensation trickled from my head to my feet. I looked down, now able to see Attor's talons around me. My hands slowly reappeared.

"Are you okay, Your Highness?"

Martin materialized at my right, wounded and bleeding. Holding his chest, he managed a weak smile.

I reached toward him. "Can you get any closer? I'll heal you."

He looked about to fall from his staff when Katu flew overhead and seized him. Martin's staff plummeted to the ground as he passed out.

"Martin!" I shouted.

Attor darted among the trees as if soaring through the open sky. How he was able to use his wings among the dense trees baffled me. He tilted left and then right. Next to the trees, Attor looked no bigger than a small bird. I glanced toward Katu, relieved to see Martin coming to. He was still holding his chest while Katu aided him with spells.

The sound of a waterfall redirected my attention ahead. As we emerged into a small clearing among the trees, I saw it—not big, but breathtaking. Lush green foliage encircled the cave-like rocks, from which sparkling flowers bloomed. A small, crystal-clear river came into view, by which Morgan stood, waving. Sparkles of light danced above the water. As Attor prepared to land, the sparkles didn't fly away, but hovered over the river. I could just make out their tiny wings flapping. It was like a cloud of hummingbirds.

After setting me down on the riverbank, Attor staggered and stumbled to the ground.

"Are you alright?" I screamed.

His breathing slowed. I examined his body, looking for evidence of a spell, and found a gaping wound at the base of his neck. Attor was bleeding out. I heard Katu land but kept my attention on Attor. I placed my hands on his neck and chanted: "Heal."

Katu brushed me aside with his wing, then stooped and licked Attor's wound, chanting words I didn't understand. Meanwhile, Morgan was already working on Martin. I trembled as I pressed my cheek to Attor's chest. I prayed for a heartbeat, for any sign of life.

Attor's wing enfolded me. "Are you hurt?"

My head slowly rose from Attor's chest. I looked to Katu, who gave a quick nod and stepped back.

"Oh Attor, I thought you were dead."

"Shut up, witch. I'm fine now."

I could hear the other dragons rejoicing as Attor labored to his feet. I spun to check on Martin, who was standing behind me, grinning. I scrambled to my feet and threw my arms around him. "You're okay?"

"I'm fine, Your Highness."

"What has happened to Magia?"

Martin's smile disappeared when he looked into my eyes. After a few long moments, he shook his head. "Don't surrender yourself to him, Thea."

I stepped back. Martin knew; he saw it in my eyes. I looked away, ashamed of the coward I'd been. I wanted to keep him from finding out just how far I'd let things go with Simon. I'd been so confident until now that Simon's spell was waning. My anger for James had seemingly dissipated. I'd been able to hold my romantic feelings for Simon at bay. Now I had to accept that the spell was stronger than ever, that it had been strengthened by Simon's little experiment.

"You are half wizard, Your Highness," Martin said. "Fear and doubt do not grow in the hearts of wizards. We are not made that way. No spell can control who you are. Don't you know, Thea, that only you have power over your heart?"

I lowered my head. There was nothing to say in my defense.

Martin lifted my chin. "Shame is connected to fear. Wizards bow their heads to no one." He smiled. "Not even to other wizards."

"But the spell is too strong."

"You are stronger."

I wanted to be as confident in my abilities as Martin was. His shining eyes exuded confidence, just like my father's. He wore his bravery like a badge of honor. Nothing scared him. I felt like that sometimes, but only when my heart was filled with rage.

"I don't think I can fight it."

"The witch in you is vulnerable, yes. But the wizard part of you can fight this, Thea. Simon has no defense against that."

Why couldn't they understand? I barely knew the witch part of me, much less my wizard side. I didn't want to talk about it anymore. "What's happened to Magia?" I asked again, hoping to redirect our conversation. "Why does it look like a battlefield?"

Martin remained silent, fury burning in his eyes. He was clearly worried.

"It's Wendell," Attor replied on Martin's behalf. "He's keeping the Secret River of Life covered with spells. They know we're trying to send Xander the energy; they cast spells on the river to prevent us from getting to it. The fools don't even realize they're killing Magia."

"What do you mean?" I asked. "How could they not know, not see?"

Martin finally spoke. "A few weeks ago," he explained, "we noticed that the sun was losing its power and the plant life had begun dying off. It was then that we realized what Wendell was doing. Curiously, he doesn't seem to realize that he's killing everything that lives. For all we know, Wendell thinks we're to blame."

"What about this place?" I asked, looking around. "Why isn't it dying?"

Martin pointed toward the fluttering lights hovering about the river. "The fairies are keeping it alive."

The fairies' sparkling lights had changed in just the few minutes since we'd arrived. They were no longer changing color; they looked tired and weak. "They're using all their magical energy just to keep this place alive."

Martin nodded, a sad smile tugging at his mouth.

"And the wizards," I said, "why didn't they follow us here?"

Martin smiled. "Because of the Onfroi."

"Onfroi?" I asked. "What's—"

An unfamiliar voice cut me off mid-sentence. "Is this the girl?"

Martin and Morgan dropped to one knee. Attor bowed his head. "Your Majesty," they said in unison.

Behind me stood a striking girl with shining green hair the color of the forest, eyes like perfectly shaped pink sapphires, and flawless milky-white skin. Crystal-like wings fanned out from her back like a peacock's. She appeared to be no older than a teenager.

A soft glow radiated from her as she smiled.

"Rise." Her voice was almost musical.

Martin rose and quickly stepped to my side. "Thea, this is Levora, queen of the Fairies." He reached behind me and placed his hands on my shoulders. "Levora, this is Thea, Xander's daughter."

Levora stared deeply into my eyes, lifted her hand, and then brushed her silky-smooth hand across my cheek. I was stunned by her magnificence. She was the most beautiful creature I'd ever seen.

"You have your father's eyes, child," she said. "I wonder if you have his wisdom, as well."

My eyes widened. "You know my father?"

She smiled, pulling her hand away. "Xander is a very dear friend to me." She looked down at my father's ring and extended her hand. "May I?"

When I placed my hand on hers, she closed her eyes and covered the ring with her other hand. An angelic smile broke across her face. "It's true," she whispered. "Our king is alive, held prisoner by a spell." She opened her eyes and smiled. "You don't know about the spell, do you?"

My heart skipped a beat. "What spell?"

"I see." She glanced at Attor.

My eyes darted from Attor to Levora. What were they keeping from me?

Martin approached the queen. "She hasn't found the leaves yet."

Her eyes met mine again. "You can't find them?"

I cast my eyes to the ground. "I haven't been able to find out where Simon is keeping them." I looked up, allowing Levora to see my shame.

Her eyes drifted skyward. "Perhaps Peter can help us."

Chapter 8
The Onfroi

The ground shook violently, and I stumbled
back. One of the tree-like giants walked toward us
holding Martin's staff, which looked no bigger than a
toothpick in the beast's gargantuan hand. He stood at
least fifty feet tall and had arms like branches. Leaves
covered most of his body. I spotted a pair of eyes
carved deep into his bark-like skin. Human-like skin
covered his forearms, and though his hands were
covered in bark, his palms also appeared human-like.
That same earlier feeling of pleasant drowsiness
returned as he neared.

The giant stooped and presented the staff to
Martin, who cautiously retrieved it. I flashed back to
the memory of the wizard growing old in the giant's
hand.

"Peter," Levora said, stepping forward, "this is
Thea, Xander's daughter."

The giant studied me closely, his golden-brown
eyes warm and friendly. He smiled and reached toward
me.

Martin swiftly seized my arm and yanked me
back. His head shot up. "Make sure you don't touch

her."

The giant straightened, looking offended. "I would never hurt the princess."

His massive voice carried like a band of trumpets. Sound waves bounced off of me and soft air brushed my face when he spoke. My drowsiness increased, calling me to sleep. I struggled to stay upright.

"Not intentionally," Martin replied.

"Be well, Martin," Levora said, stepping between the two. "Peter knows to be careful."

Martin remained glued to my side as Levora turned to Peter. "She can't find the leaves. Where do you suppose the witch Simon is keeping them?"

Peter returned his attention to me, his gentle smile putting me at ease. He was so massive and obviously had the power to do a lot of damage, yet I felt safe in his presence.

"Have you checked all your lakes?" he asked.

"Lakes?"

Peter hunched over me again. "The leaves can only survive under water in your world."

His eyes mesmerized me; I could see tiny roots inside them and see myself in his irises. "Any kind of water?" I asked.

"Any kind of fresh water—the leaves would wither and die in salt water."

"How do you know this?" I asked.

Levora spoke again. "Peter is an Onfroi, half man, half tree. They have an extremely particular diet, which makes them very helpful to us. The Onfroi have agreed to help save both our worlds."

"Both?" I asked. "I'm not sure I'm following you."

"Our worlds are connected, Thea. We share one sun, one light. If the sun goes out in our world, so it shall in yours."

An image of a snow-covered Salem flashed in my mind. "The temperature," I said, "it keeps dropping."

"And it will continue to drop if Wendell and his band of wizards are not stopped." She gestured to their surroundings. "All that lives will soon die."

"Die and save your friends, or live and save the world," I whispered. Finally my father's words made sense. But how could he keep this from me?

Levora stepped closer and reached for my hand. "Don't blame your father, Thea. In the human world, anything he talks about can change. He will never be able to tell you how you can help him. The only thing he can do is guide you."

I looked into her pink sapphire eyes. "How did you know what I was thinking?"

She smiled. "The same way I know you don't believe in yourself. I can see into your mind."

I turned my head away. I didn't like her inside my mind, sifting through all my insecurities. "How does Peter know about the leaves?"

Levora looked up at the giant. "The Onfroi feed on the leaves from the forest that rob you of your powers. Your spells cannot affect him because of this. But if he touches you, he can kill you." She looked at Morgan. "Show her, please."

When Morgan slowly raised his hand, Peter nodded and braced himself.

"Stand back," Martin warned, stepping in front of me.

Morgan sent a spell flying at Peter's massive

form. Like a lit match bouncing off the trunk of a tree, the spell floated to the ground and extinguished itself. He sent another, with the same result. I now understood why the wizards stayed away. Their magic didn't have the power to stop these giants.

Levora instructed Morgan to stop and then turned the tables. "Peter is going to show you what he can do."

Peter's feet began to grow and spread like roots burrowing into the ground. As his body grew taller, he stilled himself. He now blended in with the other trees. I would never have been able to spot him among the trees if I didn't know to look for him. I scanned the area and spotted several Onfroi that I hadn't noticed before, standing among the trees. They were guarding us, keeping the other wizards away. My sleepiness made sense now. Their scent was that of the leaves they ate, the leaves that sapped my power. They had developed a defense against the wizards. One touch from an Onfroi would drain a wizard's life in mere moments.

The earth shook violently again, and Peter reverted to earlier form. His roots withdrew from the ground and became feet again. His face was visible once more. He smiled down at me.

"Are you ready?" he aasked.

"I don't know about this," Martin said to Levora.

"What's going on?" I asked.

Attor finally spoke up. "I will remove her from him if I see that she's weakening."

I didn't like the tone of their discussion. "What are you all talking about?"

Levora faced me, her expression serious. "Peter

is going to protect you from the wizards so you can break their spells over the river."

"What spells?" I asked.

"You are the daughter of our king. When he is not here, your command must be followed. Only you can break a wizard's spell."

"Your Highness," Martin said, turning to me, "we believe you can break the wizards' spell over the Secret River of Life. You can free the energy just long enough for Magia to become strong again. Our sun needs to be replenished. If we don't do something soon, we will all die."

I looked from Peter to Levora. "What do you want me to do?"

"Attor will place you on his back and stand on Peter's shoulders so Peter can take you to the energy. We believe as long as you do not touch Peter, so long as you remain in body contact only with Attor, you will be safe. Once you get to the Secret River of Life, you can break their spell."

I breathed deeply, trying to tame my racing heart. "And how do I do that?"

Levora smiled. "Let us first determine if our plan will work. We're not certain placing Attor between you and Peter will be enough."

"So a test, then?" I asked.

"Yes," Levora replied. "To make sure that you will be safe, and to determine if your powers will work in such close proximity to the Onfroi."

I looked at Attor. "I will fly off of him if I see you getting weak," he assured me. I remembered again about the wizard whom Peter had killed, but somehow I had no fear of the massive Onfroi. They needed my help, and if necessary, I would die saving Magia.

"Okay, I'm ready."

Attor lowered himself to the ground. "Get on and hold fast to me."

I climbed onto his back and inched toward his neck. His skin felt scaly and hard in my hands. I wasn't sure what to hang on to. When Attor rose to his feet, wing-like cartilage bubbled up from the skin around his neck. I took hold of the bat-like wings and braced myself as Attor took to the air, then landed gently on one of Peter's branches. Instantly the weakness set in. I held on as tightly as I could while fighting the urge to close my eyes.

Through the haze of my lassitude, an idea occurred to me. I had once enclosed myself in a transparent, protective bubble as I walked through the forest from which these giants fed. I quickly chanted the spell and the bubble encircled me, immediately restoring my energy. I could see the wizards from here, still hovering at the edge of the forest, waiting. My earlier confidence was suddenly replaced by apprehension. I couldn't let Attor get hurt again. He wasn't immune to the wizards' spells like Peter was.

"Attor," I said. "I have an idea."

Attor lifted his great wings and flew off Peter, landing on the ground beside the group.

I waved my hand, popped the bubble, and jumped off his back. "I know how we can do this."

All eyes were on me as I explained my plan.

"As you saw just now, I can enclose myself in a protective shield. So long as I'm in the bubble, Peter can't hurt me. This way, Attor doesn't have to be the go-between, and there's less risk of anyone getting hurt."

"Your Highness," Martin said, stepping

forward, "do you think the bubble can hold both of us?"

I nodded. "I know it can."

Martin straightened, jutting out his chin. "Then I am going with you."

I hesitated, not wanting to put anyone in harm's way, but it was clear that Martin wasn't going to take no for an answer.

"Then it's settled," Levora said. "The wizards will begin their attack as soon as they see Peter. The other Onfroi will take care of them. The wizards will most likely flee to escape the Onfroi's touch. You will only have a few moments to chant your father's spell."

"But I don't know a spell that can do that," I replied.

Levora looked thoughtful for a long moment, her dainty features taking on a strained appearance. Finally she spoke: "You will return to your world and explain the situation to Xander. He will know which spell to give you."

"Tell him to send another capsule for the energy," Martin added.

A jolt of panic shot through me. "But that will take days."

Martin placed his hands on my shoulders and stared into my eyes. "Thea, we may never get another chance to get close to that energy. We need Xander here. We have to send him the energy. It's time for him to return to Magia."

I stared back at him. The thought of my father switching Simon's spell, and likely dying in the process, terrified me. Martin, sensing my anguish, softened his appeal. "Thea, if you can show your father that you can control the spell, he won't feel the need to switch it. You can still bring Simon here so the dragons can kill him and break the spell."

I lowered my head. "I don't know if I can—control Simon's spell, I mean."

"You can start by holding your head high," Martin replied. "You are a wizard—brave in every way. Do not allow a mere spell to weaken you, especially one cast by the likes of Simon."

"But how do I control it?"

"Look inside yourself, Your Highness. You will find more strength there than you ever imagined." He lifted my chin. "It's time to give Xander the energy."

Martin was right. My father's home was dying. His people needed him. Simon was the last thing my father should have to worry about right now. It was time for Xander the King to return to Magia.

"I'll get another capsule," I replied.

"You're doing the right thing, Your Highness."

"I'll be back in five days." I looked around at the group. "Will you all be okay till then?"

Levora stepped forward. "The Onfrio will keep us safe. Also, the ring will bring you back here. Martin will not have to wait near Attor's cave anymore."

"You waited for me at the cave?"

"It's the last place you used the ring," he replied. "I waited for days."

A disturbing thought occurred to me. I'd slipped the ring on at Simon's house. What if he was waiting for me when I returned? What if he held that knife to his neck again? What if I couldn't fight the spell?

"Martin, the spell, what if I—"

Martin held up his hand. "I believe in you, Thea. It's time you start believing in yourself. Go get that spell. We'll be waiting for you."

I looked around at all their faces. They were counting on me. I removed my father's wand from my jacket pocket and watched as it transformed into my stick. I took a deep breath and contemplated, staring down at the ring. I fought the fear and pulled it from my finger.

Chapter 9
Hypothermia

Simon's voice was the first thing I heard. My stick hovered above the exact spot from which I'd transported. I was surrounded by warlocks, each holding a bucket. My plan had been to fly out the moment I returned, but Simon was ready for me.

"Now!" he shouted.

The water struck me before I could make my escape. My body grew weak. I fell from my stick and onto the floor. I'd managed to drag myself to the door when a warlock grabbed my legs. I waved my hand and sent him flying only a couple of feet.

My powers were weakening with each passing second. The water had surely been taken from where Simon was storing the leaves. I could barely move. More warlocks appeared holding more buckets as my breathing slowed. I searched frantically for Jason, but he was nowhere to be found.

"Jason!" I screamed.

From the corner of my eye, I saw Simon holding the shawl. He closed the gap between us and covered me with the enchanted garment. What little energy I had left drained from my body.

"Put her in the car," Simon ordered.

I tried to fight the shawl's effects and wave my hand, but it was no use. Once again, it had rendered my arms useless. As the warlocks dragged me out of the room, Simon picked up my stick and followed us outside. The frigid winter air stung my face as the warlocks hauled me through the front door and out into snow. The temperature had dropped again. It hurt to breathe.

A piercing and familiar whistle sounded as we neared the car. Relief washed over me. Three warlocks hit the ground, arrows firmly planted in their chests. *Joshua!* Simon rushed back into the house, taking my stick with him. His men stayed behind and faced the attack. My heart leapt when I spotted the boys dashing out from the trees with Ciro. I searched frantically for Jason, who emerged from the woods with Justin at his side. A second wave of relief brought tears to my eyes.

Ciro sent a spell at each of the two warlocks holding my arms. I was stunned when the spells exploded like bombs and hit them. Justin shielded me, shooting spells from one of Jason's guns as Cory rushed to my side and pulled the shawl away.

I stumbled getting to my feet. The effects of the leaf-tainted water had yet to wear off.

Jason appeared, carrying a hose that had frozen solid. He chanted a spell, and water gushed from the opening. Jason pointed the hose at me and began washing the leaf-tainted water off of me.

Cory pulled me to my feet and stepped back. I was freezing, but I didn't care. I welcomed the freedom the frigid water had given me. I felt stronger. I extended my arm, and my stick flew out of the house and into my waiting hand. Jason tossed the hose aside, pulled out his guns, and resumed his attack on the warlocks. Cory flicked his arms to expose his weapons and joined the others.

I shivered, stick in hand, water dripping from my clothes and hair. My teeth chattered uncontrollably. I looked toward the house and knew what I had to do. It was time to face my weakness and fight Simon's spell. As the others fought, I told myself I could do this. Martin's words repeated in my head. Yet some part of me still clung to my fear.

The water dripping from my body began to freeze, forming miniature icicles that hung from my clothes and hair. I could barely feel my feet. I stood surrounded by a sheet of ice that had formed from the runoff of the hose water. As feelings of self-doubt threatened to overtake me, anger rose from somewhere inside.

"G . . . g . . . get in th . . . there, w . . . witch," I said through chattering teeth.

My heart began to slow as exhaustion set in. I fought to keep my eyes open. The sounds of the battle going on around me faded, and I barely registered the distant sound of someone calling my name. I lost sight of my friends and the surrounding trees until only the house remained in my view. Although I willed myself to take a step, my feet wouldn't respond. Once again, my fear rose to the surface. I had been so close to giving myself to Simon. Was I strong enough to fight him off this time?

My mind began to drift away. An image of James in a tuxedo, standing next to Helena, flashed in my head. My mind drifted again, this time to happier days. I was at the lake with James. We looked so in love. He rubbed my arms. "She's so cold." He held me close to him. "Get another blanket!"

Who is James talking to?

"Her hands are frozen."

His voice sounded panicked.

"Pick her up and take her to sit in front of the fire."

My father's voice. What was he doing at the lake with us? He never went outside. I heard the crackling of flames as a soothing heat brushed my face. I returned to my dream, where James wrapped me in a warm, soft blanket. I wanted to touch his face. I feared that if I opened my eyes, he would disappear.

"What was she doing in the woods again?" James asked.

Who was he talking to? How many people were in this dream?

"Stay with her while I make some tea." My father's voice again. "And please, keep talking to her."

I heard a door close and the sound of faraway voices asking how I was. Was I hurt? James' pleasant scent filled my head.

"Open your eyes, forest girl."

Forest girl?

"Come back to us, Thea. Open your eyes."

Why wouldn't he call me his love? I could feel my heart breaking as he pulled me closer.

"Don't cry," he whispered. "You're safe now."

Safe? Had I been in danger?

"Are you still cold?" James asked.

I was cold. I couldn't feel my feet or hands. My muscles ached.

"Why am I so worried about you?" James said, touching my face.

If this was a dream, I would take advantage of it. I kept my eyes closed as I lifted my hand from under the blanket and ran my fingers through James' hair, then pulled him toward my lips. "I love you," I whispered.

He kissed me slowly, running his tongue along my lips. I felt his gentle touch on my face.

"What am I doing?" he asked.

I didn't want the dream to end. I wanted to stay in his arms forever. "James," I whispered.

He stiffened. A moment later, I felt his lips gently on mine. "I'm here, forest girl," he whispered into my mouth.

"Call me your love."

"My love," he said, kissing me again.

I felt pure joy as I wrapped my arms around him. He felt so real, like he was really here. I opened my eyes. James stared down at me. I lay in his arms in front of a fireplace.

"You're still here," I said.

He smiled. "And you're back."

"Why are your eyes brown?"

He raised his eyebrows, seeming confused.

"What color should they be?"

I smiled. "The blue I love so much."

He patted my arm. "You're not quite yourself yet."

I closed my eyes and leaned my head against his chest. "I don't want to wake up."

"Do you think you're dreaming?" he asked.

"I know I am."

"Am I in your dreams?"

"Always."

"Why?"

"Because I love you."

"Since when?"

"Since the moment I met you."

I heard a door open.

"She's still a little out of it," James said.

"Has she stopped shivering?" my father asked.

"Yes, a few moments ago."

"Thea," my father said, "can you hear me?"

"Yes, Father."

He placed his hand on my forehead. "How do you feel?"

I opened my eyes and looked up. "Why are you in this dream?"

James chuckled nervously. "Like I said, she's still a little out of it."

I closed my eyes and drifted into another dream. When I opened my eyes again, I lay in bed in a sunlit room, looking through an enormous window. A pot of tea sat next to me on the nightstand. Pearl-colored furniture filled the room. Paintings hung on every wall. A vase filled with white lilies sat atop a bureau across the room.

I sat up, confused. Was I still dreaming? I couldn't recall how I had gotten here. I looked down. I was wearing pajamas, but didn't remember having changed into them.

"Oh, good," my father said. "You're awake."

I hadn't seen him sitting in the corner of the room. "What happened?"

He stood and walked to the bed. "You were in shock from hypothermia, which set in because you were soaking wet and standing in the freezing cold. Cory called. I told them to bring you here."

I hazily recalled the events at Simon's house in the woods. "How are the others?"

"Fine," he assured me. "They're staying in the

guest house. Jason is here, also."

I sighed and leaned back. "I think I blew his cover."

He shook his head. "Jason blew his own cover. When Simon ordered them to wait for you in that room, Jason snuck away and came to warn me. I'd read your note, so I already had the others headed that way."

"Ciro never left, did he?"

My father sat on the bed. "Did you really think he would listen to you?"

"Father, I have a lot to tell you. Magia is dying—"

"I know. I have already begun preparing a capsule for the energy."

I straightened. "You know?"

He smiled. "When will you learn that you can hide nothing from me child?"

"I wasn't trying to hide anything. I just hadn't had a chance to tell you yet."

He reached for my hand. "I know what you fear, but if I promise you something, will you believe me?"

I looked into his eyes. "Yes."

"If you bring me the energy, I promise I will not switch the spell. I give you my word. I will not break that promise."

I wasn't sure what to say. "I want to believe you, father."

"Thea, I wanted to switch the spell when I thought you would fall into Simon's arms. That fear is gone now."

How could he say that? I believed in myself less and less every day. "What changed your mind?"

"It's because I am certain you will find yourself. You have something Simon can't compete with. It will make you stronger than you ever imagined."

"What is it?"

He got to his feet. "You will soon find out, but until then, there will be no more meetings with Simon. He's found the spell's weakness. You will need to avoid him until you are strong enough to fight it."

"Can I ask you something, Father?"

"Of course."

"Why is Simon's spell no longer making me hate James?"

My father scratched his chin, looking thoughtful.

There was a knock at the door. "Come in, Cory," he called over his shoulder.

Cory walked in, looking relieved to see me awake. "Hey, how you feeling?" He closed the door behind him.

"I'll give you both a moment alone," my father said, heading for the door.

My eyes followed him out. He hadn't answered my question.

Cory sat on the bed. "You gave me quite a scare."

"What happened?"

"You don't remember?"

I shook my head. "The last thing I remember is Jason hosing me down."

Cory shook his head. "Man, what a mistake that was."

"What do you mean?"

"You should have seen yourself, Thea. I kept

you in my sights as we fought the warlocks. You were shivering violently, like I've never seen anyone shiver before. You kept looking toward the house like it was some sort of monster. You'd slipped into a trance or something. By the time the fight was over, your hair was a frozen mass. Even your eyelashes were encased in ice. After we brought you back here, your father couldn't even get a pulse." Cory ran his hands through his hair and leaned over. "We thought you were dead."

I took his hand in mine. "What about Simon? Did you find him?"

He shook his head. "We searched the house, but it was empty."

"Was anyone hurt?"

"Only the warlocks, and man, those guys are hard to take down. You were right about them being such good fighters. It's a good thing your father taught us some wizard spells."

"He did?"

"Yeah." Cory poured some tea into a cup and offered it to me, his hand trembling slightly.

"Cory, what are you not telling me?"

He exhaled loudly and reclaimed his seat on the bed. "I think you should know, I told James the truth. Well, sort of . . ."

My heart began to thump wildly in my chest. "Sort of?"

"Well, I didn't tell him that I wasn't really your husband. I told him that we never bonded because I felt guilty about seeing other women. I told him I'd made a mistake marrying you, that I loved you, but not in the romantic sense."

I set my teacup, still full, on the nightstand. "What did he say?"

"He seemed confused at first. He couldn't understand why I'd married you in the first place. We talked for a while. I told him a little about our history. He was sorry to hear about the breakup, but it was pretty easy to see that the news made him happy."

My heart leapt. "He was happy?"

Cory smiled. "You can erase a man's memory, but you can't erase what's in his heart. I see the way he looks at you. His heart knows it's you."

I threw my arms around Cory. "Thank you."

"I figured I'd let you tell him the truth."

There was a knock at the door, and Cory pulled away, saying, "It's James. He asked if he could see you."

"How do I look?" I asked, trying to fix my unruly hair.

Cory smiled again. "Like you can't wait to see him."

I breathed deeply as Cory opened the door. "I was just leaving," he said, walking out.

James remained in the doorway. "Mind if I come in?"

"Please do," I replied, sitting up straight.

He pulled the door closed. "How are you feeling?"

"Much better, thank you."

He looked toward the bureau. "I see my flowers arrived."

My heart began racing all over again. "You sent them?"

"Your father said you loved flowers."

"Thank you. They're beautiful."

He was holding a shopping bag. When he saw me looking at it, he held it up. "I took the liberty of buying you some clothes. We had to cut away your wet clothes before you froze to death." He set it on the bed beside me. "I hope these fit."

"You didn't have to do that," I said, peeking into the bag. I couldn't make out all of the items, but I spied a pair of black designer jeans. I closed the bag and smiled. I didn't know what to say. It was such a personal gift. I couldn't help but hope that perhaps it wasn't too late to salvage what we once had together.

"How did you sleep?" he asked.

"I had some very pleasant dreams."

A hint of a smile tugged at his lips before his expression turned serious. "I was sorry to hear about you and Cory."

"Cory and I have always been better at being just friends."

He tilted his head, genuinely surprised. "So you're okay?"

"Actually, I'm more worried about him—at least, I was."

He nodded, smiling. "Somehow, I think Cory is going to be just fine." He looked toward the door. "The others are downstairs having breakfast. Should we go down and join them?"

I placed my hand on my stomach, suddenly aware of how hungry I was. "You go on ahead. I'll get dressed and come down."

"Great. See you in a few minutes."

When he was gone, I bounded out of bed and opened the shopping bag. I held the jeans up to my hips. "Oh no." The red V-neck blouse was pretty, but way too small and not the type of top I would usually wear. I looked at the jeans again, which also now seemed too small. I threw the clothes on the bed and took a quick shower. When I returned to the room in my towel, I noticed a pair of black leather boots on the floor. I saw a note on the bed and quickly reached for it: *I forgot to give you these. ~James.*

"Since when do you wear boots?" Delia asked.

I turned to see her standing in the doorway. "James bought them for me, along with all these clothes. But they're all too small."

"Nonsense," she said. "That's what size you should be wearing."

I shot her a look. "How's Fish?"

"Back to his old self. He's in the kitchen with the rest of them." She studied me closely. "How are you feeling?"

I picked up the blouse again and quickly dropped it to the bed. "Not so good at the moment."

Delia rolled her eyes. "Put them on, Thea. They're fine."

I bit my lip and shook my head.

"I will never get you, witch," Delia said, hands on her hips. "You can face an army of warlocks, but wearing well-fitting clothes brings on a panic attack."

My jaw clenched. "They won't fit, Delia."

"Okay then," she said, gathering up the garments and shoving them back into the bag. "I guess Helena can look good for James then, because you don't seem too interested in winning him back."

When she made like she was leaving the room, I yanked the bag from her hand and dumped the clothes back out onto the bed. "Help me get ready, witch."

There was a lot of pulling and stretching, but I finally managed to get the jeans over my legs and zipped.

Delia stood back. "Have you gained weight?"

"Not helpful."

She helped me slip into the blouse, and I stepped into the boots and zipped them. She pinned up my hair using clips decorated with red jewels.

When she pulled out her make-up bag, I shook my head. "Uh-uh. No way."

"Close your eyes," she ordered.

"Ouch!"

"That's the price we pay for beauty," Delia said, plucking a hair from my brow line.

"This is silly," I complained.

"No, this is fighting dirty."

When she'd finished, Delia stood back and admired her handiwork. "Well, would you look at that."

"I'd rather not, thank you."

She laughed and fussed with my blouse.

I looked down. "It's too low."

"Not even close. Those there are your best weapon. Helena's are half this size."

"I look ridiculous."

She stepped back again. "You have curves I would kill for, Thea. You're the most beautiful size twelve I've ever seen. You're a bombshell. Why can't you see that?"

"And why can't you see that a woman of my size isn't meant to wear these clothes?"

"You listen to me, witch. There's a man downstairs who can't remember how much he loves you. I don't know what you were thinking when you picked Helena, but it will be a cold day in hell before I let her take your place." She turned on her heel and headed for the door. "Come on, I'm hungry."

When I passed the mirror on the way to the

door, a wave of panic flooded me. I felt short of breath. The clothes were so tight. I didn't know if I could do this. What if James didn't like what he saw?

"Are you coming or what?" Delia called from the hallway.

I took a deep breath and followed. Laughter echoed from the kitchen as we descended the stairs into the entryway. Delia walked through the kitchen door ahead of me. I paused at the door.

"You can do this, Thea."

Chapter 10
Wicked Cat

The laughter stopped abruptly when I walked into the kitchen. All eyes were on me. Everyone was there: Ciro, the boys, and Jason. Even Justin was sitting at the table. I felt my face flush. I wanted to run out of the room and back up the stairs. I glanced at Delia, who gave me a smile and thumbs-up.

My eyes wandered to James, who held a coffee cup halfway to his mouth. He slowly set it back down on the table as his eyes traveled the length of my body. When they met mine again, I knew I could do this.

"Good morning," I said, giving a little wave. I crossed the room carefully, trying not to fall off my heeled boots. The boys stood as I approached the table, mouths open. James quickly pulled out the chair next to him. "James was first," Fish said. It was then I realized everyone was offering me a seat.

My father walked over from the stove and handed me a plate. "I believe James is offering you a seat."

"Oh, of course," I said, slipping in next to James. "Thank you."

As the rest of the group reclaimed their seats, I

smiled at Justin, hoping against hope that he would smile back.

"You look pretty, witch," he said, winking.

"We okay?" I asked.

He nodded. "We'll be fine."

"How are you feeling?" Ciro asked.

I had no words to thank him for staying. "*Mi sinsero amigo.*"

He smiled. "*Por vida*, Thea."

"What does that mean?" Fish asked.

James spoke up. "She called him 'her sincere friend.' Ciro answered 'for life.'"

I'd forgotten James knew Spanish.

"So, how are you feeling?" Ciro asked again.

"Much better, thank you."

"I'd say *way* better," Javier said.

Cory smacked him on the head. "Eat your food."

I wished everyone would laugh again. I felt so uncomfortable. Javier and Joshua were sneaking glances at my cleavage. I could have killed Delia for insisting I wear this blouse.

"Coffee?" James asked, holding up the pot.

"Yes, please."

My father walked over to the table with more eggs and bacon. He set down the platter and gave me a smile. "I thought I was seeing your mother walk through that door." He winked and walked back to the stove.

I scooped up some scrambled eggs and transferred them to my plate. My father the wizard-king also happened to be an excellent cook.

"Delia was spot on," James said. "The clothes she picked out fit you perfect."

I shot Delia a look across the table. "I should have known."

"You can't blame Delia for everything," Fish said, glancing at my cleavage. "I picked out the blouse."

Delia punched his arm. "Close your mouth."

"I will if James does," Fish shot back.

James blushed and looked away. The group erupted in laughter. By the end of breakfast, things seemed normal again, save for James' eyes on me the whole time. Throughout the meal, his phone kept ringing, but he never bothered to check who was calling.

The third time his phone rang, Fish spoke up. "Better answer that, James. It's probably the old ball and chain. If it were me ignoring Delia's calls, I'd be in it up to my eyeballs before lunch." Once again, Delia punched his arm.

Of course he meant Helena. Nonetheless, James seemed unworried.

"I hope it doesn't keep snowing," Delia said, gazing out the kitchen window.

Several of us remained at the table long after the food was eaten, drinking tea and chatting. Once Ciro and the boys took off to the guest house, my father joined us. Jason stayed behind to catch up with Fish. I glanced at my father when Delia mentioned the snow.

He stood and looked out the window. "Your wedding day will be perfect, Delia."

She looked out again and back to my father. "I don't want to get married out there."

My father sat between us at the head of the table and patted Delia's arm. "We'll make it work."

She grabbed his hand. "No, I mean I don't want to get married without you. Who's going to walk me down the aisle and give me away if I get married outside?"

He said nothing for a long moment, clearly moved by Delia's words. For once in his life, my father was caught off guard. "It would be my honor, young Delia."

James and I exchanged smiles.

"I'll call the florist," James said, "and tell them where to put the arrangements."

"What about my dress?" Delia asked. "I still need to pick it up from the seamstress."

"I'll take you," James replied.

A thought occurred to me; I didn't have a dress for Delia's wedding. My old clothes suddenly didn't seem at all appropriate. "May I come? I want to buy a dress."

James' face lit up. "Of course. We'll all go together."

"Tomorrow morning?" Delia asked.

James threw his hands up in front of him. "Why not today?"

"Yes!" Delia exclaimed, running out of the kitchen. "Be right back!"

My father reached into his pocket. "I should give you some money."

"Actually, William," James said, "I'd like to take care of it." His gaze shifted to me. "That is, if it's okay with you."

My heart skipped a beat. James' eyes were changing color. Right before me, they had changed from brown to hazel. This had to be a good sign. But it couldn't be this easy. I had prepared myself to fight for him, but he was already brushing Helena aside all on his own. This was going easier than I ever imagined.

I stood up from the table. "I'm going to go check on Delia."

I could feel his eyes on me as I walked out of the kitchen. I hadn't made it to the stairs when someone pounded on the front door. I hurried over and opened it. It was Helena, and she was not happy. She almost didn't recognize me at first.

Her judgmental eyes scrutinized me from top to bottom. "What in the hell are you doing here?"

I grinned. "Enjoying myself."

Helena's eyes narrowed. "I see you've awoken from your nap, witch."

"I never should have dozed off."

"It's not going to be that easy, Thea." She pushed past me into James' house as though staking her claim. "He's mine."

"Is that right? Because it's been pretty easy so far."

Helena fumed, her face turning crimson. "Where's James?"

I gestured toward the kitchen. "We just finished breakfast. He was about to take me shopping."

"This was your choice, witch." Fury burned in her eyes. "You came to me, remember?"

I closed the door and turned to face her. "And now I've changed my mind."

"Consider yourself warned: I intend to put up a fight."

"I like a good fight." I stepped to within inches of her. "Want to start now?"

She turned on her heel, making a beeline for the kitchen. "James!"

Fish came out first. "What is that annoying racket?"

"Where's James?" Helena shouted.

"Lower your voice," James said as he emerged from the kitchen.

Helena abruptly changed her tone. "James, I was so worried." She rushed up and embraced him. "You didn't answer your phone."

"And that's a good reason to come in here shouting at people?"

Helena's eyes widened. "But you wouldn't answer. I was so worried."

"Please excuse us," James said, seizing Helena's arm.

He walked her outside and slammed the door behind him. Fish erupted into giggles when he heard James shouting on the porch. "Looks like you win, Thea."

I shot him a look. I'd never won a thing in my entire life. Everything I had, I'd fought for it tooth and nail. Things never went this easily for me. Tension began to build in my gut. There was no way James was just going to fall in love with me again and leave Helena. I Knew things were not going to be that easy for me.

James came back in, seeming calmer. "I'm so sorry," he said. "Will you please tell Delia I'll take care of the delivery of the dress? I have something I need to go work out."

So much for winning. "I'll tell her."

James grabbed his coat and walked out.

"He's going to break up with her," Fish said.

I looked at him. "You think?"

"I told you, Thea. You win."

I wished Fish would stop saying that. I hated Helena, but it was unfair of me to jump back into the picture and challenge her. After all, I was the one who had handed James to her in the first place.

Delia was disappointed when I told her about the change in plans. I offered to have Cory take us, but she wouldn't have it. I was sure she'd planned on pushing James and me together all afternoon.

I spent the day talking to my father. He was worried about Magia. When I asked him why it took five days to prepare the capsule, he explained that he had to grow a special mushroom first. "It takes five days to grow to the perfect size," he said. "I can't rush it. I would have you leave today if it were possible."

I also asked him if Ciro and Justin had been hunting warlocks. He assured me that they hadn't been. Although they had been searching, they'd found nothing. He also told me Ciro had been following James, making sure Simon stayed away from him. I was grateful for that. I still had no words with which to properly thank Ciro. I told my father about Simon's spell, how it caused me pain when I inflicted pain on him.

His look changed to one of worry. "What do you mean exactly?"

"When I cut him with the sword, I felt every sting. It was as if I was cutting myself."

This surprised him as much as it had surprised me. "I don't think Simon knows, though," I said.

He stood up from the table. "I know I told you I wouldn't interfere with your decisions, Thea, but I must insist that you stay away from Simon."

He received no argument from me.

After our conversation, he retreated to his room.

By late afternoon, he still hadn't emerged. I walked out into the snow-covered garden. I didn't feel like talking to anyone, and James's garden seemed like a safe place to be alone with my thoughts. As afternoon became evening, I brushed the snow off one of the benches and sat.

I was sad to see that all the flowers had died. The bitter cold had killed most of the plant life. It made me think of Magia and the horrible things that were happening there. My father couldn't get the capsule ready fast enough. I felt bad for everything Martin and the others were going through. But soon they would have their king back, and surely my father would restore Magia to its former glory.

"So you like getting hypothermia?"

James stood above me, holding a coat in one hand and my stick in the other.

"Where did you get that?" I asked.

He looked at the stick. "This was glued to your hand when they brought you back here last night. I had to peel your fingers away from it."

He draped the coat over my shoulders and reached into his pocket. "Here," he said, handing me the ring. "This was in your other hand."

I took the ring from him and enfolded it in my hand.

He sat next to me. "That's an unusual ring."

"It's my father's."

He propped up the stick between us. "So this is what you fly with, huh?"

I smiled. "I do a lot more than fly with it."

"I don't doubt that." He shoved his hands in his coat pockets. "Listen, about today, Helena and I are—"

"Thank you for letting us stay here," I said,

cutting him off. Just hearing Helena's name put me on edge.

He looked at me, a mysterious smile on his face. "You're all more than welcome to stay as long as you want."

I slipped my father's ring into my pocket. "Don't you even want to know why we have to stay here?"

He looked over his shoulder at the guest house. "It doesn't matter why."

"You're not even curious?"

"Whatever the reason," he said, scooping up a handful of snow from the ground, "if it keeps you here, I'm good with it."

"What if I'm a murderer?"

He laughed. "You wouldn't hurt a fly, forest girl."

"You don't know me very well."

James packed the snow into a ball, tossed it into the air, and caught it. "Can I ask you something?"

"I suppose," I replied, threading my arms through the sleeves of the coat.

"When they brought you here half frozen, you wouldn't respond to anyone. Your father asked me to talk to you, to let you hear my voice. In fact, he asked everyone else to leave and left me alone with you." He scooted closer to me. "Any idea why he did that?"

I tipped my head back and gazed at the clear evening sky. I didn't know what to say.

"When I was talking to you," James continued, "you whispered my name."

I lowered my head and glanced at him from the corner of my eye. "I did?"

"Uh-huh. You also said you loved me." He

inched closer until our shoulders touched. "You even kissed me."

I bit my lip. "I wasn't myself last night."

"Funny thing is," he said, tossing the snowball from one hand to the other. "I kissed you back."

I stood and turned away from him. I wanted to throw myself into his arms, but somehow that didn't seem right. I wanted *my* James back, not some man who couldn't even remember me. I felt like I was tricking him into loving me.

"Is it Cory?" he asked. "Are you afraid of hurting him?"

I turned to him and searched my mind for a way to change the subject. I took hold of the stick. "You want to go for a ride?"

He squinted up at me. "A ride?"

I released the stick, which turned on its side and hovered between us. "I want to show you something."

He looked at the stick, arching an eyebrow. "Now?"

"You scared?" I asked playfully, folding my arms across my chest.

He tossed the snowball aside and stood. "What are we waiting for?"

I zipped my coat and climbed on.

James took a seat behind me and wrapped his arms around my waist. "Well, this is different."

"Don't worry," I said. "I won't let you fall."

We flew toward the ocean under a star-filled sky. James looked down and gasped. I couldn't help but giggle. When we reached the ocean, I flew just above the water along the shore.

James reached down and let his fingers trail through the water. "This is amazing!"

I changed direction and flew back toward the lake. It seemed like the right place to continue our conversation. It was at the lake that I wanted to hear what James had to say. I planned on telling him who I was, who he was. I didn't want any more lies. It was time to come clean.

When we reached the lakeshore, James jumped off the stick. "This is what you wanted to show me?"

I tossed the stick onto the snow. "It's my favorite place in the world," I said, looking around.

He eyed me suspiciously. "Who are you, forest girl?"

I wanted desperately to tell him I was his wife and that I loved him, that I'd erased myself from his memory to save his life. But I couldn't find the words.

James tilted his head. "Why do I feel like I know you?"

I bit my lip and blinked back the tears. How could I tell him I'd given him up to a witch like Helena?

James stepped closer to me, studying my face. "Do you still love Cory?"

"Well, yes, but not like . . ." I couldn't finish my sentence. Frustrated tears rolled down my face as I fought for the courage to tell him the truth.

Concern washed over his face. "Why are you crying?"

"I don't know," I lied.

He looked into my eyes. "What are you doing to me, forest girl? What spell did you use to engrave your face onto my brain, to make my heart feel desperate without you?"

When I opened my mouth to answer, he took my face in his hands and kissed me. His kiss was gentle, his breath sweet. I was reminded again how Simon's spell was not making me hate him.

When the kiss ended, I kept my eyes closed. "Kiss me again."

His soft lips met mine, and he drew me into his arms. It was a perfect moment. I was home again.

"I don't care what happens now," James whispered. "I'd give up everything for you."

I leaned back. "What about Helena?"

"I could never make her happy. I see that now."

I opened my mouth, intending to tell him everything, but stopped short. "I love you, James."

"Yeah," he said, kissing me again. "You already told me that."

A rustling noise in the nearby woods interrupted our embrace. James shielded me behind him and pulled out his whip. "Who's there?"

I was about to reach for my stick when Kym stumbled out of the trees, breathless and covered in scratches. Dead leaves hung from her frizzy, tangled hair. She waved to us and collapsed onto the snow. We quickly ran to her. I scanned the trees but saw no one. "Kym, who did this to you?"

James peered into the trees. "Stay here."

"James, don't," I pleaded.

But it was too late. He had already disappeared into the woods.

"Kym," I said, shaking her awake, "who did this to you?"

Her eyes fluttered open and closed again. "Warlocks," she managed to say.

I threw my coat over her and took off into the forest, sprinting through the trees in a panic. "James!"

"Over here!"

A wave of relief washed over me to hear him calling from less than ten feet away. I found him standing over a pile of clothes.

He kicked at the garments on the ground. "There's no one here."

I surveyed the area. No dust piles in sight.

The sound of screeching cats sent us running back to Kym, who was suffering at the mercy of hundreds of scratching and biting felines. James lashed his whip at the cats, sending them away from Kym two at a time, but they kept returning. I approached the brawl and dragged Kym toward the lake. The cats followed, attacking her again. No amount of lashings from James's whip seemed to deter the vicious animals. I waved my hand and sent the lot of them into the trees. My jaw dropped when they rapidly recovered and ran at Kym again. I reached for my stick and lugged Kym on top of it. James jumped on behind me, and we took to the sky.

"What the hell was that?" James asked, looking back.

"I have no idea; those cats adore her."

I glanced down at Kym, horrified by what they'd done to her face. I could barely see her eyes, which had swollen almost all the way closed. Blood streamed from deep gouges in her cheeks and forehead. Within minutes, we were back at the mansion. James lifted Kym and carried her into the house and up the stairs. I dropped my stick in the entryway and rushed to the guest house to find Jason. When we returned to the main house together, Kym lay in one of the bedrooms with James standing over her, chanting healing spells.

Jason ran to his mother's side. "What happened

to her?"

"It was the strangest thing," I said, stepping up beside him. "It was her cats. They attacked her."

"Her cats?"

"Hundreds of them."

Jason reached for Kym's hand. "But why?"

James's spells worked quickly, and Kym's wounds began to fade.

"Mother," Jason said, gently shaking her. "What happened?"

Kym turned her head slightly. "Warlocks."

Jason headed for the door, his eyes filled with fury. James caught his arm. "That's just it. Thea and I didn't see any warlocks there."

"But you heard what she said."

I stepped in front of Jason, blocking his way to the door. "James is right. There were no warlocks anywhere around. We even checked the nearby woods." I glanced back at Kym. "It was her cats."

"At ease, everyone," my father said, striding into the room. "There's an explanation." My father approached the bed and shook his head. "She's been turning the warlocks into cats."

"What?" the three of us asked in unison.

My father nodded. "It's true. Her sister Donna told me earlier today. Kym has been doing this for years, apparently." He looked at Jason. "When she found out what you were doing, she upped her game, as they say. She was trying to protect you."

All this time, it had been Kym taking out Simon's men. I had to give her credit, it was a clever way to deal with the problem of Simon's ever-growing army. Unfortunately for Kym, the game, emboldened by their growing numbers, had turned on the hunter.

Jason stepped beside my father and reclaimed his mother's hand. "What was she thinking? She could have been killed."

Kym's eyes fluttered open. "I did it for you."

"But why?"

She clasped her other hand on top of his. "Because I only have one son." She gave a small, labored chuckle. "I hadn't realized how many warlocks I'd changed. I never foresaw them uniting and coming after me. Up until today, they simply followed me around, begging to be changed back. I suppose their patience has worn thin."

Jason kissed her hand and looked at James, who'd taken a seat in the chair by the window. "Have you ever hunted cats before?"

James smiled. "No, but tonight seems like a good night to start."

I stepped to Jason's side and smiled down at Kym. Somehow, I felt like I'd underestimated her.

"I'm coming with you."

"No, Thea," my father said. "You're staying here."

Chapter 11
The Power of a Witch

I gazed down at the driveway from the bedroom window and watched as James, Jason, and the rest of the boys piled into Cory's truck. I was thankful the others were going with them. Delia was furious that Fish insisted on tagging along. She tried to talk him out of it, but Fish wouldn't have it.

"I'm a man, Delia," he said. "And you're not my mother."

Hours passed and not a word from James and the boys. I sat with Kym, overseeing her recovery and periodically looking out the window. Donna had arrived not long after the boys had left and concluded the healing process with her superior medicinal spells.

Now feeling more herself, Kym's concern grew to match my own. We'd petitioned repeatedly to go and search for them. But my father remained firm, demanding that we stay put. I couldn't understand it. I knew he was worried; I could see it in his eyes. But it was past midnight and they were still gone. I made up my mind to fly out of the house and look for them if they didn't return by one o'clock.

"Does James know who you are?" Kym asked as we stood at the window together.

I shook my head. "No."

"I saw the two of you kissing." She tore her eyes away from the empty driveway to look at me. "Helena's not going to take this lying down."

I met her gaze. "I know, and I don't blame her."

Kym sighed and turned back to the window. "What's taking them so long?"

I looked out into the darkness. I could sense that Kym was just as anxious as I was to go out and search. She rubbed her arms as she gazed down at the street below.

"Why did you change the warlocks into cats?" I asked.

An evil smile spread across her face. "Cats can't talk, can they? Every warlock who became suspicious of Jason, I quickly took care of."

"Why didn't you just kill them?"

She faced me. "What makes you think I wasn't going to kill them?"

I tilted my head. "What do you mean?"

"What do you think I was doing out there tonight—feeding them?"

"What were you doing, then?"

A mischievous smile spread across her face. "Trying to make a coat."

"No wonder they attacked you," I said, shaking my head.

I could feel Kym's eyes on me and started to grow a little uncomfortable.

"You look pretty like this, witch," she said.

Her compliment took me off guard. Kym and I had never shared any particular affection for one

~ 151 ~

another. "I look like a fool."

There was a moment of silence between us as we returned our attention to the window.

"This is the most we've ever talked," she said.

I folded my arms in front of me. "None of you witches ever talk to me."

"It's hard to talk to someone who only wants to give orders."

How could she say that to me? My whole life, all I'd ever tried to do was keep them safe. This wasn't a conversation I wanted to have right now. "I'm tired of waiting," I said. "I'm going out there to go look for them."

Kym was quickly on my heels. "I'm coming with you."

I turned around. "No, you're staying here."

"I can take care of myself, witch."

"Really? Because you certainly seemed to be having a hard time taking care of yourself earlier tonight. I demand that you stay here."

Kym drew back. "You can give all the orders you want. That's my son out there, and I've been fighting those warlocks a lot longer than you have. You're not stopping me, witch."

I could see Kym wouldn't be deterred. I gave up trying and agreed to let her come with me. Halfway down the stairs, I heard my father walk out of the kitchen. He was talking with Donna and what sounded like a group of other witches.

I stopped in my tracks and held up my hand to signal Kym.

"Hurry, before she sees you," I heard my father say.

My anger flared. Once again, my father was

sneaking around and keeping things from me. I quickly descended the last ten steps and met them in the entryway. "What's going on?"

I saw the worry in my father's eyes—not for me, for something else. Donna and the other witches seemed nervous as well.

"Before *who* sees you?" I asked.

"Go back upstairs, Thea," my father said.

"What the hell is going on?" I asked.

Donna looked at my father and sighed. "Just tell her, William. She has a right to know."

I was struggling to keep my temper in check. "Tell me what?"

"Is it Jason and the others?" Kym asked, stepping up beside me.

When my father nodded, I scooped up my stick from the floor and hurried to the door.

"Thea, wait!" my father shouted.

I stopped and turned, keeping my hand on the knob. "You need them," he said, gesturing to the other witches. "Look into my eyes and know that I am telling you the truth."

The fear in his eyes set me on edge. It took a lot to rattle my father. I fought the impulse to leave the other witches behind. My father wouldn't have invited them here if he didn't have good reason.

Delia rushed down the stairs, holding her weapon. "Get out of my way, witch." She batted my hand away and reached for the doorknob herself.

I caught her arm and held it tightly while I inspected the group of witches standing across from me. "You'll be killed."

One of the witches, whom I knew only as Compton, stepped up. "We can take care of ourselves."

Compton was brave and sassy. Though centuries older, she fit in with the teenagers around town. She was known for being fearless, that much I knew. I also noticed that one could never predict from day to day what hair color she might be sporting.

I didn't know much about any of the others, aside from their names and a few superficial details. April owned a donut shop at the east end of town. Like Donna, she was tall and had a commanding presence. Her long black hair and striking dark eyes caught the attention of most of the males in town—witch and human alike. Laura, a dirty-blond, blue-eyed witch, conducted tours of Salem and told old witch tales to the tourists. Melanie, whom I'd seen at the various medieval fairs around the area, had a booth selling T-shirts and faux-designer bags. Her smile was warm and friendly, and I'd often found myself tempted to approach her. I envied how the other witches were drawn to her. Leny was the youngest of the group. With her dark hair and chestnut-brown eyes, she appeared to be of Latin descent. Like Compton, she possessed a certain fearlessness I admired. Jennifer was easily as tall as Donna, but had curves like mine. Her light-brown hair and soft curls gave her a look of innocence. She worked at a car dealership. I'd heard a rumor that she wasn't above casting spells on customers so they would buy cars from her.

I held fast to Delia's arm. "You witches have no idea what you're up against."

Laura stepped forward and stood beside Compton. "You have no idea what we're capable of, witch."

Delia managed to pull away from my grasp. "We're coming with you. Like it, or not."

"Thea," my father said, "there's no time for debate."

I could see they would have to come with me. As I held up my stick, it hit me: I could get to the woods in mere moments, but it would take a lot longer for the others to get there. "Follow me," I said, making a beeline to the kitchen and through the back door.

When we were all standing together on the patio, I looked up into the trees. "Hold out your hands."

I waved my hand. Branches separated from the trees and floated down into their waiting hands.

I faced them and chanted: "Take these witches through the sky, lift them up now so they can fly." When I waved my hand again, the branches tilted out of their hands and hovered horizontally in front of them.

Compton immediately jumped onto hers and called out to the others: "Let's go kick some ass."

One by one, the other witches followed suit.

Delia was the last to hop on. She gave me a nod. "Let's go do this, witch."

I nodded back and took to the sky in a single-file line—me at the front, Delia at the rear. I had to admit, it was a proud moment, having all these witches flying with me. It gave me a sense of sisterhood I'd never had before. I began to understand how Cory and the boys felt, living their lives for each other. They kept no secrets and told no lies. I'd always envied that. None of these witches had ever bothered with me before. I knew they resented me, and I couldn't help but wonder why they'd stepped up to help me now.

The bitterly cold air burned my face as we flew through the night. The witches didn't take long to get the hang of flying. It was as though they'd been born to do it.

Delia couldn't fly fast enough. She darted from her place at the back of the line and cut in behind me. "I'm going to kill Fish if he's not already dead!"

I was trying not to think of it, but the nagging concern about putting these witches in harm's way wouldn't leave my head.

"This is fun," Melanie yelled.

As we descended, Kym pointed to where she had last seen the cats before they overpowered her. I scanned the woods in search of James and the boys, but the forest was unnervingly quiet—not a sign of them anywhere.

We landed and searched the area. The moonlight reflected off the snow-covered ground, providing a clear view into the forest. I made my way through the trees, trying to pick up James's scent. I stopped and sighed—nothing. It was as though they'd vanished without a trace.

Kym appeared at my side. "This is the spot where they first started attacking me."

I spotted an object on the forest floor and moved toward it. It was James's whip, encased in ice crystals, as though it had been sitting there for some time. Panic sank in. What if he and the others were hurt?

A few feet away, Delia wept, having found Fish's hooks next to Ciro's machete at the base of a large evergreen. I dropped to my knees and searched through the snow. "Please don't be dead."

When I came across James's clothes, I froze, my heart thumping wildly in my chest. A few feet away, Delia's quiet tears grew into choking sobs.

"No!" Kym cried. "They're dead."

I turned to find her holding Jason's guns. Delia had found Fish's clothes, along with those of the rest of the boys. Suddenly, a loud screech sounded from deep in the forest. I was on my stick and zooming through the trees within seconds. Rage mounted within me. I could barely think straight. I was out for blood. I wanted someone to hurt as much as I did.

An assembly of warlocks was gathered just ahead—twelve of them, at least. I reduced my speed and hid behind a tree.

"Just don't kill her husband," one of the warlocks said. "We can't touch him, or the witch's spell will kill us."

They had formed a circle around eight hissing and growling cats.

"Well, which one is he?" another warlock asked.

I clamped my hand over my mouth to keep from gasping. They had turned James and the boys into cats.

"How does that feel?" one of them taunted.

"Hey, let's skin them alive!" another yelled.

I stepped out from behind the tree. "You took the idea right out of my head." I waved my hand at them. I was surprised when my spell bounced right off of them.

Laughter rippled through the group.

A dark-haired warlock wearing a red jacket called out, "It's not going to be that easy, witch."

The cats' attempts to attack the warlocks were hampered, I soon realized, by the fact that each had been tied down by one leg. I sent another spell at the warlocks, but it, too, bounced off and fizzled. A warlock seized me from behind and wrapped his arms around my body. I became suddenly too weak to fight him off. An unmistakable odor emanated from the warlock's clothes. It didn't take long for me to realize how they'd armored themselves against my spells. They had saturated themselves with the leaf water.

A second wave of rage swelled inside me. I slammed the back of my head into the warlock's face and wriggled from his grip. Another warlock was on me at once. He removed his coat, threw it over my head, and punched me in the face. I'd been struck before, but never had it rendered pain like this. He struck me a second time, and again intense pain shot through me. I could usually take a punch with a smile, but this was different. The scent from the leaves had somehow made me vulnerable to the pain. When he struck me again, I nearly lost consciousness. He pulled the coat away and smiled.

Face to face with the gray-eyed warlock, I knew instinctively that his deepest wish was to kill me.

"I've been waiting years for this, witch," he said, his eyes full of hatred. He raised his hand, made a fist, and struck me again.

I stumbled back into the arms of the first warlock, who restrained me as Gray Eyes struck me repeatedly. All the while, the cats—the boys—hissed and growled, trying to break free. Darkness began to close in. I'd lost all hope when the warlock holding me abruptly let go. I collapsed to the ground, shocked when he fell down beside me and turned to dust. My eyes shot up to catch James's whip striking another warlock. Shots rang out, and two more warlocks hit the ground. They shrieked in pain as the enchanted bullets tore through their bodies.

From my place on the ground, I looked up and spotted Delia and the other witches coming to the rescue. Compton had co-opted James's whip. April held Ciro's machete. Kym weaved through the warlocks on her stick, shooting Jason's guns. Laura jumped from her stick, putting Joshua's arrows to good use. Melanie had hold of Cory's blades and was busy cutting away heads and limbs. Leny, on foot, threw powder in the warlocks' faces, making it easier for Compton to go in for the kill. I was surprised to see Jennifer, and not Delia, using Fish's hooks.

I pointed to Gray Eyes. "Do not kill him!"

Delia kicked him to the ground, and Leny threw powder in his face. Delia chanted a spell, holding her oversized dagger to his throat. Amazingly, Donna fought off two warlocks with no weapon at all. Clearly a skilled fighter, she broke legs and necks like a warrior.

I looked around in wonder at these brave and capable women. These witches had obviously been preparing themselves for battle. I watched in awe as they worked together to kill the warlocks. Perched upon her stick, Laura knocked a warlock to the ground in mid-flight. April rushed in and sliced him nearly in two. After they had succeeded in killing the lot of them, Kym rushed to my side and helped me to my feet. I faltered, still dazed from the warlock's repeated blows.

Delia stood over Gray Eyes, waiting for instructions. "Remove his clothes," I said, wiping the blood from my mouth.

April didn't hesitate, immediately stepping in and cutting away the warlock's shirt and pants. Together Delia and April pulled him to his feet and stepped back. Leny snatched the tainted clothes and tossed them into the trees.

Instantly I felt my strength returning. I smiled at Gray Eyes. "Try and hit me now, scum."

He glanced around at the other witches.

"Don't worry," I said. "They're not going to help me."

The naked warlock spat a spell into his hand.

Kym held the gun to his head. "You won't be using magic, scum."

He closed his hand, and the spell evaporated. He stared into my eyes, swallowing thickly. "What about her magic?"

Kym looked at me and smiled. "I don't think she'll be needing it."

Gray Eyes made a fist and raised his arm. The cats' hissing and growling grew louder in the background. As I approached him, he took a swing and missed. I kicked him across the face, knocking him off his feet. I strolled around him as he lay prostrate on the cold, hard ground. "Get up, scum," I hissed.

He bounded to his feet and took another swing. I seized his fist, jerked his arm across my knee, and slammed it down hard, breaking it at the elbow. He staggered back, holding his shattered limb. He tried spitting a spell at me, but I punched him in the jaw. He slammed against a tree, and the spell escaped his mouth. I caught the spell in my hand, stuffed it back into his mouth, and forced his jaw shut. His eyes soon began to seep blood. His body shook from the pain. When he finally turned to dust, the other witches cheered.

I straightened and faced them. I wanted to thank them, to tell them how proud I was, but the fear of coming off as patronizing made me hesitate. Apart from Delia, these witches had been routinely hostile toward me. How could I thank people who disliked me so intensely? I looked at Delia and bit my lip.

She knew me too well. "A simple thank-you will do, Thea."

I looked around at each of their faces. They had humbled and honored me. "Thank you," I finally said.

"So she does know the words," Compton said.

"I told you she didn't hate you," Delia replied.

My heart sank. "Hate who?"

April gestured to herself and the group. "Us."

I looked at her, confused. "Why would I hate you?"

"You've never bothered with us," she replied.

"Or asked for our help," Melanie added.

All this time, I'd thought it was them not bothering with me. It was true I never asked for their help, but that was only because I didn't want anyone getting hurt on my account.

Laura stepped forward. "Before your memory returned, you were nice. You always said hello when any of us passed you on the street. But this Thea," she said, looking me up and down, "she's arrogant, cold, and uncaring. She can never be bothered with the likes of us."

I'd always tried to be brave and confident. I had no idea that others read those qualities as cold and arrogant. They looked up to me. Showing weakness of any kind would compromise my obligation to be there for them, fight for them. How could they run to me repeatedly for hundreds of years and call me uncaring? Before tonight, none of them had ever fought in a real battle. It was always me, the witch with the powers.

I stood before them, at a loss for words.

Delia stepped forward. "We've all made mistakes. When Thea lost her powers, you all ran and hid like cowards, so don't go pointing fingers now just because you've been training and know how to fight."

Silence

"Where was your courage then?" she asked, surveying the group. "Why didn't any of you step forward to help me protect her? Once your sons were all safe, you faded into the woodwork and left that job to the boys and me. We protected her all those years, not you."

One by one, the witches bowed their heads.

"Yes," Delia said, "she was arrogant. Yes, she was proud. But have any of you stopped to wonder why? How many of you have ever been tortured? How many have been beaten and buried alive?"

When no one answered, Delia shook her head. "Exactly. None of that happened to any of you because of what Thea was willing to endure on your behalf. So do not stand here and act like you've done nothing wrong. You all knew Simon wanted to kill her, but none of you stepped in to help until you found out he was coming after you, too."

We stood in silence, regarding each other cautiously. Tears streamed down Kym's face. Donna could barely look at me.

I took a deep breath and stepped forward. "Forgive me. Forgive me for never knowing how you felt. I never wanted to hurt any of you. All I've ever wanted was to keep you safe. I have nothing but respect for each and every one of you."

Melanie came forward, taking my hands in hers. "You are my sister now. I will fight at your side for as long as you need me to. The past is in the past. We unite as witches, but we fight as sisters."

I nodded. "Sisters."

Kym rushed forward and threw her arms around me. "My sister."

"Sisters!" Compton called out.

"Sisters!" we all shouted together.

Delia cleared her throat. "Uh, ladies, I hate to break up this tearful reunion, but Thea, can you please change Fish back so I can kill him?"

We broke out in laughter and looked over at the boys, who were pathetic and growing ever more anxious in their feline forms.

Compton jumped on her branch. "I'll go and gather up their clothes."

When Compton returned, I broke the warlocks' spell with a wave of my hand. The men writhed in pain as they retook their human forms and slipped into the woods to dress.

A few minutes later, Cory emerged from the trees, rubbing his neck. "Man, I hate animal spells."

Kym threw her arms around Jason. "The pain will wear off."

Fish stepped from behind a nearby tree and made a beeline for Delia with open arms.

"Delia, baby."

She slapped him hard across the face. He stood frozen in his tracks as the rest of us exchanged nervous glances. Delia's tears came quietly at first and quickly escalated into choking sobs.

She threw herself into Fish's arms. "Don't ever do that to me again."

Fish breathed a noticeable sigh of relief. "You have no idea how happy I was to see you tonight, baby."

"Together," she said. "We fight together." She pulled away and looked into his eyes. "Do you understand?"

"I swear," Fish said, holding up his hand. "From now on it's together or nothing."

James was the last to appear from out of the trees. Our eyes locked, and I knew then that I was done with the lie. I was also done living without him. It was time to tell him the truth.

"My love," I whispered, throwing myself into his arms.

"My Forest girl."

"Are you hurt?"

He caressed my battered face. "Shouldn't I be asking you that?"

He smiled, leaned down, and gently kissed my head. I felt him stiffen. He froze for several moments before pulling back, saying nothing. The expression in his eyes was no longer kind, but cold. I could feel him trembling as he dug his fingers into my arms.

"Are you okay?" I asked.

He slowly pulled away and stared at me in disbelief. He looked shocked. He stepped back, his rage-filled eyes still boring into me.

My heart sank; what was wrong with him? "James, please talk to me."

He tore his eyes away from me and ducked back into the woods. "I need to get away from here."

As Ciro followed James into the forest, the rest of the boys stood a few feet away, wearing the same grim expression. Cory approached me, but said nothing. He kept looking into the trees.

"What's wrong with him?" I asked.

Cory gave me a look of shock.

"You didn't just catch that?" he asked.

"What are you talking about?"

"Wow, Thea. Even I caught that," Javier said.

I looked at them confused.

"What happened tonight?" I heard Delia ask the boys.

Jason pulled away from Kym. "We found the cats. It took a few hours, but we'd almost killed them all when those warlocks showed up. We never even saw their spells coming."

I only heard about half of what Jason said. I looked back into the woods wondering about James. What was wrong with him? I started to think of Simon's spell. Was it possible it was to blame? Until now, there had been no evidence of the anger that once lived inside of us, but I saw it in James's eyes tonight. Was the spell working again?

By the time I left, I was half-crazed with worry. James didn't even know who I was, much less could he understand what was happening to him.

I didn't wait for the others. I flew back to the mansion, taking Fish and Delia with me.

James still wasn't back when we reached the house. My father waited in the kitchen with a fresh pot of tea. "No questions," he said when I entered the room.

For once, I didn't argue. I sat at the table and buried my face in my hands.

The other witches soon arrived, still talking about the fight. My father smiled to hear how their training had paid off.

"There was no fear," Melanie said, grinning.

My father nodded. "Fear only holds you back."

Fish was supremely proud of Delia. "You kicked some butt, baby."

Across the table, Javier and Compton were deep in conversation. "Why do they call you Compton?"

Compton jutted out her chin. "Because I've got street smarts."

My eyes kept darting to the kitchen door. What was taking James so long? Cory and the boys had arrived home almost an hour ago. Was he okay? *He must be terribly confused.*

Cory explained to my father the events of the night. "They figured out their friends had been turned into cats," he explained. "They must have thought we had something to do with it."

I stood abruptly when the back door opened and James strode into the kitchen.

"There you are," my father said, reaching into the cupboard for more teacups.

The look on James's face sent my heart racing. I swallowed hard as he eyed me with that all-too-familiar look of contempt. For the second time that night, my heart sank. I realized that a small part of me had clung to the possibility that I'd been wrong, that I'd misinterpreted what had happened back in the woods.

"Everything okay, James?" Cory asked.

James shot him a sideways glance. "Actually, I'm a little pissed."

My father's shot his head up. He wouldn't take his eyes off of James. "Impossible," he uttered quietly.

"Stay out of this, old man," James said through clenched teeth.

My father stared at James for a moment before nodding. "I give you my word."

James's eyes again drifted to me, his expression one of utter disdain. "Excuse me," he said, leaving the kitchen. "I want to be alone."

My eyes followed him to the door. It was time to accept the inevitable. "It's Simon's spell, Father. James's hatred for me has come back, hasn't it?"

My father looked in the direction James had left. "That's what you think this is, Thea? Simon's spell?"

"What else could it be?"

"If you have to ask the question, then you're not as smart as I thought you were."

I looked at him confused.

My father's expression softened. "Let me ask you something: Are you feeling hatred toward James?"

I shook my head. "No, but—"

I gasped. It wasn't Simon's spell. James knew. He remembered everything. I looked at the door knowing he was furious. I had to talk to him, explain why I had done this to him. I swallowed thickly and went to look for him.

Chapter 12
I'd Rather Feel the Needles

I found James in the sitting room across from his office. He sat quietly, smoking a cigar and staring into the fire.

He heard me enter the room and glanced over his shoulder. "Shouldn't you be out saving the world or sacrificing yourself?" He turned back to the fire and puffed on his cigar.

I swallowed down the hurt and stepped into the room.

"Don't waste your breath," he said. "I don't want to hear anything you have to say."

"James, please, you have to let me explain."

"There's nothing to explain." He chucked his cigar into the fire. "I understand everything."

I drew a deep breath and soldiered on. "Please, won't you at least look at me?"

He stood and faced me, his eyes throwing daggers. "Say what you have to, witch. I have a fiancée waiting for me—one you handpicked yourself."

His words pierced my heart. "Can't you see? I had no choice. I had to save you."

"Wasn't that just so nice of you," he said, clasping his hands together in front of him. "What would poor, helpless me do without you?"

The intensity of his bitterness was more than I could stand. "My love, please." I stepped toward him. "Let me explain."

"Shouldn't you be calling Cory your love?" he asked. "Isn't *he* your husband? How many times did he warm your bed, witch?"

"It's not like that with Cory. It never was."

He turned toward the fire. "Go away, Thea. I have nothing to say to you."

"You won't even let me explain? You would have died, James."

He spun around, his eyes blazing with fury. "I was dead for four hundred years, waiting for you! You sent me away and didn't give me a second thought!"

I stepped back.

"Do you even care what kind of hell I went through?" he asked. I heard the others coming out of the kitchen as his tirade continued. "I suffered without you, witch. I counted the days so I could be near you again. I thought it was over when I came back to you. I tried to show you I could protect you, be the man you needed me to be. And what did you do? You erased yourself from my memory!"

I opened my mouth again to explain, but he wasn't finished with me yet.

"I would have never done that to you, Thea." Tears brimmed in his eyes and spilled down his face. "I would have never put you through that kind of pain. No matter how bad things got, I would have never wanted to be without you. You would have been my strength."

"James, I only wanted to save you."

"No!" he shouted. "I thought we were in this together. I thought I was your husband and you believed in me. Instead you pushed me aside when you needed me the most. What's next, Thea? Are you going to erase my memory when something else goes wrong? Maybe send me away for another four hundred years?"

I tried to move closer.

"Get away from me! You had your chance. You wanted me to marry Helena? Well, you got it, witch. I should have married her in the first place. At least she can be loyal. She never stopped believing I would come back to her. Her faith in me never died. And unlike you, she never shared her bed with another man."

Cory stepped forward. "James, it wasn't like—"

"Shut up, Cory," James growled. "If you value our friendship in any way, you will stay the hell out of this."

My father grasped Cory's shoulder and pulled him back.

James glared at me. "I didn't realize it was so easy for you to go on living without me. How quickly and easily you slipped into your new life."

"That's not true!" I said between sobs. "I've only ever loved you."

"Lies! Why did you choose to have a husband at all? If you only wanted to save me, why was it necessary to crawl into bed with him?"

Once again, Cory tried stepping forward.

My father was instantly at his side. "Stay out of it. This is between them."

"I did no such thing," I replied. "How can you

~ 170 ~

think that of me?"

"I know he stayed in your apartment the entire time, Thea. He never left your side."

"Nothing happened between us, James—I swear."

James skirted around the sitting room sofa and passed me on his way to the door.

I reached for his hand. "Please, you have to believe me."

He grabbed my wrist. "I believed in you, Thea. I believed in us. But you gave me away without a moment's hesitation and went so far as to plan my future without you. I hope you're happy with your decision." He released my arm and walked out.

"James!"

He never looked back. He walked out the front door and slammed it behind him. I stood frozen in place as pain shot through my heart. I wanted to run after him, but for once in my life, I understood that James was better off without me. I had let him down, had let us down. I had made all the decisions, had tried to control everything. But what choice did I have? I couldn't let James die. I loved him too much to sacrifice him to my ongoing war with Simon.

I turned to the others, all now gathered in the foyer. My father cast his eyes downward as choking sobs racked my body.

Delia mouthed the words, "I'm so sorry," before bowing her head as well.

I dashed across the foyer and locked myself in James's study. Full of shame and regret, I couldn't face them. James had every right to be angry with me, but he wasn't right about everything. How could he think I would betray him like that? It was true that I had once wanted Cory in that way, but only when I thought he was my husband. How could James think I didn't believe in him? Couldn't he see that I was only trying to save his life?

I thought of the words Delia had said to Fish tonight: that they would fight together, always together. If he was going to die, she wanted to die with him. I realized I never gave James that same courtesy. My thought had always been that I would die without him. What I didn't realize was that he wanted to die with me.

I slid down the door and buried my head in my hands. I was starting to see all the harm I had caused. I had never meant to hurt anyone, especially James.

I sat for hours in the dark. Delia knocked a few times, but I couldn't bring myself to open the door. I wasn't ready to face anyone yet. I fell asleep sometime around dawn.

Two hours later, I opened my eyes to the smell of coffee. A new day brought new hope. Maybe James would be calmer and we could talk. Maybe he was ready to listen. I could tell him how wrong I was for not believing in him, and in us, and explain why Cory had posed as my husband. When I opened the study door, I heard voices in the kitchen. I could hear James, and he sounded happy. Hope rose inside me. My heart raced as I imagined our tearful reunion. I smoothed my hair as much as I could and prepared to face the new day.

Moments later, I walked into the kitchen and froze. Helena sat next to James at the table. They were having breakfast together. James slowly leaned back and gave me a cold look. There was a moment of silence before he stood. "Would you like some more coffee, my love?" he asked Helena. He glanced at me, leaned down, and kissed the top of her head. I steadied myself against the counter, fighting the impulse to attack her.

Helena smiled and reached for his face. "Only if you kiss me first," she replied, offering her lips.

I stormed out of the kitchen and straight up into Delia's room, where I began ripping off my clothes.

"What are you doing?" she asked.

"I look like a damned fool, Delia." I pitched the clothes across the room and pulled the pins from my hair.

She sat up in bed. "What's going on?"

I stomped into the bathroom, scrubbed my face, and returned to the room. "Helena's downstairs having breakfast with James."

Her eyes grew wide. "That hag is here?"

I opened Delia's closet and began searching through her clothes for something that might fit.

"What are you going to do?" she asked.

"For starters, I'm leaving this house. If he wants to be with her, I won't stand in his way."

I walked out and slammed the closet door when I couldn't find anything to wear.

"So you're just going to run away? You're going to let that witch win?"

"He doesn't want me!"

Delia shook her head. "He's angry. What if he had erased your memory or sent you away? How would you feel?"

I leaned against the closet door and stared up at the ceiling. "I don't give a damn about him anymore."

"Ha! Nice try." She tossed aside the covers and swung her legs over the side of the bed. "You're in pain. And for the record, it's okay to not have all the answers."

I walked across the room, plopped down on the bed, and leaned my head on Delia's shoulder.

She rubbed my back. "You know, this reminds me of certain times when your memory was gone. You would break down like this whenever you got scared. The thing to remember, Thea, is that it's okay to be scared."

I buried my head in my hands. "What am I going to do, Delia? He hates me."

"He doesn't hate you. He's angry. There's a difference. And for what it's worth, James doesn't know what to do, either."

"I think I've lost him. I'd rather feel the needles than lose him."

"So get him back. Do whatever it takes, and don't stop until he believes that he can trust you again. And another thing, it wouldn't hurt to show him a little more of that witch that walked into the kitchen yesterday morning." She reached down, picked up the red blouse from the floor, and threw it at me.

"Go get your man, witch."

There was a knock at the door.

Delia snatched her robe from a nearby chair and tossed it to me. "Put that on."

On the other side of the door stood my father. I sighed in disappointment. Some small part of me had actually believed it might be James, coming to find me so we could talk and work things out.

"There is a woman here to see you, young Delia. Should I send her up?"

"Is it Connie?" Delia asked.

"Yes, I believe that's what she said her name

was."

"My dress!" Delia wasted no time. She was out of the room like a shot.

My father stood in the doorway, looking more somber than usual. The anguish in his eyes brought up a new wave of anxiety. I lowered my head. He sighed and walked away.

Delia startled me when she rushed back into the room a few seconds later. "Come on, Thea," she said, practically breathless. "I want you to be with me when I see my dress for the first time. Connie is here."

I looked at her happy face. I realized what I was doing. I refused to cloud Delia's happiness. Here she was spending all this time and energy trying to cheer me up, when she was getting married tomorrow. I wasn't going to let her worry about me for another minute.

I mustered a smile. "Connie Ouellette?"

"Yes!" Delia gushed. "When James flaked out on our shopping date, Connie offered to deliver the dress here, in person."

Connie was known for a captivating smile that rarely—if ever—left her face. She was unfailingly warm and inviting, even to warlocks. She didn't like their ways, but believed they could change with her help. She owned a store called the Magic Mirror in Bristol, Rhode Island. Another witch with a talent for seeing the future, Connie was never at a loss for customers. She also made clothes that were stylish yet unique. It was easy to understand why Delia had insisted that Connie be the one to make her wedding dress.

It did my heart good to see Delia so excited about her wedding. She'd spent so much energy warning Fish and James to keep it simple, it had been difficult to discern whether she was actually looking forward to the event herself.

I hurriedly dressed and followed her down the stairs. As Delia chatted excitedly along the way, it occurred to me that I hadn't gotten her and Fish a wedding gift. Once again, I had been so awash in my own problems that I'd allowed them to block out everything else in my life—including my friends. Thankfully, an image of the perfect gift lit up in my mind. I would make Delia's wedding day more special than she had ever imagined and show her how much she really meant to me.

Connie stood in the foyer holding a long garment bag. She flashed us her famous smile. "There's more in the car."

Delia clapped her hands together.

I'd never seen Delia so happy or so giddy. Fish had somehow managed to bring out her softer side.

"Hi, Connie," I said, giving her a hug.

"Thea, my angel," she said, kissing my cheek. "How are you?"

"I'm fine. You look radiant as usual."

Connie's long blond hair was piled atop her head in her usual attractive style. "I have some things in the car for you as well." She smiled and winked.

"For me?"

"You're a witch, sweetie. It's time you start looking like one."

Delia ran back in, holding too many garment bags to count. "There's more in the trunk." She started up the stairs. "Some of it's for you, Thea!"

I tilted my head. "Why would you bring clothes for me?"

"James called me yesterday. He said to spare no expense."

I gazed at the kitchen door as Connie continued.

"I had to use spells to finish them all in time. He said to deliver them here when I was done."

A fresh wave of agony engulfed me. I felt lower than I had the previous night, if that was possible.

"Are you okay, sweetie?" Connie asked. "You look a little pale." As I turned to face her, concern rose in her kind eyes. "I take that back; you look a lot pale. Is there anything I can do?"

I shook my head. "I'll go get the rest of the bags from the car."

I felt like running the moment I stepped onto the porch. I longed to escape James's house, and my shame. Just yesterday, James had loved me. He had asked Connie to make clothes especially for me—to spare no expense. Twenty-four hours later, everything had changed. He couldn't look at me without disdain in his eyes.

I was lifting the bags out of the trunk when Helena emerged from the house. She approached me and peered inside the trunk. "Looks like someone had to buy secondhand."

I slammed the trunk, nearly catching her face. She drew back, eyes wide.

"Should I open it again?" I asked. "Next time I won't miss."

Her eyes narrowed. "You don't scare me anymore, witch. He'll hate you forever if you lay a hand on me."

I stepped closer to her. "Who said I needed to use my hands?"

Helena leaned down, her face inches from mine.

"Go ahead, witch. Knock yourself out."

An odd sensation swept through me. Usually Helena turned into a coward when I challenged her.

From the porch, Fish said, "Need help with the bags, Thea?"

Helena shot him a look over her shoulder. "Can't you see we're talking, scum?"

"No," Fish replied, approaching us. "I only see Thea sniffing some trash."

Helena placed a hand on her hip. "You'd better watch what you say to me, little man."

"Or else what?" Delia descended the porch stairs and approached our little insult party.

Helena sniffed and returned her attention to me. "We'll finish this another day, witch."

"Why wait?" I replied. "I'm free right now."

She flipped her hair over her shoulder. "Maybe you should try begging. James might forgive you if you get down on your knees."

"The only begging is going to come from you, Helena. Right before I kill you."

"You're never getting him back, you dirty witch. He loves me now, and we're getting married." She paused, smiling. "He's going to cast the divorce spell and forget all about you."

I fought off the urge to kill her and smiled back instead. "What are you afraid of, Helena? That I'll crawl back into his bed and take him from you? Because if that's the case, you should be worried."

Helena's lips quivered as she raised her arm. She was actually thinking about taking a swing at me. I had to give her credit. She seemed to have developed some moxie since our last run-in. Still, I was looking for any excuse to kill this witch. I closed the gap between us, again overtaken by the same peculiar feeling.

"Helena, go home!" James boomed from the porch. "I'll pick you up later."

As he approached us, a smile spread across Helena's face. "Yes, my love." Her eyes remained on me as she spoke in her sickeningly sweet voice—the one she reserved only for James. She turned on her heel and strolled down the driveway. She blew James a kiss before getting into her car and driving away.

I turned to face James. His eyes were dark and empty, no longer possessing even a hint of blue. His glare sent a chill snaking down my spine. Who was this callous and unkind man? This couldn't be my James. I nervously glanced at Fish and Delia, who remained safe on the sidelines.

"Just so we're clear," James said coldly, "you and I are finished. You have no ties to me anymore, and soon you will be free to do whatever you want. But until then, I want you to stay out of my way. I don't want to see you. I don't want to talk to you. I don't want to even hear your voice if I can help it." He walked back inside without another word.

My temper flared, getting the best of me. I fought the impulse to wave my hand and cast that divorce spell he wanted so badly.

"Thea!" Delia stopped my hand in mid-motion. "I know that look. Don't be stupid."

I turned away and brought the rest of the bags inside. When I spotted James walking up the stairs, I dropped the bags and told him, "I don't want these. You can keep your gifts and give them to Helena."

James stopped and turned. Meanwhile, Connie

stood quietly by the front door, her eyes darting nervously from James to me.

"You can burn those clothes, for all I care," James replied. "Helena doesn't need hand-me-downs from the likes of you."

I approached the bottom step, fuming. "Why don't we end this once and for all?"

He stepped down a stair. "Are you suggesting we kill each other?"

Delia and Fish walked into the house. When Fish tried to gently lead me away from the confrontation, I batted him away. I noticed Connie tiptoeing toward the kitchen.

I glared at James. "Cast the divorce spell now."

His earlier expression of mock delight transformed into a nervous smile. "Is that really what you want?"

"Didn't you tell Helena you wanted a divorce?"

For a long moment he remained silent, his hands balled into fists. "Yes."

"Then why wait? If you want to be with her so badly, cast it now."

His eyes remained locked on mine, though he said nothing. I had called his bluff.

I rose to the next stair. "Do it, coward."

Delia approached me from behind. "Thea, stop."

My pain wouldn't allow me to think straight. James's cold hatred was changing me back into my former wicked-witch self.

Finally he smiled and walked down a few steps. "Why don't you take the easy way out, Thea? Go ahead, erase my memory and make the problem just go away."

"I was trying to save your life!"

"What life? You think you handed me a happy life? You think I deserved to be alone for four hundred years? Who the hell do you think you are, witch? What gives you the right to choose a life for me, to hand me over to another witch like some sort of dog?"

I didn't know what to say. He had it all wrong.

"I regret the day your memory came back," he continued. "The memory-free Thea was scared; she needed me. She would have chosen death over living without me. There isn't a force on this earth that could have changed her mind. She's the witch I love. She felt like a real woman in my arms. I was all she needed, all she wanted. I never felt more wanted in all my life. You'll never be that Thea."

My insides burned. "Is that what you want?" I shouted. "A scared, insecure witch incapable of thinking or taking care of herself?"

"You'll never get it, will you? That scared girl was more of a witch than you'll ever be."

I watched in silence as he disappeared up the stairs. My temper had calmed, leaving only pain behind. I really had lost him. James didn't love me. He loved her. He was in love with a ghost, a ghost I couldn't bring back.

I turned with the intention of leaving the house. Delia's tear-filled eyes stopped me. What was I doing? I was ruining the happiest moment of my best friend's life. Somehow I had to push my own pain aside.

I managed a smile. "Let's go try on that dress."

Delia furrowed her brow and turned to Fish. "Why don't we delay the wedding?"

Fish's eyes widened. "What?"

"Just until the dust settles." She gave me a

sympathetic smile.

"No," I replied. "You are not postponing this wedding, Delia. I'm fine." I picked up the bags from the floor. "Come on. Help me try this stuff on." My voice trembled as I spoke, but I blinked back the tears and held my head high.

Connie emerged from the kitchen, waving us down. "Wait for me, ladies."

The three of us headed up the stairs and into Delia's room.

I dropped the bags on the bed and peeked inside the one closest to me. "Do you think the clothes you made will fit me?" I said, trying to sound cheerful.

Connie glanced at Delia, a concerned look on her face.

Delia appeared at my side. "Are you sure we should—"

I turned to her. "Delia, I'm fine."

She smiled and nodded.

We spent the day trying on dresses. James's name was not mentioned once. Connie was a true artist. I hated wearing dresses, but her work was so exquisite it would have been a shame not to wear them. She had a flare for sixteenth-century style. She held up my bridesmaid dress, which was a plush red color with cap sleeves. I was thankful it wasn't too long, but panicked a little when I saw the bodice—a gold corset that tied in the front.

"Okay, ladies," Delia called from inside the closet. "Are you ready for this?" Delia emerged wearing her wedding dress. The sight of her took my breath away. The chiffon fabric flowed with every step she took. The empire waist was accented with two cobalt blue stones, and the cap sleeves gently hung off her shoulders. Crystal beads were sewn into the split-front white overlay.

She lifted her arms and turned in a circle. "How do I look?"

I couldn't put into words how beautiful she looked. I imagined her hair up with white roses nestled here and there. "Oh Delia, you're breathtaking."

She looked down at the dress. "It's not too much?"

I shook my head. "It's perfect." I gestured to the mirror. "See for yourself."

Delia closed her eyes. "No, I don't want to."

Connie and I exchanged puzzled glances. "But why not?" Connie asked.

She wrung her hands. "Tomorrow; I'll look into the mirror tomorrow."

Connie looked over the dress, smiling. "Well, it doesn't seem to need any further alterations, so I believe my work here is done."

Delia's eyes popped open. "I can't thank you enough, Connie."

"No need to thank me. This is what I do. And I love what I do." She glanced at her watch. "But I'm afraid I really must be going." She leaned over carefully and pecked Delia on the cheek.

She blew me a kiss before slipping out the door and closing it behind her.

Delia looked at me. "So, should I wear my hair up or down?"

"Doesn't matter," I replied. "You'll look stunning either way."

She nodded and bowed her head, suddenly seeming nervous.

"What is it?" I asked.

She looked up, her eyes glassy. "I've never done this before, Thea. What if Fish doesn't like that part of me?"

I sat in the chair next to the mirror. "Part? What part?"

She sighed. "I know I once threw myself at James, but this is different. It really matters to me what Fish thinks. He's been with human girls before. He knows what to expect. What if I do it wrong and he doesn't like it?"

"Would you believe me if I said that you'll know exactly what to do?"

She looked at me, confused. "What do you mean?"

I thought of the first time James had taken me in his arms. The fear had melted away when he held me. With every kiss, I had worried less and less about what to do and simply gave into my desire for him. I knew instinctively how to touch him, how to please him.

"Do you love him?" I asked.

Her eyes brimmed with tears. "With all my soul, Thea."

"Then let your love guide you. Surrender to your love for him."

My own words crystallized how many mistakes I had made. I'd never surrendered myself to James and our marriage. Only in his arms did I give him complete control. I knew he would take care of me, keep me safe and protect me, just as I would do for him. But why would I hesitate to surrender completely to our love?

By the end of the day, I was actually excited about the wedding. I went about preparing the spell I was planning for Delia's wedding gift. After her conversation with my father, the wedding's venue had changed from the garden to the ballroom, but I knew that in her heart Delia had always imagined an outdoor wedding.

After everyone had gone to bed, I tiptoed downstairs and into the ballroom. Two hours later, I slipped back out and started for the stairs, but paused. A stream of light beamed across the entryway floor, coming from the open door of James's study.

Against my better judgment, I peeked inside the room. James sat with his back to the door. Cigar smoke drifted toward the ceiling. I struggled to see around his high-backed leather chair and zeroed in on an object sitting atop the cabinet behind his desk. My heart thumped inside my chest. It was a painting of me holding a bouquet of flowers. I knew the portrait well; it had been painted on the day of our wedding. It used to hang in one of the upstairs bedrooms. James had cast a spell on the artist so he wouldn't miss a single detail of my face.

My eyes filled. How happy I looked then.

He'd stood next to the artist the whole time. I kept asking him to come and sit with me, but he refused. He kept repeating that he couldn't believe I belonged to him. "I want this moment engraved on my brain forever," he'd said.

Now he took a sip of brandy—not a typical habit for him—and another puff from his cigar. He stared at the painting. "You broke my heart, Thea."

My knees nearly gave way beneath me. I wanted to rush in, kneel at his feet, and beg his forgiveness.

He drained his drink and refilled the glass from a bottle that sat on the cabinet. "I would have taken care of you."

I backed away from the door and tiptoed up the stairs. I had caused James so much pain. But I felt hopeful. He still had feelings for me. Maybe it wasn't too late to save our marriage after all. Somehow I would find a way to win him back.

I went to bed knowing what I had to do. Tomorrow I would begin showing James how much I needed him.

Chapter 13
The Big Day

Nearly a foot of fresh snow had fallen during the night, and many of the roads were closed. The florist and caterers were stuck in Boston. I was unworried. My father and I snapped into action. There would be plenty of food for the guests—if the guests were able to make it, that is.

My father was decidedly tense, at least to my eyes. He did his best to mask his worry, and the others hadn't seemed to notice. But I knew him too well. He was consumed with thoughts of a dying Magia. I peppered him with questions in an effort to get him to open up, but to every inquiry he simply raised his hand and replied, "Not today."

My father had distanced himself from me. Since the day he'd returned my memories of James, he had avoided talking to me, except for giving me orders. He could barely look me in the eye anymore, and kept his mind blocked from me at all times.

Resentment was beginning to set in. He had promised me no more lies and no more secrets, but here he was keeping things from me again. If I dared to ask a question about James, he merely replied, "I'm not getting involved."

Cory and the boys had distanced themselves from me as well. I felt very alone. Were my friends punishing me? I sought out comfort from Justin, only to have him walk away. I tried to be humble, but couldn't seem to find the girl I had been when my memory was gone.

After helping my father in the kitchen, I returned to my room. I dressed for the wedding and went back downstairs to find the musicians waiting in the foyer. I was grateful they had been able to make it through the snow. I led them to the ballroom and opened the doors. They walked in and immediately praised the décor, curious as to how I could pull off such a thing.

"Magic," I replied, winking. I slipped out quietly and left them to set up.

I hadn't seen James or Fish all morning. My father informed me that James had agreed to help Fish prepare the guest house for his wedding night. I could only imagine what Fish had in store. Delia was upstairs with Connie, getting ready. Joshua and Javier were shoveling the front walk. Cory was busy setting up tables.

I stood guard by the ballroom doors. On his way back into the house, Joshua tried to peek inside.

I shooed him away. "Not until the ceremony."

I fidgeted in my dress, which felt too tight. My exposed cleavage made me uncomfortable. Connie had done my hair in an up-do with curly tendrils framing my face. I looked like I belonged at one of those medieval fairs.

I was glad when Justin arrived and offered to

watch the door for me. I was curious about what Fish had done to the guest house. I treaded carefully through the snow across the backyard and peeked my head through the door of the cottage. I stared in awe at the transformation—from guest house to a honeymoon suite.

Huge pillows were strewn all over the floor, and there must have been a thousand candles scattered about the room—magically lit to keep them from melting. A spell had been cast to make the ceiling look like a clear night sky, complete with stars and comets. I was tempted to reach up and touch them.

"Well, what do you think?"

I gasped and turned to Fish as he emerged from the kitchen. "You startled me. I didn't realize you were still here."

"Sorry. Well . . . ?"

I giggled. "Oh, of course, it's amazing."

My heart fluttered when James came into the room behind Fish. He saw me and did a double take. I wanted to tell him how handsome he looked in his tuxedo, but he looked away before I could say a word.

"You think she'll like it?" Fish asked.

"She's going to love it."

Fish eyed my gown. "You look very pretty, Thea." He turned to James. "Doesn't Thea look pretty?"

"Excuse me. I have something to attend to." James brushed past me, avoiding eye contact, and headed back to the main house.

Fish shrugged.

I stuck around and helped him put the finishing touches on the room. A magical night awaited Delia.

"I even made sure there's enough food here for

three days," Fish said. "Delia's not going anywhere."

I laughed and left Fish to get dressed. It was almost time for the ceremony, and the guests would be arriving soon. My father had disappeared from the kitchen. I presumed he was upstairs getting ready.

I relieved Justin at the ballroom doors and tried to make conversation with him, but he made some excuse about needing to find Ciro. Fish approached me about ten minutes later and asked me to check him over. I had no words to tell him how handsome he looked dressed all in black, Delia's favorite color. Fish's boyish face beamed.

I wrapped my arms around him. "You're going to make her so happy, Fish."

"I plan on making her happy all night."

I stifled a giggle. "Be patient with her; she's nervous."

"Patient?" he asked. "I'm going to tear that girl apart, Thea."

I was still laughing when I heard someone yell, "Sister!"

I spun around to see a young boy running toward me. I felt like the lowest of the low. Immersed in my problems, I had forgotten all about Steven. I had saved him the night of the battle, then erased his memory and woven myself into his life as his sister.

He ran into my arms. "When did you get back?" he asked. "I missed you."

I glanced at James. Steven couldn't remain here after I erased myself from James's memory. I realized at this moment that I didn't even know where my father had sent Steven.

He watched me nervously. "Can I come back now?"

"You never should have left," James said, shooting me a dirty look.

I wrapped my arms around Steven again. "Of course you can come back, sweetie. And I promise never to leave you again."

He pulled away. "Where did you go?"

How could I tell him I had forgotten all about him? "I had some things to sort out."

"Auntie Delia said you were sick."

"When did you see Auntie Delia?"

"She comes to see me every day. So do the guys."

Fish avoided my gaze, which only fueled my self-hatred.

"Steven," James said, "your room is just as you left it. Why don't you go up and get ready for the ceremony?"

"Can I say hello to Auntie Delia?"

James nodded. "She'd like that, I'm sure."

James handed Steven his suitcase, and the boy lugged it up the stairs.

"The next time you feel like toying with people's lives," James said, "leave that boy out of it."

My stomach lurched. "But I never thought— "

"That's the problem, Thea," James said. "You never think about how your choices will affect others."

"I never wanted to forget him."

"But you wanted to forget me, right?"

"James, I made a mistake. How can I show you how much I regret it? If you would just let me explain things to you."

He looked up the stairs and back at me. "If you're truly sorry, give that boy his life back. Return the memories you stole from him. Let him make his own choice about whether or not to live with you. Don't choose his life for him."

He walked away before I could respond. He was right. How could I have not taken into consideration how my choice would affect Steven? I didn't even think of what would happen to him when I had my father erase James from my memory.

"He's been living with Sharron," Fish said.

I sighed and nodded. "I'm so sorry, Fish."

"He asked for you every day. We told him you were sick and couldn't come see him." He rubbed my arm. "But he's been okay."

"Stop trying to make me feel better. I don't deserve it."

"Let's talk about this later, okay?" Fish said, throwing his arm around my shoulder.

"I messed things up so bad, Fish."

"It's never too late to fix things."

"But I don't know how."

He turned to me. "I'm going to say something, and I don't want you to take it the wrong way."

When I lifted my head, Fish smiled. "What is it?" I asked.

"I always knew James would remember you. He told me so many times how his love for you could break a million spells. You're so busy blaming yourself for everything that you don't realize he's waiting and hoping to see that you have the same faith in him. He fought for you, and now he wants to see if you'll fight for him. He needs to see if you need him as much as he needs you."

I looked down. "James doesn't want me."

"Delia didn't want me either, but look where I am today."

The ringing of the doorbell saved me from responding to Fish's last comment. I didn't know how to show James what he needed to see.

Fish opened the door, and together we greeted the guests. I was happy to see my new friends—my sisters. Sharron arrived a little while later. I noted that Pam was curiously missing from the milling guests.

Everyone was dressed simply, just as Delia had requested. Only James and Fish were wearing tuxedos—Fish's idea, no doubt. I felt overdressed compared to the simple sweaters and skirts the other witches wore. I wanted to rip Connie's extravagant, low-cut creation off me and slip into something less obvious.

All my worries about the dress drifted away when Cory strolled in, also wearing a tux. His green eyes sparkled. There was something about Cory; you couldn't help but stare into his eyes when he looked at you.

"Cory, you look so handsome."

He looked down. "This old thing?"

I giggled. "Why are you wearing a tux?"

"Didn't you hear? I'm giving away the groom."

I stared at him. "You're what?"

He chuckled. "Fish asked me to give him away. I think it's his way of saying that he's sorry for not asking me to be his best man."

"You ready, Dad?" Fish asked, walking up to us.

Cory smiled and placed his hand on Fish's shoulder. "Do we need to have that talk about the birds and the bees, son?"

"Not to worry, Pops," Fish replied. "I've made nest and honey before."

Cory and I burst into laughter.

James approached us. "What's so funny?"

"You know," Fish said, "you ask that question a lot."

James nodded. "And I miss the joke a lot, too." He gave me a sideways glance. "I think the bride is ready. Is it okay to let in the guests?"

I nodded, turned, and opened the doors. The guests gasped in unison as they entered the ballroom.

Fish peeked inside, and his mouth fell open. "What in the world?" he muttered. He entered with James at his side, both gazing in amazement.

The ceiling was the sky, with soft clouds floating amongst the blue. Rays of sunshine streamed down onto the maples that grew from the floor. Birds sang high up in the trees. The chairs were crafted from trees stumps, and ivy hung from them along the lavender-lined center aisle. The floor was covered in grass, with patches of wildflowers and mushrooms spread about.

"When did you cook this up?" Cory asked.

"Last night," I replied. "Delia had always planned on an outdoor wedding."

"And outside she'll be," Fish said. He embraced me. "Thank you, Thea. She's going to love it."

"My pleasure, sweetie."

"This is so cool," he said, looking around.

James, who hadn't said a word since we'd entered the room, turned to me. "Is this the place where we were married?"

"It was the most beautiful place in the forest."

He looked around again. "I always thought so, too."

Cory patted my back. "It looks amazing, Thea."

Steven walked in with Jason, Ciro, and Justin. "Wow," Steven gasped.

Justin's mouth dropped. "God, I wish I was half wizard."

"Trust me," I replied. "You don't."

When Connie came down the stairs, we all took our places. I stood at the front of the room with Cory, James, and Fish. Connie took her place between us and pulled out her spell book. She looked toward the stairs.

My father appeared at the top of the stairs with Delia on his arm. He looked dashing in his suit. His eyes sparkled as he pecked Delia's cheek.

Delia wore her hair gathered to one side, with a simple white rose pinned into it. The light from the window above the front door reflected off her dress, making it appear more beautiful than ever. She held a simple bouquet of white roses in her hand.

The musicians began to play, and the guests rose to their feet. Fish's mouth dropped open as his bride slowly made her way down the stairs with my father at her side. James put his hand on Fish's shoulder and smiled. Fish swallowed thickly and nodded at James.

When they entered the ballroom, Delia stopped. Tears rolled down her cheeks as she took in the room. She looked down the aisle at me. "Thank you," she mouthed.

I smiled as she walked down the aisle, her eyes never leaving Fish. When they reached the altar, Delia kissed my father's cheek. Cory reached for Fish's hand and offered it to my father.

My father smiled and placed Delia's hand in Fish's. "Take care of her, son."

Fish gave him a nod. "I will, sir."

Delia turned to Fish as Connie addressed the room. "I have been given the honor of uniting these two in life," she began. "As of today, Fish and Delia will be one. They will share one heart, one soul. No amount of time will shatter their love. They will be united in this life and the next."

I couldn't tear my eyes away from James as she spoke those words. It came as a surprise when James met my gaze and didn't look away.

"A spell will unite them," Connie continued. "But their love will forever keep them together."

Connie nodded to Fish.

Fish took a deep breath and exhaled. He looked into Delia's eyes. "I, Kris Fisher, give my life to thee. I cast the spell and give to you, all that lives in me. I will be your husband, protector, and a friend. I will fight beside you and defend you to the end."

Tears filled Delia's eyes as she delivered her vows. "I, Delia Williams, give myself to thee. I cast the spell and give to you, all that lives in me. I will be your wife, protector, and a friend. I will stand beside you till the bitter end."

When they clasped hands, streams of energy passed between them. Delia closed her eyes as Fish's energy entered her hands. I could almost see them becoming one.

I looked back at James, whose gaze hadn't wavered. I knew what he was thinking. No one had shared this moment with us. It had been just me and him. There were no guests, no food, no dancing, not a single moment of celebrating with our friends, but somehow, it hadn't mattered. The only thing I had ever wanted was him. My life was complete when I was with him.

I turned my eyes to Connie, who opened her spell book and asked for the rings. Once James had placed the rings on the book, Connie chanted a spell and offered the rings to the happy couple. When Fish slipped the ring onto Delia's finger, he kissed her hand. He looked at Connie. "Can I kiss her yet?"

We all giggled. Cory reached over and punched Fish lightly on the arm.

Connie nodded.

Fish drew Delia into his arms, tilted her back, and looked into her eyes. "Hello, my beautiful wife."

Their lips met, and the room erupted into applause. When Fish finally let her breathe, Delia burst into tears of happiness. Fish turned and offered his hand to James, but James pushed it aside and gave him a hug.

Cory stepped up to Fish. "You did good, kid."

Delia threw her arms around me. "Oh Thea, I'm so happy."

"You deserve this and more," I replied.

Javier approached and hugged Fish, lifting Fish's feet from the floor. "You did it, man. I'm so happy for you."

Joshua joined the group and wrapped his arms around Delia and Fish. "I love you guys."

"Shut up, Ginger," Fish teased.

We all burst into laughter when Fish swept Delia up into his arms and started walking out. "Be right back!" he called over his shoulder.

No one could stop laughing.

The look of horror on Delia's face was priceless. "Now?" she asked. "Right now?"

"And later, too," Fish said, kicking open the ballroom doors.

The giggles continued all through dinner as we waited for the happy couple to return. Fish had waited so long for this moment, who could blame him? James celebrated with the rest of the boys. They must have opened six or more bottles of wine in the hour since Fish had taken off with Delia. Ciro already seemed a little drunk, and the rest of them weren't far behind.

When Mr. and Mrs. Fisher finally returned, looking a mess, the entire room burst into laughter all over again. Delia was smiling from ear to ear. Fish looked relieved. James stood and held up his glass.

"To the happy couple!"

A round of applause broke out amid the laughter as everyone toasted the disheveled newlyweds. Delia smoothed her hair and smiled sheepishly. I couldn't help but noticed how she was glowing. She looked utterly happy.

Fish shook hands with James. "Sorry, buddy," Fish said. "I had a four-hundred-year itch to take care of."

James threw his head back and laughed. "I'm happy you finally scratched it, kid."

Fish raised his eyebrows. "More than a few times."

James laughed again and raised his glass. "I would like to make an official toast to the happy couple."

He was a little drunk. I'd never seen him like that before. Fish and Delia sat as James took the floor. He walked to the middle of the room, stumbling a bit. "When you fall in love," he began, "you want to give everything to that person. Any dream they have, you want to make come true. Anything they desire, you want to put within their reach.

"What you don't do," he said, glancing my way, "is push them away from you. You never hurt them, you never leave them, and you never lose faith in them."

Delia glanced at me and nudged Fish.

"Who gives their husband up to another witch they don't even love?" James slurred. "I'll tell you who, this witch right here." James pointed to me while taking another swig of his wine. "The vows we heard today meant nothing to her. She never stood behind me or next to me, only in front of me."

Fish and Cory got to their feet, but Ciro was already there. "James, come sit down."

James pushed him away, spilling wine onto Ciro's shirt. "I'm okay, amigo. I just have a few more words for my sorry excuse for a wife."

Cory joined Ciro's effort to lead James out of the room. James pushed Cory. "Take her, she's all yours. But don't come running to me when she throws you away like a used rag."

"James, you're drunk," Cory replied. "You don't know what you're saying."

James stumbled toward Cory. "Oh, I know what I'm saying. That witch gave you what she never wanted to give me—her respect. All she ever gave me was a little piece of ass. Then again, I guess she gave that to both of us."

Pressed to his limit, Cory punched James square in the face. James fell back and hit the floor.

Cory tried going after James again, but Ciro held him back. "Don't you ever talk about her like that again!" Cory erupted.

Ciro dragged him off into the foyer while James slowly rose to his feet, staring me down the entire time. I didn't know what to say. I had known he was angry, but this was different. He hated me. I could see that now. The love we shared was gone. I had done too much damage.

James finally looked away and walked out. A moment later, I heard the front door open and close.

After a moment of awkward silence, Fish stood and raised his glass to Delia. "To my beautiful bride."

We all raised our glasses. "To the bride!"

Fish was determined not to let James's outburst spoil the day. He took Delia's hand and led her to the dance floor. Soon everyone was dancing and smiling again. I kept checking the door, hoping James would run back in and beg me to forgive him. But that never happened. James never returned to the wedding.

Cory later apologized to Delia and Fish. James's name wasn't mentioned for the rest of the day. The bride was passed along until she had danced with all the boys. When Fish snuck her away to the guest house again, the guests started to leave. I couldn't wait to take off the dress and hurried upstairs to change. I was thankful to find a pair of old jogging pants and a sweatshirt and threw them on. It was time to help my father clean up. One quick wave of my hand would put the house in order again.

I was coming out of my room when I saw James walking down the hallway with his arm around Helena. He was so drunk, she was practically holding him up. They passed me without a glance. James's eyes were glazed over. I'd never seen him so drunk.

They stopped in front of the bedroom we had once shared. James slowly looked at me and back at Helena. A single tear rolled down my cheek as he kissed Helena and opened our bedroom door.

I couldn't help myself from calling out. "Please, don't, James."

He paused, closed his eyes, and guided Helena into the room. Helena looked over her shoulder and gave me a wicked smile as James closed the door behind them.

When I saw the light disappear from under the door, my heart died.

Chapter 14
Death Valley

I tore my eyes away from the door and started for the stairs. My world was crashing down around me. My body was numb. I could barely feel the floor beneath my feet. I felt only pain traveling through every part of me. When I reached the bottom step, I sat down and stared ahead of me, seeing nothing.

My father walked out of the ballroom and approached the stairs. "I didn't hear you come down."

My gaze remained fixed ahead.

"What's wrong?" my father asked.

I couldn't answer him. I buried my face in my hands and began to cry.

"Thea, look at me."

The shock on his face when he looked into my eyes told me that he knew. He looked up the stairs. "What has he done?"

Cory walked out of the kitchen covered in snow. "Hey, have you guys looked outside?"

My father turned to him. "What do you mean?"

"The snow, I've never seen it so heavy before. You can't even see the guest house from the back patio."

My father hurried to the kitchen. "Thea!"

I wiped my face and rose to my feet. In the kitchen, I followed my father's eyes out the window. It looked like the heavens had opened up. The snow fell so fast I couldn't tell if it was night or day.

My father turned to me. "You must leave now." He rushed out of the kitchen.

I followed him up the stairs. "But the capsule, it's not ready."

"You'll have to leave without it."

Cory followed close on our heels. "What's going on?"

When we reached my father's room, he scratched out a spell on a piece of paper and handed it to me. "Here, this is the spell you'll need. You must leave at once."

"But the capsule—"

"There's no time."

Cory snatched the paper from my hands. "I'm coming with you."

"No, Cory," I said. "You're staying here."

"Don't bother, Thea. I'm not taking no for an answer."

There was no talking him out of it. I hurried to my room, grabbed the ring and the wand, and threw on a coat. When I reappeared in the doorway of my father's room, he ushered me in and closed the door. "Quickly now!"

Cory grasped my arm, and I pushed the ring onto my finger.

Normally I would have gazed around me in wonder as we spiraled into my father's world, but this time I kept my head down, trying hard to redirect my thoughts from James to Magia. I held back the tears for as long as I could, but my emotions got the best of me. My heart was breaking into a million pieces.

Cory pulled me into his arms. "It's going to be okay. I don't know what's going on, but I'm with you."

I didn't bother to explain that I was crying for James. I just buried my face in his chest until we reached Magia. I quickly pulled away when the scorching-hot air hit us. It felt as though Attor was blowing fire our way.

Cory wiped his forehead, which was already damp with sweat. "What the hell?" He removed his huge winter coat. "Where are we?"

"Still in Magia," I replied, slipping out of my own coat. "This is just another part of it."

He removed his wool sweater. "Why is it so dam hot here?"

I looked up at the sun, which was dimmer than the last time. Where was all this heat coming from? It felt like we were inside an oven.

Cory peeled off another layer. "It's got to be a hundred and thirty degrees here." He was already half undressed, wearing only his jeans.

I looked around for the others, but they were nowhere in sight. "I don't understand. Where are they?"

"Attor!" Cory called out.

The greenery had turned brown and dry. Most of the massive trees leaned to one side, their leaves drooping and nearly dead. I searched for Peter but couldn't locate him among the trees. The rushing river was little more than a slow-flowing creek. The falls had run dry. The fairies were gone.

"What the hell is going on?" Cory asked.

I shook my head. "I don't know."

"Attor!" Cory called out again.

We separated and searched the forest. The heat made it impossible to do anything with any kind of speed. Walking soon became an arduous task, and the jogging pants I wore were not making things any easier. I was drenched in sweat. I thought of using my stick to fly, but I couldn't chance Wendell spotting us.

I stumbled through the trees, snagging my clothes on the dried branches. I could no longer stand it. I removed my pants and, soon after, my shirt. For once in my life, I didn't care that I was out and about half naked. I picked up my father's wand and kept searching. Intense thirst soon set in. If I didn't find them soon, I would have to leave and get some water. I made my way back to where we'd arrived.

"Thea, I think I found something," Cory called out.

I stopped in my tracks. "Where are you?"

"Over this way!"

I followed Cory's voice and found him standing near the dried-up falls. The look on his face reminded me that I was walking around in my bra and underwear. I didn't care. It didn't even faze me that he, too, had undressed down to his boxers.

"What did you find?" I asked.

He pointed up at the rocks. "A tunnel."

I could see the strange rocks more clearly now that the water wasn't cascading over them. A cool breeze met my face as I examined one of the holes more closely. I couldn't tell how far back it went.

"What do you see?" Cory asked.

"Nothing, but it's cool in there."

"Get in, Thea," he said, helping me up.

He climbed in behind me. The tunnel was small and cramped.

"Thea, let me crawl in front of you."

I looked back to find Cory averting his eyes from my backside. I laughed and let him pass me. We both sighed in relief when the cool breeze hit us.

I leaned my back against the cool wall. "I'll never complain about the cold again."

Cory laid on his back. "Or the snow," he added.

We laughed, enjoying our respite from the intense heat.

"Why is it so hot out there?" Cory asked. "What happened to this place?"

I told him what I knew.

He was disturbed to learn that Wendell's war was affecting our world as well. "So that's why all the snow?"

"Yes, that's why I have to break the spells the wizards cast on the river."

"Don't they realize what they're doing?"

"Martin seems to think not."

Cory got on all fours. "We'd better find Attor and get to that river."

"You're not going there with me."

"I got news for you, lady. You have no choice but to take me with you."

"What do you mean?"

"I memorized the spell and threw the paper away." He smiled and began moving forward again.

I crawled behind him, shaking my head. I saw an opening a good distance away. The tunnel became damp as we neared the opening. It soon became clear that water lay ahead.

"Man, am I ever dying of thirst," Cory said.

The tunnel ended in a huge cave with a few inches of water on the ground. Cory called it a cavern. A dim light shone down over the cave's opening. Cory said the water was from the rain.

"Is it safe to drink?" I asked.

"Guess we'll find out," he said, scooping up a handful.

I quickly followed suit and filled my palms with water.

"Take it slow," Cory warned.

"But I'm so thirsty." I filled my palms again.

Cory stood and looked around. "Look, there are hundreds of tunnels just like the one we used. There's no telling which one they could be in."

I looked at all the holes in the walls. "What makes you think they're in any of them?"

"Are you kidding? We were only out there five minutes, and we couldn't take it. I'd be willing to bet they've found an even better place than this cavern."

A thought occurred to me. I scrambled to my feet. "If the others are trying to stay cool, maybe Wendell and his army are doing the same."

"Are you saying you think they're in these tunnels?"

"No, I'm just saying they're not out there."

Without thinking, we both jumped back into the tunnel and returned to the sweltering heat. It felt like the temperature had risen since we crawled into the tunnel. My throat was so dry; I longed to go back to the cave for more water.

Cory coughed. "This place is an absolute oven."

I held the wand up and waited for it to turn into my stick. But the wand didn't respond. I waved my hand at a tree, and a branch flew into my hand. "Hop on."

I was taking a big chance by flying, but Cory was right. If we couldn't take being out here, neither could the wizards. The air made it almost impossible to breathe. I searched the trees, hoping to spot Peter, but all I could see for miles was dying forest. The trees seemed to have thinned out. Perhaps Peter and his people had also moved to a cooler place.

I didn't know my way around Magia, and I had no idea how big it was.

When we flew into the part of Magia we'd been to before, Cory gasped. "What happened to this place?"

I didn't answer. I was too busy keeping an eye out for wizards. I passed the edge of the forest where they had waited during my last visit, but the coast was clear. When we neared the magical lake I loved so much, my mouth fell open. The lake was pure mud— dried and cracked. Dead fish lay on its surface. The stench of death permeated the air.

"Are we too late?" Cory asked.

I flew faster, searching frantically for any signs of life. Why had I waited so long to come back? Why hadn't I insisted my father give me that spell right away and returned to Magia that same day?

"Hold on, Cory," I said, soaring over a mountain. The heat was nearly unbearable now. It intensified as we neared the river. Attor's cave soon came into view. The forest adjacent to his cave remained untouched, the leaves as green and lush as ever.

"Don't go through there," Cory warned.

I flew high into the clouds and over the top of

the forest. "What the hell is that?" Cory asked, pointing down.

Below us, streams of energy flowed back and forth over the river, so strong we could actually hear the spells buzzing.

"The wizards' spells."

"Is that the river?"

"I think so. Attor told me once it was just beyond the trees."

I hovered above the river, the heat from the spells making it impossible to remain still.

Cory grasped the branch. "We're going to fall."

I saw a safe place to land near the river bank. We jumped off the branch and right back on when our feet hit the blistering ground.

Cory struggled to breathe. "I can't take this."

"Tell me the spell—hurry!"

After Cory relayed the spell to me, I looked down at the river and chanted: "I break this spell and free the land, your king removes it with my command."

I waved my hand and sent the spell into the river. A sound like breaking glass crackled in the air. Cory and I watched in awe as the wizards' spells lifted, spiraled toward the sky, and exploded like a Fourth of July fireworks display. Millions of tiny sparkles whirled upward and into the sun.

The ground rumbled as clouds formed and released sheets of cool rain. The wind blew like a tornado. The sparkles coming from the water felt like grains of sand hitting my face. The branch spun wildly.

"Thea!" Cory shouted.

I reached for him, but he lost his balance, fell into the river, and was quickly sucked under. Attor's talons snagged me before I could jump. "Let go!"

I kept screaming Cory's name as Attor flew. I was about to wave my hand when he set me down at the river's edge.

"Stop screaming, witch. I will go and retrieve your friend."

Panic consumed me as Attor flew up and dove into the water. When they didn't emerge right away, I cried, "Cory!"

The wind died down. The sun once again shone brightly over Magia. Minutes passed, and there was no sign of either of them. I stood trembling at the water's edge, tempted to jump in. I screamed Attor's name and waited.

I was about to dive in when I felt a stabbing pain in my back. My head hit the ground with a thump. A loud buzzing filled my head, and pain traveled through every part of my body. I could no longer feel the ground under me. I could move my eyes but nothing else.

A pair of feet and two long brown talons appeared in front of me. It was one of the guards. He turned me over onto my back and threw what looked like clay over my hand. The clay encased my hand and turned to stone. They were trying to prevent me from removing my father's ring. The guard snatched my father's wand from my other hand and ordered his cronies to search me.

"She's not wearing clothes," one of them said.

"I don't care," the guard replied. "Find that capsule."

I felt hands along my body. I squeezed my eyes shut when the guard put his hand under my bra. He brushed over my breast and moved down toward my underwear.

He paused and looked up at the guard. "I can't do it, Porteus."

The one named Porteus pushed him away. "She broke her spell for a reason." He searched me himself, making sure to cover every inch of my flesh. I kept my eyes closed until it was over.

He towered above me. "Where's the capsule, witch?"

When I didn't answer, he leaned over and grabbed my ankle. My body convulsed from the shockwaves his hand sent through me.

"Where is the capsule?"

"I . . . I didn't bring it with me."

His eyes narrowed. "Why did you break your spell over the river, if not to steal the energy?"

"It wasn't my spell."

"We shall see, witch."

He lifted me from the ground and flung me over his shoulder. I looked toward the river as Porteus mounted his staff. Neither Attor nor Cory had emerged yet. I tried waving my hand, but the buzzing grew louder. "I'm going to kill you." I closed my eyes, trying to tune it out. I thought my head would explode. "Make it stop!"

Porteus laughed. "You are no wizard."

"Go to hell."

"It is you who will go to hell, witch."

"It wasn't me, you idiot. It was the wizards."

He stopped in mid-air and pulled me off his shoulder, his touch sending more waves of pain through my body. He held me up by the neck. "What do you speak of, witch?"

I looked into his big red eyes. He had the

features of an owl, with colored feathers covering most of his face. "Are you blind, or just stupid?"

He tightened his grip around my neck. "I will ask again, what do you speak of?"

I could barely breathe. "The wizards bound the river with a spell, not me."

He drew me closer until I could smell his putrid breath. "The wizards would do no such thing."

"They would and they did. I broke their spells."

His eyes flared with anger. "That was your spell!"

"You're hurting me."

His unnerving smile revealed foul yellow teeth. "This is nothing compared to what the wizards will do to you." He squeezed my neck harder. "They'll kill you for what you've done."

"All I've done is break the wizards' spells that were killing Magia."

"Why would the wizards cast a spell over the river if they knew it would kill us?"

"Why don't you ask Wendell that question?"

He heaved me over his shoulder again and flew away. The buzzing in my head intensified when the other guards caught up to us. One guard threw a net to Porteus, which he used to restrain me. He tied the net to his staff and flung me over it. I dangled at his side, sighing when the painful shocks finally stopped. I threaded my fingers through the net and surveyed the surroundings.

Magia was coming back to life. The sun's rays had awoken the forest. Flowers sparkled again. Shades of green spread across the land. I heard the water cascading over the falls as my lake—restored to its former beauty—came into view.

You did it, Thea.

Behind me, there was still no sign of Attor or
Cory. I wouldn't give up hope, but things were not
looking good. I prayed they'd seen the guards and
come out at another part of the river to avoid them. I
tried to scrape the clay from my hand, but the shocks
returned with a vengeance when the guards caught me.
All the while, Porteus kept me dangling from his staff.
I thought I would fall at any moment.

The guards flew past the village they had once
taken me to. I saw a mountain like the one where Cory
and I had found the tunnels—a massive rock dotted
with holes. As we approached a particularly huge
tunnel, the guards glided into it with ease. The cool air
washed over me as we ventured inside. It took me only
seconds to realize where the wizards had taken refuge.

When Porteus stopped abruptly, the other
guards looked at him, confused.

"Is something wrong?" one of them asked.

"No," Proteus replied. "Go tell the wizards the
girl removed her spell. I will wait for them back at the
village."

The guards exchanged puzzled glances. They
finally nodded and continued through the tunnel.

I didn't know what to think as Porteus made his
way back toward the tunnel's entrance.

"What are you doing?"

"Silence, witch. I don't have much time."

"Where are you taking me?"

Ignoring my question, he flew back to the
village and flung me to the ground. He opened the net
and dragged me out, then placed the tip of his tail into
my ear. "This is going to hurt."

Pain like I'd never felt before surged through

my body. I couldn't scream. I could barely breathe. Porteus peered into my eyes, searching for God knows what.

After what seemed like an eternity, he removed his tail from my ear and threw the net back over me.

"Wendell is going to kill you."

I looked up at him. "You know, don't you? You know it wasn't me."

"Silence, witch. The wizards don't know about our ability to see truth."

"You have to help me. Remove this cast from my hand so I can leave."

He looked up to the sky. "It's too late. They're coming."

Chapter 15
The Dungeon

Wendell was drawing near with his army of wizards in tow. Upon closer inspection, the wizards appeared weak and tired, their eyes dull and their frames frail. Wendell's hair had grayed completely, and his eyes were lined with dark circles. He grasped his staff with what little strength he had, looking as though he would tumble off it at any moment. I wondered if Martin and the others had fared as badly.

Wendell landed with a thump and staggered over to us. "Did she take the energy?"

"I found no capsule," Proteus replied.

Wendell craned his neck to the guard. "Did you search her?"

"Yes, sire. She had nothing."

Wendell peered down at me. "You're about to die, witch."

I tried again to remove the clay from my hand, with no success. As I raised my other hand to wave it, the painful shocks returned. Porteus eyed me intently, gesturing with his head toward the arriving guards. I understood then that they, not Porteus, were the ones causing my pain.

Slowly the village filled with people, all weakened by the wizards' spell. Their faces were drawn, their expressions angry. I was the enemy. They blamed me for what Wendell had done. Once again, he had lied to them. I tried in vain to tell them the truth. When I opened my mouth to speak, the painful shocks returned, rendering me silent and convulsing. I covered my head as one of the guards pulled me out of the net and threw me at Wendell's feet.

"Bring me a dagger," Wendell said, glaring at me.

I staggered to my feet, but Wendell kicked me back down.

"Any last wishes?" he asked.

I lifted my head and glared. "I was about to ask you the same question."

"I don't think you're in any position to threaten me, witch."

"Kill her!" a wizard shouted from the crowd.

Wendell faced his subjects. "Do you doubt me now, brothers? Have I not shown you the true enemy?" He pointed at me. "She cast the spell that nearly destroyed this land. I warned you this would happen."

"We see now, Your Majesty," one of the wizards replied. "She did indeed come back to steal the energy, just as you said."

I had believed that all the wizards together had cast that spell over the river, but I now knew that Wendell had worked alone.

"Make her surrender the ring to you, sire," another wizard called out.

Wendell nodded and turned to me. "Of course, the ring."

I screamed as shocks seized my body. I vaguely

sensed myself being dragged across the ground. When I opened my eyes, I lay on a wooden table in a dark dungeon. Chains restrained my hands and feet. The clay on my hand had been removed. I struggled to free myself, once again racked with the pain of the shocks.

"Do you know what that pain is?"

I lifted my head and peered into the darkness. Wendell stood across the room, flanked by two guards. He looked himself again. He'd been to the river and replenished his powers.

"It's the guard's defenses," he said. "We know how to stop it. Our minds are too strong to be controlled by pain. It's clear your father never bothered to teach you that." He approached the table and smiled. "I shall thank him for that one day."

He trailed his fingers along my face. His touch felt like a thousand daggers penetrating my skin. My screams pleased him.

Without looking back, he said, "Leave us."

After the guards left the room, Wendell leaned over me. "Surrender the ring to me."

I looked into his eyes, a glimmer of hope rising inside me. "You can't take it from me, can you?"

He clenched his jaw and sniffed.

I spat in his face. "That ring is never leaving my finger!"

He wiped his face and smiled, placing his hand over my forehead. A gasp of pain escaped me.

"Your father's shield grows weak," he whispered in my ear. "I'm going to enjoy torturing you."

"G . . . go to hell."

He pulled his hand away and walked to a box on the floor. "Did you know there is a part of the body that feels pain more intensely than any other?" He opened the box. "Simon knows of it. I'm the one who told him." He pulled out three long needles. "I told Simon about a lot of things. I even taught him a spell to render your father useless." He walked back to me. "You see, wizards can be killed in your world. Our defenses grow weak in the human air—something your father has learned the hard way."

He placed the needles by my feet and continued. "I should have been king. I was next in line for the throne. But Xander decided to have a daughter, an heir. My chance at becoming king just floated away. And that's where Simon comes in. Your father was a fool to bring that witch here. He was even more foolish when he began leaving Simon behind in Magia. He never suspected the evil thoughts going through that boy's head." He held up one of the needles and inspected it. "But I did. I began to mold Simon, shape him in my image. While your father was busy falling in love, I was busy turning Simon against him."

He placed his hand over my ankle. "I must say, I was disappointed to see you were still alive. Simon made a very special promise to kill you. But I'll deal with Simon later. Right now I have a question for you." He held up the needle again. "Is your father really alive?"

"Yes."

He turned the needle in his hand as tiny steel barbs popped out of it. He held the tip to the needle up to my foot and pushed it in.

"Please, no!"

He left the needle in place and grabbed another. "Let me explain something to you. It's not possible for your father to be alive. No one can survive a black spell." Once again, he placed his hand over my ankle. "So I will ask again: Is your father still alive?"

"N . . . no," I lied.

"Very good. Now I want you to command the ring into my hand."

"Never."

I felt the agony of the second needle, a thousand times more painful than Simon's. My screams echoed off the dungeon walls. Wendell waited patiently until my cries of pain ceased. I saw where Simon had acquired his signature lack of empathy.

"Surrender the ring to me, witch!"

"N . . . no."

He pushed in the last needle.

"Father!" I screamed.

Wendell returned to the box. "I see that three needles will not be enough for you." He pulled out five more and fanned them in his hand.

"No!" I cried.

The dungeon door opened, and Porteus walked in. "Sire, the Onfroi are back."

Wendell's face went pale. "Where are they?"

"A few miles from the line, sire."

Wendell rushed to my side, holding the needles over my face. "Surrender the ring to me!"

I narrowed my eyes. "Go to hell, Wendell."

Fury filled his eyes. He scurried down the length of the table and thrust all five needles into my foot at once. I gasped from the pain. Darkness clouded my vision. "Surrender it!"

I couldn't scream. I couldn't cry. As I slipped into shock, I could see Wendell's fist striking my face over and over again, but I felt nothing. I looked up as I drifted away. Wendell's voice faded. As the darkness closed in around me, a single stream of light shone on a figure standing in the distance. *Father.* He held out his arms, calling for me to come to him. I ran to him.

"Close your eyes," he whispered.

"Yes, Father." I felt his arms around me as I drifted further into blackness. I felt something bouncing off my body but couldn't see what it was. My father held me tightly as a cold, sharp object was dragged along my stomach.

He pulled away and took my face in his hands. "Come back to me, Thea."

"I will, Father. I will."

A tearing sound broke through the haze, and I opened my eyes. Wendell stood above me, dagger in hand. His chest heaved. His hands were covered in blood. Porteus stood behind him, mouth agape.

"Why won't you die?" Wendell shouted. He turned to Porteus. "Take her to the cave."

Porteus nodded and removed the chains from my hands and feet. I had no strength with which to pull the ring from my finger. It was my only chance of escape, but I was too weak. There was pain, but I was too exhausted to react to it. Porteus lifted me from the table, but unlike before, he didn't fling me over his shoulder. He held me in his arms and let me lean my head on his chest. I spied the puddle of blood left behind on the table and wondered how long Wendell had been beating me. I looked down at my body, now saturated in blood.

Deep gashes lined my stomach. Every breath I took sent more blood gushing from the wounds. I couldn't understand how Wendell could cut me open without me feeling it. I closed my eyes and thought about my father, allowing myself to believe that he had helped me. The comfort of his arms had shielded me from the pain.

Wendell waited at the door of the dungeon. "Take her to the cave, and don't leave until I come for you."

"Yes, sire," Porteus replied.

I could hear the commotion in the village as people frantically asked Wendell what to do about the Onfroi. Porteus quietly mounted his staff and flew away with me.

I looked up into his red eyes. "Why didn't you help me?"

He ruffled his feathers. "I just did, Your Highness."

I moaned and tried to heal myself, but my magic was weak. I couldn't focus my mind long enough to render a successful healing spell. I was dying. These would be the last moments of my life.

I wanted my last thoughts to be of James. He was my greatest love. I would die loving him. I wished him nothing but happiness and prayed he would find peace in his life with Helena.

"Hang on, Your Highness. We're almost there."

But I knew it was too late. I thought of Cory. I couldn't leave him trapped here in this world. Even if he was dead, the ring would find him and bring him back when I removed it. I looked down at my bloody hand. It took every ounce of strength I had to reach for the ring. I had to do this for Cory. The boys deserved to say their goodbyes. With one last effort, I pulled off the ring.

The wind blew backwards. Porteus, who had maintained his grip, spun into the vortex with me. I sighed in relief. I heard a voice getting closer and closer. I soon saw Cory being pulled in with us. He slammed into Porteus's back with a thud.

Cory turned and quickly backed away, his eyes widening. He looked at my feet and shot his head up. "Put her down!"

Porteus held fast to me. "You will have to kill me first."

I extended my hand to Cory. "It's okay."

Cory grasped my hand and stepped closer, he shook his head in horror. "For the love of god, what have they done to you?" His eyes filled as they drifted up to meet Porteus's piercing gaze. "I beg you, let me hold her."

Porteus hesitated and looked at me.

I nodded slightly.

Carefully he handed me over to Cory, who gathered me in his arms and burst into sobs. "My god, Thea, look what they did to you." His body trembled as he tried to heal me.

I knew it was too late. I slowly looked up at him. "I love you, Cory. You're my greatest friend."

"No! Do not say good bye. Please, Thea."

"Tell James I love him. Tell him I believe in him."

"Thea!" Cory cried.

I closed my eyes and felt the ring slip from my hand. I prayed that my father would not blame himself. He had done all he could to change the outcome of my fate. I regretted never having been able to find the leaves. I had wanted desperately to set him free. I prayed Porteus would find some way to help him.

"She's gone," Porteus said.

Cory held me to his chest and sobbed. "I'm so sorry, Thea. I'm so sorry."

I wanted to tell him I was still here. I could still hear him, I could still feel him. The wind slowed to a stop. I heard the ring bounce onto the floor. We were back in my father's room, but I couldn't hear his voice. I tried to open my eyes so I could see him one last time, but it was no use. I was drifting further and further into darkness.

I felt Cory sink to the floor, his tears wetting my face. A moment later, I heard the door open.

"Thea!" James yelled.

I felt James gently pull me from Cory's arms. "No, no," he murmured, holding me to his chest.

"She's gone," Cory said.

"No!" James cried. "Please no." He chanted a healing spell, his sweet breath caressing my face, his body trembling as he rocked me. "Come back to me, Thea."

Trapped inside a lifeless body, I fought to communicate any way I could, but I couldn't break through.

I felt James's gentle touch on my cheek. "I'll be right behind you, my love. Nothing will ever keep us apart again." His lips were on mine. "I love you."

His words gave me permission to let go. I could die happy, knowing he loved me. As I drifted toward darkness, the sound of James's sobs brought back memories of my father after my mother died. His cries of agony were as though his heart had died with her. I had never wanted to cause James that kind of pain. I had only ever wanted to make him happy. If I could only touch him one last time.

"Did you see that?"

Cory's voice.

"She moved her hand."

"She's alive," Porteus said.

"William!" James shouted.

James, Cory, and Porteus broke into simultaneous chants.

"William!" James shouted again between spells.

The pain began to fade. I felt a single tear roll down my cheek.

"Don't leave me," James cried. "Please don't leave me."

"William!" Cory shouted.

"Go bang on that wall," James said. "Tell this thing to help you."

I heard a scuffling sound, and a moment later, pounding on the wall of my father's room.

"William!"

Cory gasped, and then silence.

"Your Majesty," Porteus said.

"Your Majesty?" Cory replied.

"Bring her in here," my father said. "Quickly."

He sounded out of breath. What was wrong with him? They carried me across the room, but to where?

"There on the floor," my father said.

"William," Cory asked, his voice panicked. "What's wrong with your stomach?"

My father's stomach; now I knew. We were more deeply connected than I could have imagined. My father had taken the brunt of my pain from Wendell's violent blows.

I tried desperately to open my eyes. "Father . . ."

I felt his fingers brush my face. "I'm with you, daughter. I am always with you."

"Please save her, William," James cried.

I felt another set of hands on me. "What are you doing?" Cory asked.

"Heal her, son," my father said. "Wish her back to the way she was."

"What?" Cory replied. "I don't have the power to do that."

"I can't hold on to her life much longer," my father said. "You must heal her."

"William, I'm half human. I don't do things like that."

"You do now," my father replied.

The room fell silent.

"Just do it!" James yelled.

"She's going to lose her baby if you don't hurry," my father said.

"What?" James gasped.

Baby? Memories flashed in my mind of me placing my son's soul into the crystal. Why hadn't I remembered this before? How could my son be at risk if he was safe inside the crystal? Panic set in. What had my father done? Things started to make sense: why my father was always trying to feed me, why he didn't want me fighting the warlocks. But why would he move my son and put him in harm's way?

The desire to live grew inside me. I would protect my son at all costs. Why wasn't my father retrieving him and returning him to the crystal?

Take him out!

"We're losing her," my father said. "You must heal her now."

"Heal her, or I'll kill you!" James shouted.

Cory's trembling hands hovered over my stomach. "Heal." He gently ran his hands over my arms to my hands, and from my hips down to my feet.

One by one, he removed the needles.

"Careful," James said.

Nothing mattered but our son. I clenched my jaw as Cory carefully withdrew the needles. I could take any amount of pain if it meant saving my son. But why couldn't I open my eyes? I felt desperate to know if they had saved my son. If my son was lost, I would hunt Wendell down like an animal, torture him, and kill him.

"I'm sorry, William," Cory said. "I've done everything I can do."

There wasn't a needle in the world that could match the pain in my heart. My son was dead. My life was over. Not even James could give me a reason to live.

Their voices faded as I sank into the darkness with my misery.

Chapter 16
Greed and Revenge

I remained in darkness for countless days. I heard voices around me, but felt no compelling reason to open my eyes. I ignored James's cries and drifted further into isolation. Something had changed inside me. This new kind of hell had painted my heart black; it was easier to hate than to love. Love caused pain. Hate turned pain into madness—a madness I willingly embraced.

I opened my eyes to the room I had once shared with James, the same room where James had bonded with Helena. I sat up in bed and gasped. Throbbing pain pulsated through every inch of my body. My father's healing tea sat untouched on the nightstand. I searched the room and was relieved to see that I was alone. I swung my legs over the edge of the bed and placed my aching feet onto the cool wood floor. I lifted my foot and surveyed the damage, shocked to see that my feet were still bruised, as though someone had smeared them with black paint. I ran my fingers along the stitching. It had been days; why hadn't they healed?

I pushed myself up from the bed and stood, shaking off the agony. The only thing on my mind was getting my hands on my father's ring. Wendell would not live to see another day. I took two excruciating steps forward and stopped, drawing a deep breath to combat the dizziness. James had restored the room to how I remembered it—filled it with glittering flowers and signs of our love. But nothing he did now could change what had happened. My son was dead, and James was a bonded man. Any hope of reuniting with him had died with our son.

I shuffled to the door, trying to ignore the pain in my feet. I felt so weak and wondered how long I had been in that bed. I opened the door and peered down the hallway. I had to get to my father's room and retrieve the ring—but quietly. My father would surely stop me from returning to Magia.

I tiptoed down the hall and heard voices as I approached my father's room. I stopped short of the door and listened.

"What do you mean I'll be back to normal in a few days?" Cory asked.

My father chuckled.

How can he be so happy right now?

"Human air will destroy what the river has given you," my father said. "You will be back to being half human in no time."

"Why hasn't that happened to Thea?" Cory asked.

"She's not half human, is she?" my father answered. "The river can't take what it never gave her. She will always be half wizard. No amount of human air will ever take that from her. She is the first of our kind to be born here. Her body has learned to adapt to this world."

"What if she had fallen into the river with me?" Cory asked. "What would have happened then?"

There was a pause before my father answered.

"I have wondered that myself."

"You don't know?"

"I have an idea, but it's only speculation, of course."

"What if that Wendell guy recasts the spell on the river?" Cory asked.

"Wendell is not that foolish," my father replied. "The wizards will guard the river, now more than ever."

"Martin said they would have died if Thea hadn't broken Wendell's spells."

"Are they safe now?"

"I think so. When Attor pulled me out of the water, he took me back to the mountain where Thea and I found the cave. Attor shuttled Martin and Morgan to the river. I thought they were dead; they looked so weak. Those fairy things said the Onfroi had gone looking for water, but that they would return now that the spell was broken. When Martin came back, we searched for Thea. Before I knew it, I was sucked into the vortex." Cory paused, then snapped, "Stop hitting me with that thing."

"I can't control how my tail moves," Porteus replied, his tail hitting the floor with a thud.

"I'll make you a potion," my father said. "You will have to take human form until Thea can take you back."

"I have nothing to go back to, sire," Porteus said.

Silence. I inched closer to the door and leaned in.

"I can't believe you're a king," Cory said.

"Share that with no one," my father replied.

"Sire," Porteus said, "why did you never come

back to Magia?"

My father sighed. "It's a long story."

Anger swelled in my heart every time my father spoke. I blamed him for my pain. He had taken my son out of the crystal. I would never forgive him for that.

"I want to understand, sire," Porteus said. "Why did you bring that boy into our world?"

He was referring to Simon, of course. I waited, my ear against the door. I also wanted an answer to that question.

"The first time I saw Simon," my father began, "he'd been left on the streets of London by his human father. The boy couldn't understand why his father had abandoned him and left him on the streets to starve. I soon realized that he had no idea what he was. The fact that he was half witch had been kept from him. I began to help him. I showed him what he was." He sighed. "I felt sorry for him. His father had done this unspeakable thing. I took him to Magia in hopes that he would forget the nightmare he had lived through. Years passed, and he adapted well. But when I met Thea's mother, I began to leave him behind in our world for periods of time, and things changed. At the time, I didn't realize that Wendell had taken Simon under his wing in my absence and was molding Simon into his puppet.

"When I married my wife, I planned on taking her back to Magia with me. But, of course, I had to introduce her to Magia gradually. Our word would enchant her if I didn't take things slowly. At some point, I began to sense the danger. It kept me up nights and nagged at me for months. My gut told me someone was betraying me, but I wasn't sure who. When my wife told me she was with child, I knew I had to stay in the human world until I found out who the traitor was. I found a way to stay strong. I wasn't as strong as I was in Magia, but strong enough to protect my family."

Silence, and then: "What happened, sire?"

My father drew a deep breath and exhaled loudly. "One day Simon came calling at our home in this world. Needless to say, I was astonished to see him. I had never taught him the spell to leave Magia.

"Anyway, he told me that Wendell had kicked him out, and I foolishly believed him. I gave him a place to stay and let him eat from my table. Over the course of his stay, I saw the changes in him. And I didn't like the way he looked at my daughter. When he asked for her hand in marriage, I knew what he was up to."

"What did Simon do?" Cory asked.

My father's voice trembled as he spoke. "Human air had rendered me weaker than I realized, and Simon had gleaned just enough power to cast a black spell on me. It was then I realized who had betrayed me. Only a wizard could have taught Simon that spell—the only wizard who wanted me out of the way. Wendell was next in line for the throne. If I died, he would become king. Wendell needed me and my daughter out of the way, but Simon knew I would be hard to kill. That's when he decided it would be better to kill my wife. He understood that if he took something I loved, he would then be able to control me. It was the only way for the black spell to work. And once he had control of me, he could command me to her grave."

"Why didn't you kill him, sire?"

"I tried, but Wendell had taught Simon very

well. Simon protected himself with a wizard shield. My weak spells had no power to penetrate it. He escaped and disappeared. I knew Simon was waiting for the spell to work its evil. I searched for him for months, but when I saw the vision, I knew I had to come back and help my daughter."

"You searched for months?" Porteus asked. "How is that possible? The black spell would have put you in an endless sleep within days."

"Simon is not a wizard, Porteus. The spell he cast was weak by wizard standards. I was able to fight it for months, something Simon hadn't counted on. It gave me time to prepare, time to save my daughter."

Silence again. I straightened as a plan began to formulate in my head. When their voices resumed, I leaned toward the door.

"Why would Simon ask for your daughter's hand if he planned on killing you?" Porteus asked.

"Don't you see, Porteus?" my father replied. "Simon needed me to give him my daughter. He was never going to let Wendell be king. Simon had grown greedy; he wanted it all. If I agreed to let him marry my daughter, Simon would one day be king. He came armed with the black spell and had planned to cast it only after I said yes."

I couldn't believe it was going to be this easy. At last, Simon would have a purpose.

"Sire, you went back to Magia several times with your daughter. Why did you never go to the river and get strong again, or warn the wizards about Wendell?"

"The wizards were guarding the river by then," my father replied. "Wendell had turned them against me. And I was weak. What good would it do Thea if they killed me? I used what powers I had left to prepare her, to block the way out of Magia."

"And the ring will not take you there now?" Porteus asked.

"The ring no longer works for me. I have surrendered it to my daughter."

I heard Porteus' tail flapping. "I wanted to help her, sire, but Wendell would have killed me."

"You don't have to explain, Porteus. You did what you had to in order to get her out of there. Lying about the Onfroi was brilliant, by the way."

"You were there?" Cory asked.

"Yes," Porteus replied.

"Why didn't you stop him?"

I heard a scuffle and imagined Cory going after Porteus.

"It doesn't work that way, Cory," my father explained. "The guards can't attack a wizard. Our orders must always be obeyed. Wendell would have destroyed Porteus if he dared to speak up for Thea."

I stepped away from the door with my father's story repeating in my head. Simon wanted the throne, and he'd made it perfectly clear by now that he would do anything to get it. I finally had a weapon—Simon's greed. I would have my revenge, and Wendell would die.

Every step away from the door was more painful than the last. I clutched the railing as I descended the stairs. At the front door, I looked back. I was leaving the old Thea behind. She was dead, and she was never coming back. I opened the door and stepped out into the darkness.

Chapter 17
The Black Witch

The snow soothed my bare, aching feet. A cold gust of wind blew through my nightgown, but I could barely feel it. All I could feel was the pain of losing my son. How could a mother forget her own son? After I punished Wendell, I would find a way to punish myself.

I gazed at my surroundings. The snow had finally stopped falling, and everything was covered in white. The plows that had managed to get through before the wedding had left a wall of snow along the street. Cars parked along the curb had been buried. It appeared that the town had lost power, since the only light came from the moon reflecting off the snow. I looked back at the mansion's lit window, certain that spells were powering the house in the absence of electricity.

I walked to the gate and pulled it open. My blackened heart cared little for the life I was leaving behind. I had nothing left to lose, nothing left to fight for. I had already lost it all. Revenge was my only desire. I would pay any price to get it.

I walked down the middle of the snow-lined street. The town had come to a standstill. Not a single soul could be seen. I must have broken Wendell's spell just in time. The air was milder than it had been earlier in the day, but my feet were numb by the time I reached town.

My mind focused on Simon. He had the enchanted leaves and desperately wanted to rule Magia. I was going to take him there. Simon's warlocks would finally get their chance to kill the wizards. Those old fools had done nothing to help me, and I wasn't going to help them.

I sensed Simon when I neared my apartment. My eyes scanned the neighborhood. He was in the old man's house again, the one I passed in the mornings on my way to the bakery.

Simon's the old man.

I seethed at my own stupidity. I should have known. Simon had a talent for changing form.

I walked up onto the porch, waved my hand at the front door, and stepped inside. Simon's scent flooded the darkened room, which was lit only by firelight. Blankets lay in front of the hearth, as though someone had recently slept there. I warmed my hands in front of the fire, dropped to my knees, and waited. Simon would find me sooner or later.

I thought of the many ways I intended to torture Wendell, smiling to myself at the thought of slicing him open. I didn't want to kill him right away. I wanted him to suffer like I was suffering. I was still staring into the fire when I heard Simon walk in from the hallway.

I turned and smiled. "Hello, my lord."

He glanced over his shoulder, looking for his warlocks.

"Oh, you won't be needing your precious

minions tonight," I said, getting to my feet. "I'm not going to hurt you."

He eyed me from top to bottom, his eyes stopping at my bare feet.

I smiled. "I left in a hurry."

He tilted his head, mystified by my presence. "What are you doing here, witch?"

"Looking for you."

A nervous smile tugged at his mouth.

"I told you," I said, taking a step toward him. "I didn't come here to hurt you."

He eyed me suspiciously, his gaze traveling the length of my body. "I'll ask again, why are you here?"

"I need your help, my lord."

His face twisted in confusion. "You came to *me*, for help?"

I nodded. "I came to give you what you've always wanted."

Fear flashed in his eyes. He glanced over his shoulder again.

When I took a step toward him, he took a step back. "Remember, if you kill me, you die with me."

What a coward Simon was when his men weren't around to protect him. This was going to be too easy.

"Now Simon, how could you assume such a thing? As I said, I only came to give you what you've always wanted."

He stared at me, his terrified eyes exposing his true spineless nature.

"Who is this scared little boy I'm looking at?" I asked. "Where is the cold Simon I've grown to love?"

"You caught me off guard, witch."

I smirked. "You wouldn't be scared if you had

any real power."

I moved closer to him. This time he didn't back away.

"I can give that power to you." I brushed my hand along his cheek. "I will see to it that you are feared and respected."

He grabbed my wrist and held it. "What are you up to, witch?"

I smiled. "I'm looking for a king to rule beside me, my lord."

His eyes widened. He released my hand and again scrutinized my clothes, looking confused.

He obviously needed convincing. I would have to prove that I meant business. I stepped back, pulled my nightgown over my head, and let it drop to the floor. "Do with me what you will."

His mouth opened and closed. He studied me suspiciously. "Why now?"

"Because I need you."

"Need me for what?"

"To help me rule Magia."

His lips quivered. He looked over his shoulder and back to me. "Wait here," he said, and disappeared into the hallway. When he returned, he was holding the shawl. Now that he had his weapon in hand, his demeanor changed. He offered me the garment, an evil smile spreading across his face. "Put this on."

Once I donned the shawl, I would be at Simon's mercy. But the fear of what he had done to me the last time had vanished. I had nothing to lose now. If Simon bonded with me tonight, I would gladly pay the price if it meant killing Wendell. I was too weak to go alone into Magia. Wendell would have the upper hand. I needed Simon and his precious leaves to go with me.

I snatched the shawl from his hand. "If it will make you feel safe, my lord."

His face contorted in shock as I slipped the shawl over my shoulders. I staggered forward. "Please get me a chair."

He gathered me in his arms and set me on a couch across the room. "Why are you doing this?"

"Because I need you to believe me." I closed my eyes as my body grew weaker. "Do you want to be king or not?"

"What do you want, witch?" he asked, kneeling at my feet.

I gazed into his dark, suspicious eyes. "Revenge."

He smiled. "I don't think your plan is working."

"Not against you."

"If not me, then who?"

"Wendell."

Simon's smiled disappeared. He looked down, grabbed my ankle, and looked at the underside of my foot. He released my ankle and found my eyes again. "I see Wendell has left his mark."

"Yes. And now I want to leave mine."

"And you think I'm going to help you?"

"You will if you want to be king."

He sat on the couch and crossed his legs. "Do you really think I'm that stupid, witch?"

"At this moment, I think maybe you are."

"Really? And why is that?"

"Because you don't believe me."

He threw his head back and laughed. "And tell me, what else did Wendell do to you?"

I had nothing to hide anymore. What did it matter now if Simon knew the truth? "He killed my son." A single tear rolled down my face.

Simon's smile faded. He leaned in and studied my face. "You were with child?"

More tears spilled down my cheeks.   "Yes."

"The crystal," he muttered.

"Yes, my lord."

"That was your secret?"

I nodded.

"How did Wendell get his hands on the crystal?"

"My son wasn't in the crystal—not anymore." I cast my eyes down.

Simon followed my eyes and nodded. "I see." He pulled the shawl from my shoulders and smiled. "Tell me more about being king."

The numbing heaviness of the shawl lifted. Simon snatched my nightgown from the floor and handed it to me. I pulled it over my head. "So you believe me now?"

He slowly paced the floor in front of me. "I do, witch, and I'm going to tell you why. I once tortured you for information, and you surrendered nothing to me. I had no idea you had placed something else besides your powers into that crystal. You were willing to die to keep that secret from me." He stopped and turned to me, smiling. "I can only imagine what you'll do to Wendell." Once again, he knelt at my feet. "The question is: What are you willing to offer me for my help?"

I met his gaze. "If you help me, I'll marry you."

His eyes danced with a mixture of shock and delight. He reached up and ran the back of his hand along my face. It was strange how his touch diminished the pain. With every touch, he lifted me out of my hell. Simon was no longer the bad guy. He was my savior. I was ready and willing to pay any price he set to get what I wanted.

"Will you make that promise in blood?" he asked.

Once a promise was sealed in blood, it could not be broken. If the promise was broken, the blood of those who had taken the vow turned to dust. I wasn't worried; I would keep my word. The ritual was rumored to be dreadfully painful. But I was determined to endure it. "Yes."

Simon gasped. "You really are angry."

"I want all the wizards dead."

He chuckled. "That makes two of us, my angel."

"So you'll help me?"

"I'll do more than help you, witch. I'll drag Wendell to your feet."

I got to my feet. "I want him to suffer."

"I can arrange that," he replied, stroking my hair.

I leaned into him. "I want him to beg for his life."

"I give you my word, you will hear him scream."

I pulled back and looked into Simon's eyes. "I want to feel his blood on my hands."

Simon drew me back into his arms. "Consider it done." He crushed his lips to mine. I wrapped my arms around him, knowing I'd won. At last, I would know the secret of the leaves and use them to bring Wendell to his knees. Nothing else mattered. I was angry, bitter, and unable to contemplate the consequences of my actions. Only here in Simon's arms did I feel remotely alive again.

Simon's spell was suddenly the best thing that had ever happened to me. In his arms, my pain drifted away. I wouldn't have to fight anymore. I would surrender who I was and accept my future. The darkness would take care of me. Never again would I suffer heartbreak or be expected to solve everyone's problems. Finally I would be free.

I felt Simon's heart thumping as he kissed me. He moaned as I ran my fingers through his hair. When he pushed me away, I stumbled back, stunned. At first he looked angry, but soon he laughed. I stood back, perplexed by the sudden change in his mood. I was ready to give him whatever he wanted.

He pulled out his phone, a strange expression washing over his face. "Get in here." He snapped the device shut and stared at me for a moment. I was going crazy wondering what he was thinking. "I have to be careful with you, witch."

Has he changed his mind? "What do you mean?"

He ignored the question. "You have a promise to seal, remember?"

I was startled by a knock at the door.

"Just get in here!" Simon shouted.

The door opened, and a tall warlock with long, dark hair and a sword strapped to his back strode in. His choice of attire—cargo shorts and a T-shirt—stood out. It was odd to see anyone dressed like that this time of year. He had enormous calves and appeared very fit. He wasn't burly like most other warlocks, but was intimidating nonetheless. His stone-cold expression never wavered as he awaited Simon's orders.

"Toby," Simon said, "draw your sword."

The sound of the sword breaking free of its sheath echoed through the room. It resembled a Samurai sword. I closed my eyes, knowing what was coming. Pain had never deterred me before, but this was going to be difficult.

Simon caressed my face. "Now what was that you said about marrying me?"

I opened my eyes.

Simon smiled. "You should blame your father for this. He should have said yes when I asked him for your hand in marriage."

I glanced at the sword-wielding warlock and closed my eyes again, bracing myself for the pain.

"You can do it, my angel," Simon whispered. "Just picture Wendell's body at your feet."

I drew a breath. "I'm ready."

I heard footsteps and felt the sword's blade on my neck.

"Make the promise," Simon said.

Swallowing down my fear, I tried to remember the details of the ritual. A vial of blood was given to the person to whom the promise was made, and that person kept the blood until the promise was fulfilled. If the promise was fulfilled, the blood disappeared. If the promise was broken, death awaited the promise maker.

"Make the vow," Simon repeated.

With the blade pressed against my neck, I made a fist and chanted: "Shadows of darkness, spirits of hell, wake up and listen to the words of my spell. In blood I make a promise to wed this man one day. If that promise I do break, with my life you make me pay."

The blade slid across my neck like a feather. There was no pain, only the feeling of warm blood streaming down my chest. I opened my eyes as Simon held the vial to my neck. He filled it halfway, extended his arm, and nodded. The warlock held the sword above Simon's arm and made the cut.

The moment Simon's blood mixed with mine, my body twisted and contorted in pain. I dropped to the floor, screaming, as the pain seared into me. I wanted to rip away my own skin. It was as though fire ran through my veins. The spell worked its magic, marking my blood for death. I would be held accountable for my promise. I had summoned the demons and embraced the darkness. My life would never be the same.

I screamed until my mind wandered into a dark place, a hell populated by demons. Fire flamed from burning cages filled with lost souls. They reached for me through the bars, begging me to help them. A dark witch stood in the distance. I sensed that I knew her and studied her closely.

She's me.

She had dark eyes, and black clothing hugged every curve of her body. Her long, flowing hair was neither knotted nor tangled. She held out her arms and beckoned for me to come closer. I was mesmerized by her eyes, which looked so happy. This godforsaken place didn't bother her. I wanted that peace; I needed it. I inched closer, and she smiled and wrapped her arms around me. I closed my eyes and felt the two of us becoming one. The pain in my heart disappeared.

When I opened my eyes, she was gone, and I was wearing her clothes.

The demons had also disappeared. The cages were empty and the flames extinguished. A single ray of light shined into the chamber above my head. When

I reached for it, my mind was abruptly pulled away.

Chapter 18
The Spell Book

I heard the crackling of fire and opened my eyes. I lay on my stomach with my cheek to the floor. I was drenched in sweat. My heart raced as I lifted my head and looked around the room. An ugly feeling permeated my being and would not leave. Rage coursed through my veins. Something inside me had changed. There was no pain, no suffering. I had found peace in the darkest of places.

I got to my feet, trying to make sense of where my mind had just been. Had I just made a deal with the devil? I didn't care. If it meant Wendell would die, it was well worth the cost of my soul.

The house was empty. Where had Simon gone? I looked down at my nightgown, now covered in blood. I brought my hand to my neck and ran my fingers across the bandages.

A slip of paper lying on a nearby table caught my eye. It was a note from Simon: *I'll send for you.* But why had he left? My need to be with him stirred inside me, stronger than ever. I was even starting to think that making Simon king wasn't such a bad idea. We could be together forever. Once the wizards were dead, we could rule Magia the way we wanted. I smiled at the thought.

I made my way around the little house, peeking into each of the rooms. I was hoping to find some clothes to wear. I couldn't walk the streets in my blood-soaked nightgown. A man's long winter coat hung in a closet by the front door. I threw it over my shoulders and slipped my arms through the sleeves. My apartment was only a few blocks away. I would have to stop in there and change. I scrounged up a pair of men's shoes and slipped my feet into them, but screamed in pain and threw the shoes across the room. I waved my hand, hoping to heal my feet, but it had no effect. Wendell's magic was too strong.

I ventured back out into the snow and walked toward my apartment. The lights were on when I arrived. Frustrated, I stood in the driveway, eyeing Cory's truck. Cory seemed like a distant memory now. I tried to imagine his face, but couldn't. I stepped up onto the porch as he appeared in the building's doorway, with James behind him. Both stared at me, unable to hide their shock.

"Thea, where have you been?" Cory asked.

"Out finding myself."

He and James exchanged uneasy glances.

"You should come home with us," Cory said.

I looked at James, who avoided my gaze, his face drenched in shame. Although I was tempted, I decided not to argue with them. I needed an opportunity to secure my father's ring.

"Can I change my clothes first?" I was having a hard time keeping my tone civil.

Cory nodded and opened the door for me. I heard them on my heels as I made my way up the stairs to my apartment. I found it odd that they weren't questioning me—not a word about the bandages or my blood-stained nightgown.

Behind me, Cory muttered to James, "What's wrong with her eyes?"

An unexpected feeling of grief washed over me when I entered my apartment. There were so many memories here. I thought of Sammy, of the many times he'd walked in here, smiling. I shook the sentimental thought from my head. My old life was full of pain. I didn't want any part of it.

I hurried to my closet and pulled down some clothes. "I'll be right out!" I called. I didn't like the way the skirt and top fit me, so I waved my hand and made some adjustments. I looked into the mirror at the new me and smiled. The clothes that had been dowdy and loose now hugged every curve of my body. Delia was right: not everyone had curves like mine. My eyes were different, too, now darker and glossy. I was pleased with my new look.

When I walked out of the bedroom, James slipped his phone into his pocket. *Probably talking to Helena*, I thought. His eyes traveled my body.

"You don't have to hang up on your girlfriend on my account," I teased.

"I . . . I wasn't talking to her."

I reached for a pair of shoes, praying they wouldn't hurt my feet. "So when are you getting married?" It was strange how my connection to James had vanished. I'd presumed I would still have at least a little feeling for him, but I felt nothing. "Will you be having a big wedding?" I grimaced as I slipped my feet into the shoes, but I pulled myself together and ignored the pain. Why was it taking them so long to heal?

"I'm not marrying Helena," James replied.

"Huh. That's too bad. I like weddings."

"Thea, please. I didn't mean to hurt you."

"Hurt me?" I said. "You freed me, James. I've never been happier."

He kept looking into my eyes, perplexed. "I know you're in there, Thea. I still love you."

I tilted my head. "You love me? Is that why you took Helena into your room? What were you trying to show me, then?"

He stepped closer. "I made a mistake. I was angry."

I smiled. "And now I'm angry with you."

"Please forgive me, Thea. I never meant for things to go this far."

I laughed and shook my head. Cory and James glanced at each other. When I finally composed myself, I said, "Just so we're clear, you and I are finished. You have no ties to me anymore, and soon you will be free to do whatever you want. But until then, I want you to stay out of my way. I don't want to see you. I don't want to talk to you. I don't want to even hear your voice if I can help it."

James looked down. "I'm sorry for ever saying those words to you."

"Give him a break," Cory said. "He's been worried sick about you."

"I can't imagine why. All I ever gave him was a little piece of ass."

"Stop it!" James shouted.

"Don't like the new me?" I asked, placing a hand on my hip. "Too bad."

"This isn't you," Cory said.

"It is now."

Cory grabbed my wrist. "What is wrong with you?"

I yanked my arm away. "Isn't it obvious? I woke up."

"What happened to your neck?" James asked.

I reached for my coat and stood by the door. "Can we leave now?"

We rode back to the mansion in silence. I was too busy battling with myself to make conversation. I tried to ignore James's scent from my seat in the back of the truck. I didn't want to think about him anymore, having convinced myself that I no longer loved him. But every time his scent filled my head, I found myself on the verge of falling apart. It had been easy back at the apartment, but here, in close quarters, I could feel my broken heart. I'd never had a chance to respond to James's betrayal. I had left for Magia before I could fully absorb what he'd done during and after the wedding. Now the pain was crashing down around me like a landslide.

"Can't you drive a little faster?" I rolled down the window and breathed in the fresh air. James's scent was softening my resolve.

"Are you okay?" James asked.

I closed my eyes at the sound of his voice. I pictured his blue eyes looking down at me. I held back my tears with what little resolve I had left. I was frustrated and angry with myself. *Damn!* Why couldn't I rip him out of my heart?

"Let me out of the car!" I screamed.

Cory braked, and I jumped from the car, my mind spinning with emotions I couldn't control. Nearly breathless, I pictured Helena in James's bed and saw James kissing her neck.

As James followed me, I shouted, "Leave me alone!"

"Let me take you home."

I shook my head. "Why did you do it, James? Why did you hurt me like that?"

"Do you think you didn't hurt me?"

"Why do I keep having to explain this? I was trying to save you!"

"I would rather be dead!" he shot back.

I slapped my hands to my head. "Why did you bond with her?"

"I don't know!" he shouted. "I thought you had bonded with Cory. I wanted to hurt you. I wanted to make you pay for what you'd done. I made a mistake, a horrible mistake."

Cory jumped out of the truck. "Tell her why you thought we had bonded, James."

"I don't care why!" I ran in the direction of the house. We were only a few blocks away. I had to get the ring and return to Simon. Being close to James was making me weak. I had to get away from him.

"Thea, stop!" James said, running behind me.

I waved my hand at a branch, jumped on, and took off, sighing with relief as the pain-numbing anger returned. I wiped away my tears. I would never allow my heart to become weak like that again. The thought of James dying brought me added relief. It made perfect sense. He was the reason for my pain. If he was dead, I would be free. I thought about turning back and killing him now, but I knew I didn't have it in me. I would have to overcome my love for him first. Perhaps I could ask Simon about the spell. Why did I no longer feel rage when I was around James? Killing him then would have been easy.

I jumped off the branch and stood in front of the mansion. Getting past my father wasn't going to be easy. I had to make it to his room and retrieve the ring. Maybe I could fly there? If he was downstairs, he would never even know I had been there. I snatched the branch from the ground and hopped on.

Moments later, I was inside and searching for the ring. I spotted the huge book on my father's table and paused. It had an embossed leather cover and a broken sterling-silver latch, and looked to be hundreds of years old. The cover was pulling away from the binding. I was surprised to see the words *Holy Bible* printed on the cover. I had never known my father to be a religious man. I opened it carefully and ran my hand over its fragile pages, which were edged in gold leaf. My eyes widened as the scriptures faded and were replaced with spells written in my father's own hand, spells he no doubt wanted to remember. He had taken precautions, knowing the dangers of the Earth's air.

Every page I touched revealed a new spell. It was like finding a pot of gold. I would take the book to Simon. He would be pleased with my find. I could only imagine the kinds of spells we could cast on Wendell and the other wizards.

I found the spell my father had used to heal me when I had touched the enchanted baseball bat—a tea recipe full of leaves I'd never heard of. I turned the pages. Most of the spells were foreign to me, but one caught my attention. It was titled *True Love*. The rest of the page was blank. I wondered why my father had never finished it.

"You'll be writing the words to that one yourself."

I spun to face my father, who stood in the doorway, his expression severe.

His eyes drifted to the open window. "Do you mind closing that?"

I glanced over my shoulder. I had to leave it open so I could make my escape with the book and the ring—if I found it. "I think I'll leave it open for now, if you don't mind."

He smiled. The window slammed shut. "It was more a demand than a request." He walked into the room, pausing when he noticed the bandages on my neck. A grave seriousness came over his face. He ripped away the bandages, and his face twisted in anger when he saw the wound on my neck.

He struck me across the face, something I had never thought him capable of. I stumbled back, stunned, with my hand pressed to my cheek.

"What have you done?" he shouted.

I trembled before him, unable to find the words. When he struck me again, I fell against his desk and onto the floor. There was no time to react before he reached down and wrapped his hands around my neck. I clasped my hands over his, but his grip on my neck tightened.

"I'd rather see you dead!" he shouted, his eyes full of fury.

I thought of waving my hand at him, but something held me back. "William!" James shouted.

"What have you done?" my father repeated, tightening his grip.

James jumped between us and tried to pull my father's hands away. "You're going to kill her!"

Cory arrived soon after and worked from the other side, hitting and tearing at my father's hands.

"William, she can't breathe!" James shouted.

"Damn it, William!" Cory shouted.

"He killed your mother!" my father screamed.

He was like an animal. Nothing James or Cory did could stop him. His hands were like two iron clasps around my neck.

"He killed your mother!" he repeated.

Without warning, he released his grip and stumbled back. An unfamiliar man had entered the room and tossed my father aside.

"I'm sorry, Your Majesty," he said to my father.

I lay on my back, gasping for air. When my father came at me again, Cory stepped between us and dragged me toward the door.

"You have doomed us all!" my father shouted, and sent James and the strange man flying across the room.

Cory helped me to my feet, and together we ran into the hallway. I dropped to the floor when my father waved his hand at me. Cory tried helping me up again, but my father sent him into the wall. I stared at my father and inched backward. He exited the room, fury flaming in his eyes. "Why?"

"What would you do to avenge my death?" I asked, my voice barely audible.

He regarded me with disdain. "You hear everything and see nothing, Thea. I can't help you out of this one."

I smiled. "I don't need your help, Father. Simon will do what you never could."

"Foolish girl!" He lunged at me.

My hand sent him flying back into the room. I jumped to my feet and broke for the stairs.

"You're not leaving this house!"

Again, he sent me to the floor.

I tried to fight his magic as it dragged me back toward the room. I couldn't let him touch me again. He would no doubt find a way to keep me there. I held out my hand. "Stick!"

The door to my room flew open. My stick came flying into my hand, I sent my father crashing into his desk. I grabbed the spell book, waved my hand at the window, and flew out into the night.

Chapter 19
The Leaves

I felt I had won a war as I soared over Salem. I held onto the book as if it were a trophy. All my father's secrets would finally be revealed. My mind fantasized about the power I could glean from the book. I would rule Magia, and the human world as well. No more hiding or pretending to be human. I would bring the human world to its knees.

I was changing fast. The promise I had made to Simon was bringing out the evil in me. My thoughts raced nonstop. I thought of nothing but getting what I wanted, and I would destroy anyone who got in my way. Suddenly being the most powerful person in all the world seemed a perfect fit for me. How could I have not seen that before?

I would still need to return for my father's ring. But I first needed to think of a way to get past him. I had no doubt that he'd hidden it from me, but his magic couldn't stop me. I would burn the house down to find it—even kill him if I had to.

Kill them all, said a voice inside my head.

I smiled at the thought of killing my friends, but James would be the first, of course. I had to sever our connection before it could weaken me again. I would save my father for last. He would pay for taking my son out of the crystal. How could I have been so blind? He was never trying to help me. All the secrets and lies made perfect sense now. He wasn't trying to stop Simon; he was trying to stop me.

Kill them all, the voice said again.

I replied with joy: "Yes!"

Something inside me was trying to fight the darkness, waging a war in my head. The old me was trying to save the man she loved, but the new me wanted no part of him. He had betrayed me and thrown it all away. How could the old Thea want to save him after what he'd done? I flew faster, trying to shake the thought of James. He was my only weakness, it seemed. Now, more than ever, I wanted to kill him.

I flew deep into the woods, hoping to find somewhere safe to hide the spell book. I would keep it there until Simon sent for me. I pictured his smile as I presented it to him. He would love me more than ever.

"Simon," I said, flying faster.

I spotted a promising hiding place down below and began my descent. The area was sheltered from the snow and covered in brush and weeds. It would be hard to get to, but I had to try. I would bury the book there and come back for it later. My skin tingled as I thought of the spells the book would reveal to me. I would be more powerful than ever. Even my father would be no match for me.

I tramped through the brush like a mad woman. I had lost my mind to the darkness. The promise I'd made to Simon had sealed my fate. My heart was black, my soul dead. It was like my past life had never happened. I didn't think of my friends, and James would soon fade from my memory, too. I would see to that.

I pushed the thorny branches away as if they were soft twigs. My body felt no pain. My anger guided me. I felt greedy, my thoughts consumed with power. I wanted everything. Maybe I would use Simon to kill the wizards and simply take it all. The thought made me smile. I didn't need him. Why would I share what I could keep for myself? The darkness drove me mad with the desire to have it all. All I could think of was implementing my plan to conquer the world. Plan after plan sifted through my brain, each new one giving me more power and taking me further into darkness.

I found a safe spot to bury the spell book and began to dig with my hands at the frozen ground. Voices filtered through the air, and my head popped up. I listened closely, fearing that my father and the others were on my trail. I squatted down low as the voices got closer. Relief washed over me when I saw that one of them belonged to Simon. I stood with the intention of calling out to him, but quickly crouched back down. Helena walked at his side.

What is she doing here?

"I don't get it," Helena said. "Now you're going to marry her?"

"Call it an unexpected turn of events," Simon replied.

I left my stick and the spell book behind and followed them. Simon carried a big plastic bag in each hand.

"But you said you would kill her," Helena said.

"Nothing has changed, my pet," Simon replied. "She will be dead after the marriage is performed. I will have no use for her after that." He laughed. "The impulsive little witch made it too easy for me."

It seemed Simon and I had similar plans for each other after the wedding. How could I have been so blind as to think he ever really loved me? A wave of anxiety rushed through me. My head began to spin. I stopped and steadied myself, peering at the two of them through an ice-covered bush.

"What about James?" Helena asked, stepping around a patch of snow. "You said you wouldn't hurt him."

"You wouldn't have to worry about that if you had done what I asked," Simon replied.

I followed them until they arrived at what looked like a large hole in the ground. I looked closer. The hole was filled with moving water. All the lakes in New England were covered in a solid sheet of ice, but this watering hole was somehow impervious to the freezing temperatures.

The leaves.

Helena shivered and pulled her jacket closed. "I still can't figure out how you got her to make a blood promise to you."

Simon ignored her inquiry and dropped the bags on the ground. He wore his jeans and hiking boots. His new, casual attire now made sense. He came here regularly to take water from the leaf-infested pond. He leaned down and pulled a plastic gallon container from each of the bags.

"You were supposed to kill her," Helena whined.

Simon stood and slapped Helena's face. "And you were supposed to bond with James!"

Helena held her cheek. "I told you, he was too drunk. He kept calling me by her name until he passed out. But at least he thinks we bonded. I made sure we were both naked when he woke in the morning."

That news should have made me happy, but I felt nothing.

"Thinking is not enough," Simon snapped. "He can ruin my plans in a moment if he bonds with her again. Their connection is too strong."

"But she made a blood promise to marry you."

Simon slapped her again and she fell to the ground. "You stupid witch. You know nothing about the power of love. That witch handed him right to you. That's why I went looking for you in the first place. You missed your chance to take it all away from her. If she ever finds out you didn't bond with him, she will run back to him in an instant. Her blood promise to me will mean nothing if she's willing to die for him." Simon reached for one of the empty containers and tossed it in front of Helena. "Get up and fill this, and be careful with the leaves." He removed clothes and ropes from the bags. He threw the items at her feet as she peered down into the water.

I heard the crackling of leaves behind me and ducked deeper into the brush. The warlock named Toby approached them, carrying more bags. His sword was still strapped to his back. Five warlocks followed closely behind him, all carrying similar bags.

"Put everything over there," Simon ordered, pointing to a spot next to the watering hole.

I couldn't help but wonder what else they had with them. I squinted, watching as the warlocks removed more empty containers from the bags. Unbeknownst to Simon, Toby and the other warlocks exchanged furtive glances behind his back.

Simon pushed Helena into the water. "Start

filling, witch."

The warlocks continued their curious behavior as Simon passed the full containers. One warlock took a swig from one of the containers. "I wish we had a wizard to practice on," he said, taking another drink.

Once upon a time, Simon had told the warlocks that he was a wizard and that I had taken his powers. I knew that sooner or later the warlocks would get wise and turn on him when they realized they had no need for him. I was surprised Simon hadn't seen this coming. Warlocks were nothing if not greedy. Simon was unwittingly giving them what they wanted. I smiled, delighted at the opportunity to watch mutiny in action.

One of Toby's men stepped up to Simon. "I know where we can find a so-called wizard."

"You would dare turn on me?" Simon replied.

"Why should we help you?" the warlock asked. "The witch will be no match for us, not after drinking this water. Maybe we'll have her take *us* to this magical land you go on about incessantly."

The warlocks laughed.

"Funny how this water doesn't make you weak, Simon," said a young-looking warlock. "It works on the witch, but not you?" He scratched his head and looked at his partners. "Why do you think that is?"

"I told you, the witch took my powers."

The young warlock smiled. "The witch didn't always have powers, and whatever touched that water worked on her."

Simon's eyes widened. He was caught, and he knew it. "I won't be questioned like this. Get back to the others, and I'll deal with you later."

The young warlock smiled wider. His eyes

changed color every time he blinked—from blue to green to hazel. "I'm a little tired of taking orders from you, Simon. You make promises you can't keep." He glanced around at the others and held up a container of the leaf-tainted water. "I don't think we need you anymore."

I fought the urge to jump out from the brush and help Simon. The thought of the warlocks harming him was nearly unbearable.

"You think that water will last forever?" Simon asked, laughing. He pointed at the container in the warlock's hand. "The effects fade quickly, son."

"Well, we'll just do what you do, Simon. Come back and get more."

The warlocks erupted in laughter.

An evil smile spread across Simon's face. He reached down and picked up an empty container. "Be my guest," he said, throwing it at one of the others.

The warlock with the changing eyes gave his partner a nod. "Go ahead."

The other warlock nodded back and headed to the water. When he leaned down to fill the container, he was thrown back with a jolt.

Simon chuckled as the warlock scrambled to his feet. "Do you think me a fool?" Simon asked.

When the warlock didn't answer, Simon kicked him into the water. The warlock screamed and disintegrated. The other warlocks took a step back when a cloud of dust rose from the water and dissipated into the air around them. Helena looked down at the water in horror, shivering with cold and fear.

Simon gazed at the other warlocks, smiling at the one who had drunk from the container. He pulled a silver object from his pocket and held it to his lips. When he blew into it, leaves flew out of the water and spun into the air, almost as if looking for something. They gravitated toward the warlock and clung to his body, squeezing the life from him. The other warlocks dropped their containers and stumbled back. Simon threw his head back and laughed when the man turned to dust. The leaves hovered in the air for a moment before returning to the water. Helena screamed and stumbled out of the way.

Simon smiled at the warlocks. "Anyone else care to take a drink?"

The warlock with the changing eyes took another step back. "What's wrong, Netiri?" Simon asked. "Are you scared of my wizard spells?"

Netiri didn't answer. He only looked into the water, horrified.

"Would you like to see another spell?" Simon teased. "Or do you have something else you would like to inquire about?"

The one named Netiri glanced at Toby and shook his head.

"Good," Simon said. "Go and tell the others there has been a change in plans. I'll meet them later when I'm done here."

"Yes, my lord," Netiri said.

I gazed at the object in Simon's hand. A dog whistle? Why would the leaves react to that? Then it hit me: the whistle caused them pain. It was the same pain my wizard energy caused them. But why hadn't they attacked me? I wasn't but eight or ten feet away. Why only the warlocks? None of this made any sense.

I watched as the warlocks reclaimed their containers. They held them away from their bodies as if carrying bombs. Simon laughed as they left. He slipped the whistle into his pocket and tossed more containers at Helena. Something in his dark eyes alerted my suspicion. I couldn't tear my gaze away from those eyes. I saw his hunger for power in his evil stare. His incessant planning and scheming made sense to me now, because I shared those same feelings. My eyes were as dark as his. Wendell's words rang out like a bell: *Simon made a very special promise to kill you.*

I squinted, examining Simon's neck. I clapped my hand over my mouth when I spotted the scar. He'd made a blood promise to Wendell to kill me. *Big surprise.* Simon was so predictable. But I wondered if he could predict what I was going to do next. Simon thought himself a skillful double crosser, but he hadn't seen anything yet. I knew where the leaves were now. I didn't need him anymore.

I smiled to myself. My revenge on Wendell would start sooner than I had expected.

"I'm getting cold," Helena said.

Simon pulled her to dry ground, where she stood shivering and turning blue.

"Why did the warlock die like that?" she asked.

Simon smirked. "You witches can be so stupid sometimes. You can't even see the obvious."

"What is that supposed to mean?"

"Nothing," Simon said, throwing her a coat, "Time to get out of here. I have a bride waiting for me."

When I was sure they were out of earshot, I slipped from behind the brush and checked the area, making sure Simon and Helena were gone. Then I stepped toward the water cautiously, unsure of how close I could get before I felt its effects. My eyes lit up when I was able to see the leaves below the surface. Just as in Magia, they were green and lush. Nothing seemed to have affected them. I reached down and carefully tried to bring them to the surface. When my knees threatened to buckle under, I quickly backed away.

How was I going to get at them? Simon had called Helena stupid for not noticing the obvious. Could it be that only a woman could safely enter the water? Simon had made sure the warlocks would never steal the leaves from him, but he had never counted on me finding out his secret. I searched my mind for the perfect candidate to help me steal them. Once I had them in my possession, I would leave for Magia immediately—without Simon. With the leaves on my side, Wendell would be no match for me.

And I knew just who would be holding the leaves. It wouldn't be hard convincing Delia to go with me to Magia, and I could easily kill her after Wendell was dead. I would come back and kill them all. But none of this would be possible without the ring.

I waved my hand at the surrounding area. Simon would not find this spot again. I rearranged the trees and changed the shape of the ground around the watering hole. I moved the rocks and paths to another part of the forest. I waved my hand at a huge boulder and set it down over the hole.

Once finished, I went looking for my stick.

Chapter 20
The Secret Room

I buried the spell book in a safe place and flew back to the mansion. My mind raced with anticipation. I couldn't wait to see the look on Wendell's face when I confronted him. I would start with his eyes, ripping them out with my bare hands. I would take pleasure in his screams, and perhaps even find needles of my own with which to pierce his feet. I would hold his still-beating heart in my hand before he closed his eyes forever.

My father's ring was suddenly the most important thing in the world. I was determined to get my hands on it. Eventually, I would have to kill my father. He stood in the way of my happiness. It was his fault that any of this had happened in the first place. He had killed my son, and with him the only reason I had left to fight. My blood boiled thinking of how my father had tricked me. I would make him tell me why before I stabbed him through the heart.

The mansion was mostly dark when I flew into the backyard and hovered at the far end of the patio. Only the kitchen lights were still on, which meant my father was likely not in his room. He was waiting for the prodigal daughter to return. But his daughter had other plans. While he lingered in the kitchen, I would sneak into his room and find the ring. Maybe I would even find more treasures scattered about.

I flew up to his window and peered in. The room was dark. I took my chances and climbed in through the window, leaving my stick hovering on the ledge. I searched frantically for the ring, rummaging through my father's desk with little success. I was searching through his dresser drawers when something hit my back. I collapsed to the floor, an awful buzzing sound filling my head. *Porteus.* Frozen in pain, I saw only my father's feet as he strode into the room.

"Drag her to the wall," my father said.

I tried to push the pain aside when Porteus grabbed my hands, but the buzzing intensified, as did the pain.

"Don't fight it, Your Highness," Porteus said.

I looked up at him. Porteus was the unfamiliar man who had been in my father's room earlier. As my father had suggested, he had taken a human form. His appearance threw me. Somehow, I had never envisioned him so handsome, with blond hair and emerald-green eyes. He hauled me across the room and stopped at the opposite wall.

My father moved closer, his hands clasped behind his back. "If she moves, give her more pain."

"Yes, Your Majesty."

My father towered above me. "Were you looking for this?" he said, holding up the ring.

I reached for it and was immediately slammed back to the floor. I shook violently as the shocks traveled through my body. The buzzing in my ears was so deafening I could barely hear my father talking to me.

"Don't worry," he said. "I'm going to give you the ring."

I met his stony gaze.

"But first I'm going to show you something."

He walked to the wall and touched it with his palm. The floor vibrated as the wall slid aside, revealing a kind of door. There was no knob or handle, only an image of the door on the wall. A soft white light poured from its edges. When he touched it again, streams of energy emanated from the opening.

"Pick her up," he ordered.

Porteus lifted me into his arms. My father looked to the wall again as the beams of energy wrapped itself around us. My body radiated in its light. A strange sensation consumed me as the energy pulled us to the other side of the door. I was blinded for a moment, but my eyes quickly adjusted as we reached our destination.

For a moment, I thought I was in Attor's cave. There were precious stones encrusted in the walls. I saw memories of my father's past in each of them. I soon realized that this was the room Attor had told me about; my father had found a way to stay in touch with the place he had come from. Now I knew where he spent most of his time. This was where he'd hid when Simon's men had searched the house.

The room was quite small, but somehow felt spacious. Flowerpots were scattered about, and the flowers in them bloomed and glistened just like in my father's world. I heard the sound of a waterfall and felt the crisp, clean air on my face. Even the strange light from Magia's sun loomed above me. I felt transported, like I was really there. My father had captured Magia's splendor within these four walls.

He reached for one of the stones on the wall. "Put her down," he said, facing us.

I was still looking around in awe as Porteus set me down. He was no longer shocking me. I thought of nabbing the ring from my father's hand, but thought better of it. How would I get out of here?

"I know you're angry with me, Thea," my father said, "but I want you to know why I did what I did."

I glared at him. "You mean why you moved my son out of the crystal, the only place he was truly safe?"

"I did it to save James. I knew you would never forgive yourself if you killed him. I discovered too late the effects your son would have on you. I was desperate to save you both and just didn't see it. I forgot how powerful a mother's love can be. There would have never been a need to cast Attor's spell on James if I had realized that sooner."

"What are you talking about, Father?"

Porteus moved closer, poised to shock me if I tried anything.

"Haven't you noticed that the anger is gone?" my father asked. "Haven't you wondered why you don't hate James anymore?"

I looked away, because he was right. It never made sense how the murderous anger had just disappeared.

"That was your son," my father said. "He did that."

My eyes narrowed. "And you killed him."

I dropped to my knees in unbearable pain, clasping my hands to my head, as Porteus threw out the shocks. When I could no longer take it, I collapsed.

~ 268 ~

My head hit the floor with a thump.

My father leaned down and placed the stone he had been holding next to my head. "You have a choice to make. You can come into the light, or you can walk back into the darkness. I don't want to kill you, but I would rather see you dead than see you lose yourself."

I stared into the stone and saw myself in James's arms, my body covered in blood. We were in this very room. Cory was kneeling beside me. My father leaned down and touched the stone. Their voices came ringing out of it.

"Heal her, or I'll kill you," James shouted at Cory.

Cory placed his shaky hands over my stomach. "Heal." The open wounds on my stomach sealed themselves. He moved his hands across my arms, to my legs, and down to my feet.

"Careful," James said.

Cory removed the needles and placed his hands over my feet. "Heal."

My feet didn't respond.

"Heal," Cory repeated. He looked up at my father. "I'm sorry, William. I've done everything I can do."

My father nodded. "Wendell poisoned the needles. I will have to stitch her feet."

I trembled as the truth hit me. They had been talking about my feet. It wasn't my son Cory had apologized for; it was for not being able to heal my feet. My head spun as dizziness overwhelmed me. My breathing became labored. The enormity of my mistake came crashing down around me.

The room filled with light, and I heard a door slam. The buzzing in my head faded away. I scrambled to my feet. I was back in my father's room, but my father and Porteus were nowhere to be seen.

I ran to the wall and pounded. "Father!"

I couldn't think straight. What had I done?

"Father, please," I cried. "You have to help me." I turned and slid down the wall. I wanted to die. I held my hand to my stomach. "I'm so sorry." How could I have let this happen? What was I going to do now? I slammed my head against the wall. "You stupid witch."

I stood and banged on the wall again. "Father, I'm begging you, please help me!" But he never emerged. I was on my own. I had to find my own way out of this. I ran my hands through my hair. "Think, witch, think!" What could I do? I had put myself into the worst situation possible. I had accepted the dark thoughts that the darkness had given me and relished them. I had desired to kill my friends, my father, and even my love to get what I wanted—power.

I reached for my stick and flew out the window. I had to expel the darkness from my head. I had to think of a way out. If I didn't do something soon, the darkness would win.

An idea flashed through my mind—a possible way to find my strength again. The mere thought of it helped clear my head.

I flew back into the woods. I had to destroy Simon's leaves, but how? Nothing in this world was strong enough to combat them. I searched my mind for some way to vanquish their power. I breathed deep as a plan began to form in my mind. I retrieved the spell book and flew back out into the night, wiping the tears from my face. I was full of regret. The thought of my son being killed had compelled me to do unspeakable things.

There was only one person who could help me. I should have placed my trust in him from the very beginning. Even Simon knew how strong our love was. James was my greatest strength. Next to him, I could fight the devil himself. He was the only one who could pull me out of this darkness.

The plan brewing in my head began to take shape. I would have to outsmart Simon. I had made things harder on myself by giving Simon his blood promise. Fighting Simon's spell had been difficult, but fighting against the darkness was going to be damned near impossible.

I had become my own worst enemy.

The evil thoughts that lived in my head were not going to just disappear. Already the battle had begun inside me. The black witch wanted no part of the life I was trying to get back to. I was determined not to let her control me.

But I now had an edge in facing off against Simon: I knew how his mind worked, because I had joined him in the darkness. I understood the desire the darkness brought out: to get what one wants, no matter the cost. I could almost guess Simon's next move. I could feel his evil thoughts running through me. They were the very same thoughts I was having now. The darkness had wrapped its arms around me just as it had with Simon so many years ago. We shared the same dark eyes, and now the same dark desires.

Like Simon, I wished I had an army to help me. *Simon's army.*

My plan was gathering strength and falling into place. The more I thought of James, the clearer my thoughts became. I remembered the warlocks from earlier—the ones who had stood down after witnessing the demise of their friends. They had their doubts about Simon. Maybe I could use their suspicions to my advantage. I was determined to find them. They couldn't have made it far on foot.

I flew through the woods in search of them. Simon himself was nothing but a lowly coward; his only real strength was in his men. But if a few of his men doubted his legitimacy as a wizard and a leader, surely there were more who felt the same. I would find them and turn them against him. The warlocks hated me, but they were about to hate Simon more. If there was one thing I knew about a warlock, it was that they loved power. If they knew Simon had no real power to give them, they would turn on him in an instant.

There was one thing I was sure of: I couldn't break my blood promise to Simon. If my son was to live, I had to live.

I zipped through the trees, searching for the warlocks Netiri and Toby. My plan would begin with them. I was confident I could convince them of Simon's deceit. The question was: Would they be willing to help me? I needed them if my plan was going to work. If they agreed to help me, my father would finally be able to return to his home. I was attempting the impossible. Tradition had demonstrated, time and time again, that witches and warlocks couldn't get along. But I had to find a way to change that.

The hardest thing to change would be me. Evil now coursed through my blood, and it wasn't going to let me go without a fight. But I knew a black witch who might be able to help me. She, too, had once made a blood promise, and I knew for certain that the promise had never been fulfilled. I would seek her out and beg her to help me if need be. Only she had the answers I sought. I would have to look in the darkest of places and somehow compel her to give up the secrets of hell. It would be the ultimate test of my true character.

I flew faster through the woods as my plan came together. I spotted the wayward warlocks running through the forest at a good clip. I flew just above and behind them, waiting for my chance to pounce. I had to bide my time. So long as they held the leaf-soaked water, I had to keep my distance. I saw my chance when Toby and Netiri set down the containers to rest. I waved my hand and sent the warlocks flying away from the tainted water. Before they could get to their feet, I flew by and scooped them up onto the stick.

They were kicking and shouting and trying to pull out their weapons as I maintained a grip on their shirts.

I flew high into the sky. "Stop fighting, or I'll let go," I shouted.

The warlocks looked down and grasped the stick. "I'm not trying to kill you," I said.

"Sorry," Toby replied, "but we can't say the same about you." He spit a spell into his hand.

I kicked his hand, and the spell sailed down into the forest. He spit out another and held it in his hand.

I began my pitch. "Simon's not a wizard!"

He glared at me, the spell spinning in his hand. "He's not even a warlock."

Toby's eyes narrowed. He closed his hand and extinguished the spell.

Netiri kicked at his partner. "What are you

doing?"

I flew toward the ground and sent them tumbling and rolling to their feet. They pulled out their weapons as I landed in front of them. Netiri threw a spell at me, but I raised my hand and waved it away. When they both came at me with their swords, I ran up a tree and dodged their weapons. I didn't want to kill them. I needed them to hear me out.

"You filthy witch!" Netiri said, running up after me.

Branches blew away from the tree as Toby stood beneath it, throwing more spells. A sound like matches being lit resonated through the air. I waved my hand and sent Netiri to the ground.

"Toby," I shouted, "I know you know I'm telling the truth."

"I believe no witch who makes a blood promise," he shot back.

Netiri jumped to his feet. "Don't listen to her lies."

I pressed on, determined to make them hear me. "You both know I'm right. Simon has been lying to you."

They ignored me again and spit spells at the tree trunk. How stupid were these warlocks? Did they not understand that I could have killed them by now? I jumped from the tree and waved my hand, raising them ten feet in the air and throwing them back to the cold, hard ground. I waved my hand again, and roots rose up through the earth and covered them like snakes.

I stood above them. "You two are starting to piss me off."

They kicked and tried to free themselves.

I glared down at them. "Do you want to live, or would you rather be crushed to death?"

"Go ahead and throw your death spell, witch," Netiri said.

I rolled my eyes, Delia style. "You idiots, there's no death spell. Simon scared you all into helping him. I can kill you both with any one of my spells." I waved my hand at the tree. They gasped when the tree splintered into thousands of tiny pieces. They gaped at me with fear in their eyes.

"Are you ready to hear me out now, gentlemen?"

"Spit it out, witch," Netiri hissed. "What do you want?"

"Just a moment of your time," I replied.

Toby elbowed Netiri. "Let her talk."

Toby did believe me. I waved my hand and released them both. They scrambled to their feet and retrieved their swords, which they brandished with shaky hands.

"Are all warlocks carrying swords now?" I teased.

Netiri turned his sword in his hand. "Mine is called a Katana, and I'm going to kill you with it."

"Shut up, Netiri," Toby said. "I want to hear what the witch has to say."

"You believe this witch?" Netiri asked.

Toby pointed his sword at his partner. "Shut up." He returned is attention to me. "Why should we believe you?"

"Because you know I'm right."

He held out his sword. "You killed my friend Jack. You tricked him into believing you. You will not do the same to me."

"Jack was my friend," I replied. "He didn't die by my hand; he died by yours."

Toby squinted. "What are you talking about?"

"He turned himself into a cat to hide from Simon. But you all decided to practice spells on him."

"You lie!" Toby shouted.

"No," I said, shaking my head. "He died knowing the truth about Simon. And he wanted nothing more than to share the truth with all of you."

Toby lowered his sword slightly.

"He talked to you, didn't he?"

"Don't listen to this witch," Netiri said.

Toby ignored him. "The day we captured you," he began, "Jack told me everything, but I didn't believe him. But since then, I've been watching Simon closely for any sign that Jack could have been right."

"Why didn't you believe him?" I asked.

He thought for a moment. "Simon does unusual things. He casts spells I've never heard of before. His magic is foreign to me. I know no warlock who can do the things he does."

"That's because he's not a warlock," I replied. "And he's no wizard, either. He's a half-human witch who, under the tutelage of two very powerful wizards, learned some very powerful wizard spells."

Netiri looked at Toby, incredulous. "Simon is half human?"

"Yes," Toby replied.

Netiri lowered his sword. "Why didn't you tell me?"

"I wasn't sure until just now."

"You only said he wasn't a wizard," Netiri said. "You never said anything about him being half-human scum."

"I told you," Toby said, "I wasn't sure."

Netiri's eyes began changing colors. "We've been taking orders from a half-human witch?"

When Toby didn't answer, Netiri turned on his heel. "He dies today."

"You can't kill him," I said.

"Give me one good reason why not, witch."

"Because I need your help."

Netiri smirked. "Why in hell would we help you?"

His eyes were so unusual, the colors changing faster and faster. They had a distinct sadness about them. He had a boyish face like Fish.

"Do you really think Simon doesn't have a plan in place in case you turn on him? And now he knows you're onto him. You will all surely die if you confront him now."

Toby and Netiri glanced at each other. They knew I was right.

"What do you want from us?" Toby asked.

I laid out my plan step by step.

When I finished, Netiri shook his head. "The warlocks hate you. You've been on a warlock killing spree, and I can't see how you're going to convince them to help you. I don't even know if I want to help you."

He had a point. I had killed a lot of warlocks. "I killed those who wanted to kill me. I can't change that. But I can give them the revenge they want. Their friends died because Simon lied to them—about me. Greed made them believe Simon, and greed compelled them to hunt me down."

Netiri glared at me, his eyes spinning rapidly through their colors. "You know nothing about us, witch. Don't you dare stand there and judge us."

"You judge me," I replied. "You judge my friends. You judge humans and anyone or anything you feel doesn't belong in this world. What makes you so perfect? How are you better than a half-human witch?"

"Because they're scum, and we're not."

"Why? Because they were born half human? If that's your only reason, then you're more foolish than I thought."

It became more and more clear that Netiri's eyes spun colors in direct relation to his level of anger. "We're done talking, witch. We'll keep our word and talk to the others, but we can't make any promises."

"That's all I can ask."

Toby replaced his sword in its sheath. "One more question: Why come to us for help?"

I thought for a moment. "You all may be greedy, but you're also brave. You were born to lead, not follow. Simon may not see that, but I do."

"And what happens when Simon is dead?" Toby asked. "Are we to follow you instead?"

"Why should you follow anyone?" I replied.

Toby eyed me with what looked like respect and nodded.

"Thank you," I said. "I'll wait for your word."

"We make no promises, witch," he replied. "But if they agree, we'll be there."

"Please assure them that no harm will come to them."

Toby and Netiri laughed.

"We'll see you later," Toby said, turning away.

I grabbed my stick and took to the sky. I had one more stop to make before I faced my father. For the first time in my life, I was about to ask the witches for help. I flew straight to Donna's shop and was surprised to find them all there. When I walked into the store, Melanie, the smiling witch, clasped her hand to her mouth.

Kym shook her head. "You stupid witch."

My eyes gave away what I had done. They were dark, empty, and glaring. Compton stepped back as I approached them. Donna got to her feet and forced a smile. "H . . . hello, Thea. What brings you here?"

I hung my head, wanting to hide the outward symbol of my deepest regret and shame. "I need your help."

"We can't help you out of a blood promise," Kym replied.

My hands balled into fists. I fought the impulse to slap her. My mood suddenly grew dark. I could feel the evil taking over. "I don't have much time, witch," I said through clenched teeth. "Will you help me or not?"

"What do you need from us?" Donna asked. She drew in a breath when our eyes met. "Oh, Thea, what have you done?"

I bowed my head again. "I've made the biggest mistake of my life."

"What did you promise?" Kym asked, her tone softening.

I could barely find the words. I was so ashamed. "I promised to marry Simon."

Gasps sounded throughout the room.

"Were you out of your mind?" Kym asked.

I willed myself to stay calm and looked up. "If you want to help me, meet me at the mansion in one hour. I'll tell you my plan when you get there. I'll understand if none of you show up."

When there were no replies, I walked out. I didn't expect them to help me, but I had to ask. The more people I had on my side, the harder Simon would fall.

Chapter 21
Stronger Than Any Spell I Know

I retrieved the spell book from the woods and flew back to the mansion, praying that James would be there and that he would be willing to hear me out. When I saw his car in the driveway, I sighed in relief. Just as quickly, my fear came rushing to the surface. No doubt my father had already told him what I had done. I prepared to beg James for forgiveness if necessary. I couldn't lose him again.

I walked around the back and peered into the kitchen. Cory and Jason sat across from each other at the table, talking. They jumped to their feet when I walked through the door.

"Oh my god," Jason muttered.

"I told you," Cory said. I knew they were talking about my eyes.

I moved aside when the back door opened again. I kept my head down as Delia and Fish walked in. I felt like I hadn't seen them in days.

"Where have you been?" Delia asked.

She gasped when I lifted my head.

Fish cringed. "Ew, you look all creepy, Thea."

"You stupid witch!" Delia snapped. "What have you done?"

"She looks like Satan's daughter," Fish said.

Joshua and Javier walked in. I ignored their similar horrified reactions and slammed the spell book on the kitchen table. I could think of nothing contrite to say. My impulse was to be rude, but I had to fight it.

"Where is James?" I asked.

"He's not home," Cory replied, avoiding eye contact.

I was scaring them, that much was clear.

Delia yanked my arm. "How could you be so stupid? What did you promise him?"

"Don't piss her off, Dells," Fish warned.

Delia pushed his arm away. "What did you promise him, witch?"

I smiled. "I promised I would marry him."

This was bad. I couldn't stop the words pouring from my mouth. I hated Delia for daring to yell at me. I wanted to bring her to her knees and make her beg forgiveness. Instead, I asked sarcastically, "Will you be my maid of honor?"

Delia's eyes widened. She was speechless; they all were. I had to get out of there. My big plan to find James and ask for his help started to fade as my mind compelled me to go back to Simon. The compulsion was nearly too strong to resist.

"Where is James?" I shouted.

"He's upstairs," my father said, walking in from the foyer.

I spun to face him.

"I knew you would choose the light," he said.

I didn't know what to say. I lowered my head in shame.

"Look into my eyes, Thea."

I shook my head. "I can't."

"Look me in the eyes so that I may know for sure that you are still there."

He crossed the room and lifted my chin with his fingers. He stared into my grotesque eyes for a long, tense moment. "You will always be my daughter," he said. "I will not allow the darkness to take you away from me. I will fight until my last dying breath to save you."

I threw myself into his arms, sobbing. "I thought he was dead. I thought my son was dead."

He kissed my head as I wept in his arms. "I know, Thea. I know."

"I'm going to fix this," I cried.

He held my face in his hands. "I have no doubt that you will. And I am going to help you."

"I don't deserve your help."

He smiled. "I forgive you, Thea. And James will forgive you. I can see in your eyes that you finally understand how powerful love is. You are nothing without him. Go to him. Find out what makes you strong."

I looked into his eyes and knew he was right. James kept me strong, kept me fighting. He should have been by my side this whole time. I should have never sent him away. He was my husband, my love, my life. The boys and Delia should never have had to protect me. It should have been James—always James.

"He's waiting," my father said.

I walked into the foyer and looked up the stairs. I swallowed down my pride and began to walk up. I was going to humble myself. For the first time in our relationship, I was going to put my life into James's hands. The door to his room—our room—seemed a million miles away. What would I say? Better yet, would he even want to hear me out when he learned what I had promised Simon?

I stopped at his door, taking in his scent. I took a deep breath and opened the door. The moment I walked in, I wanted to leave. The black witch inside me wanted no part of this. She was angry and resentful.

I pushed aside my dark thoughts and searched the room for James. He was sitting in front of the fireplace with his head in his hands. He hadn't heard me come in. When I closed the door behind me, his stood and turned. Even with the worry on his face, he looked like an angel. I thought of the first time I had laid eyes on him. I couldn't stop thinking of him after that. He had played the starring role in my dreams and in nearly every thought I had. Even before my memory of who I was returned, James was all I had ever thought about.

At that moment, I realized something. His books—he had sent me messages in his books. He had wanted to show me he could save me, that he was the only hero I ever needed. I could see that now. All his stories ended the same way: the hero fought the villain and saved the girl. I had savored every happy ending he wrote.

I pushed the black witch further away. It was getting easier to keep her at bay. I stepped away from the door, expecting to see a look of horror on James's face when he looked into my eyes. Instead his gaze was tender and understanding. He didn't react like the others. He bowed his head. "This is all my fault."

"You know what I promised Simon?"

He lifted his head and looked directly into my eyes. "Simon will have to kill me before I surrender my place as your husband."

I was stunned. "You're not angry with me?"

"How could I be angry over a promise you made out of pain?" He closed the space between us. "I never meant to hurt you, Thea. Helena means nothing to me."

"I have something to say to you," I said.

"Is it goodbye?"

Yes! a voice screamed in my head. I shook it off and stared into his sparkling blue eyes. "It's something I should have said to you a long time ago." I looked down at my hands. Suddenly the old Thea was back. That familiar nervous feeling washed over me as I wrung my hands. "I made a mistake sending you away all those years ago. If you had done that to me, I would have died of a broken heart. My need to save you controlled every decision I made. What I didn't realize until now is that I was the one who needed saving." I looked up at him. "Even when I couldn't remember you, I longed for you. I felt my life truly began when you came back to me. I've never felt safer than when I was in your arms. It's only then that I feel nothing can touch me. You give me a sense of protection no one else can. When I'm with you, I can face the world. Without you, I'm lost and alone. No amount of power can give me what you do."

I took a deep breath. "I know I really messed things up, James. I don't know if you can ever forgive me. I'll regret what I've done for the rest of my life. But I want you to know, I can't fight this battle without you. You're the one who keeps me strong. I never realized how true that was until today." I reached for his hand. "I need you, James. I need you to fight by my side."

He closed his eyes. "How I wish you had

spoken those words to me sooner. I've waited four hundred years to hear them." He ran his hand through his hair and looked away. "I don't deserve to hear them now."

"Because of Helena?"

He looked down. "Yes."

I tapped my head to pull out a single memory and flicked it into the air. He looked at the memory cloud, confused. I waved my hand and let the truth be known.

Helena's voice echoed in the room. "I told you, he was too drunk. He kept calling me by her name until he passed out. But at least he thinks we bonded. I made sure we were both naked when he woke in the morning."

"You see, James," I said, "you never—"

His kiss cut me off as he slammed me against the nearby wall and crushed his lips to mine. My head exploded with rage. The witch inside me was furious. I tried to ignore her, but she was making it very hard.

"No!" James said when I tried to push him away.

We fell to the floor. James climbed on top of me and held my hands over my head. He looked into my dark eyes. "She's mine, witch. It's time for you to leave."

I tried not to fight him as he kissed me again. His lips were sweet, and his body felt like heaven next to mine. Our lips never parted as he ripped away my clothes. The darkness was losing its hold on me.

"I love you," I cried. "I love you."

"Thea," James said, letting go of my hands.

I wrapped my arms around him, pulled him closer, and gave in to my desire.

We became one again. Our bond felt stronger than ever. The black witch inside drifted away as I melted into his arms. She was not welcome here. I was safe now. I was home.

"My Thea," James whispered.

He trailed his fingers along my back as I lay naked in his arms on the floor. I felt truly happy for the first time since I could remember.

"I can't get used to your eyes," James said. "They're so dark."

"Would you rather I not look at you?"

He lifted up my chin, his blue eyes gleaming. "Don't ever stop looking at me, my love." He kissed my head and pulled me closer.

"I think I scared Fish," I said.

He laughed. "There's no way you could scare Fish as much as Delia does."

"Delia . . . she was so angry with me."

"She'll be fine. Just give her a little time."

I closed my eyes and inhaled his scent.

"It's going to be hard keeping the black witch away," I whispered.

"I'll chase her away like today, my love."

I smiled.

"Is it me, or does the doorbell keep ringing?" James asked.

I sat up. "They came!"

"Who?" James asked.

I bit my lip. "Do you trust me?"

"More than ever, my love."

I told him my plan, and he agreed to it without hesitation. He truly surprised me. I thought he might disagree with the most difficult part.

When I was done explaining, he jumped to his

feet and started getting dressed. "This should be interesting."

"Thank you," I said, looking up at him.

"Why are you thanking me?"

"For believing in me again."

He smiled and helped me to my feet, then pulled me into his arms. "I've got news for you, Thea. I never stopped believing in you."

I threw my arms around him. "I love you."

"Thank you for remembering that."

Epilogue

I sat at the kitchen table across from Delia and Fish. The witches had agreed to help me. Now I waited to see if the warlocks would show. I was hesitant to tell Delia and Fish about my appeal to Simon's army. They already thought I had lost my mind.

James and my father had been holed up in my father's room since the witches had left. For once, I didn't question their reasons. I trusted them both, more now than ever. They had called Cory and Jason into the room a few minutes ago. Fish was going crazy wondering what was going on.

My mind was still lost in the memory of my reunion with James. I could still smell him; his scent covered every inch of my body. I couldn't wait to run back into his waiting arms.

We had spoken to my father before venturing downstairs to meet with the other witches. My father surprised me by agreeing to the plan. I told him about my earlier meeting with Toby and Netiri, and how they had agreed to pass along my proposal to the other warlocks. Neither my father nor James were thrilled about it, but agreed we needed them. My father had no doubt that they would agree to help us.

After my father left our room, James pulled me into his arms. I basked in the pure happiness of his smile, which reflected my own joy. The black witch hadn't reared her ugly head in hours, as though I had never made the blood promise. James's love restored my strength. Wrapped in the safety of his arms, I felt the nightmare floating away.

"What can you possibly have to smile about?" Delia asked.

Fish snapped his fingers in front of my face. "Is she sleeping?"

My eyes fluttered open. I hadn't even realized that I'd closed them. I could think only of running back into James's arms and staying there forever. I imagined his beautiful body waiting for me.

"Ew, close them again," Fish said, making a face.

I smiled. "I missed you, Fish."

Delia rolled her eyes. "I'm surprised you can smile at all."

Fish rubbed my arm. "Leave her alone, Dells. Can't you see Creepella is daydreaming?"

I laughed. Fish always found the humor, even in the worst of times. "Is that my new name?"

He shielded his eyes as he sank down in his chair. "Until your eyes change back . . . yes."

I sighed. "Are they really that bad?"

He straightened. "Uh, is Helena a douchebag?"

Fish and I laughed together.

"Well, I'm glad you two think this is funny," Delia said. "How do you plan on breaking this blood promise to Simon?"

I turned to her, winking. "Who said I was going to break it?"

"This isn't a joke," she said, getting to her feet.

"Delia, calm down," Fish said. "Creepella knows what she's doing."

When we laughed again, Delia stormed out of the room.

Seconds later, Delia screamed. Fish jumped to his feet, sending his chair tumbling back onto the kitchen floor. He couldn't run out of the kitchen fast enough. His hooks were out before he reached the door. By the time I made it out to the foyer, James, Cory, and Jason were barreling down the stairs.

The warlocks Toby and Netiri stood in the open doorway, observing the rising panic.

Fish grabbed Delia and pushed her behind him. "Stay there."

Joshua stormed in, his bow and arrow at the ready.

"Don't hurt them," I shouted as I moved to stand in front of the warlocks. Netiri raised his sword, and Joshua pointed an arrow at his head.

"Are you out of your mind?" Delia asked.

I raised my hand. "Stand down, Joshua."

James stepped up beside me. "Everyone just calm down."

"Thea," Fish shouted, "move out of the way."

"No, you need to stop."

James stepped into the middle of the entryway, his hands raised. "Everyone just relax."

The tension rose further when Javier walked in and drew his weapon. Toby pulled out his sword in response.

"Stop!" James shouted. "These men are guests in my house. No one is going to touch them."

"Go ahead, you half-human scum," Netiri

yelled at the boys, "come and get us."

Fish threw one of his hooks, but I waved a hand to stop it. Meanwhile, Toby ran at Javier.

"No," I shouted. I waved my hand again, sending everyone but James, Cory, and Jason to the wall. They hung high above our heads, kicking and trying to get down.

I walked to the wall and addressed Toby and Netiri. "I'm sorry. I should have told them you were coming."

Netiri glared at Fish from the corner of his eye.

"Let me down, Thea," Fish said. "I think that warlock wants to play marbles with me."

"Shut up, Fish," Cory said.

I ignored Fish and looked up at Toby. "Did you talk to them?"

"No. We thought it best not to."

My heart sank. "But you gave me your word."

"I know, witch. But we knew they would never agree to help you."

I threw up my arms in exasperation. "Then what are you doing here?"

Toby and Netiri glanced at each other. "Simon gave orders to storm this house," Toby said. "He said to bring the butler to him."

"What?" I said, stepping back.

"That witch Helena told him about a butler that James has working for him. Simon wants to talk to the man."

Trying to mask my distress, I looked at James.

"Don't worry, my love," he said. "They'll never find him."

I looked at Delia and the boys, knowing full well that if the warlocks were to enter this house, they would kill my friends without hesitation.

"We can't stop all of them," Toby said. "But we'll stop as many as we can."

"There will be no need for that." My father was standing at the top of the stairs, wearing a coat and hat.

I hurried to the staircase. "What are you doing?"

"I'm leaving with these gentlemen," he replied as he slowly descended. "I believe someone by the name of Simon wants to speak with me."

My eyes widened. "Are you crazy?"

"Let them down, Thea," he said, gesturing to the wall. "There will be no need for Simon's army to storm this house if I leave with these two men." He paused, staring at me intently. "Think about your friends."

I folded my arms across my chest, determined not to let him pass. "I can't let you go."

He smiled, and a soft buzzing went off in my head. It wasn't my father. *Porteus!*

"Put them down," he repeated with a twinkle in his eye. "Oh, and I left something for you in my room."

When he reached the foyer floor, I threw my arms around him. "Be careful."

He spoke quietly into my ear. "I can take care of myself, Your Highness."

I waved my hand at the warlocks and set them down on the floor. "What will you tell Simon?" I asked. "He'll grow suspicious when you show up with the butler."

"That's easy," Netiri replied. "All we have to tell him is that we wanted to impress him, so we came alone. He'll believe it."

I arched an eyebrow. "Does this mean you're helping us?"

"Helping *you*." He looked at Fish. "Not them."

I nodded, giving them a small smile. I needed all the help I could get.

As Porteus left the house with Netiri and Toby, James pulled out his phone. I released the others from the wall.

"Ciro will be here soon," James said, closing his phone. "Justin is coming with him."

"We'll hold things down here," Cory said. "You two had better hurry."

"What the hell is going on?" Delia asked.

Cory ignored her. "You two get out of here. I'll explain it to them."

I hugged him. "Take care of them, Cory. We'll be back as soon as we can."

"Good luck, Thea," Cory replied. "We'll be here waiting."

"I'll never be able to thank you enough, my friend."

He smiled, his green eyes shining. "You can thank me by finally ending this."

"I promise I will."

James and I sped up the stairs into my father's room. He turned to greet us, his expression serious.

"Will Porteus be okay?" James asked.

My father nodded. "Porteus will be fine—better than fine, actually." He turned to me. "I'm proud of you, Thea. Your plan never even crossed my mind."

My eyes filled. "I'll get you home, Father."

He embraced me. "You understand that Simon's spell will seem like nothing compared to this, don't you?"

"I can do it, Father. I have my son to think about now."

He placed the ring in my hand. "I'll be waiting." He turned to James. "I can't think of a man with more honor and dignity than you. Thea has made the right choice."

"It is I who is honored, William."

My father nodded and stepped back. "Go. I'll be waiting."

James took my hand. "You're sure about this?"

I smiled and squeezed his hand. "For the first time in my life, I'm actually sure about something."

He nodded and I looked down at the ring. I gave my father one last glance before slipping the ring onto my finger. In an instant, we were gone.

49848624R00165

Made in the USA
Charleston, SC
05 December 2015